Whistlin'
Stardust

Sara McFerrin

Dedication

Born in 1918, one of five children, Margaret Jones grew up in the Burstall community near Birmingham, Alabama. In 1943, she married Charlie Bell, who supported his family by working in coal mines. Margaret helped by working various jobs as they raised their daughters, Elizabeth and Elaine. Both girls attended the Tuskegee Institute, and Elaine also attended Booker T. Washington Business College in Birmingham.

Mrs. Margaret Bell is the epitome of a Southern lady, a charming Southern Belle in every sense of the term. Her soft–spoken drawl, sharp wit and intelligence, crowned with a beaming smile, have cheered and inspired me. Margaret is a cherished, bright spot in my life.

Margaret, at age ninety-six, still lives near Birmingham in the house that she and Charlie lived in. She goes to church as often as she can, and still drives to nearby destinations.

"Margaret, this one's for you." - Sara McFerrin

Acknowledgments

A very special thanks to Richie White for sharing the load and making the task easier; to Grace Howard, a self-proclaimed non-reader, who read the first draft as a favor to me, and then encouraged me to keep going; to my husband Phil for his patience and encouragement; to my smart and capable daughter Geni, on whom I can always count to put the finishing touches on my projects − thanks ever so much! And, thanks to Barbara Klyce and Nan Bishop, who cheered me on at the very beginning when Glover was a jumbled mess of ideas.

Jamie Claire Joyner went the second mile. Her invaluable advice and expertise are so greatly appreciated. Thank you, thank you, Jamie.

Chapter One
Getting to Know Glover

Click! The wall switch shot a surge of electricity to an overhead fixture in the Daniels' tiny spotlessly clean kitchen as it silently awaited another day of non-stop activity. Soon aromas of perking coffee, baking biscuits, and sizzling bacon would be like a warm, comforting hug to jump start a new day.

Glover Daniels moved quietly to the icebox, careful not to awaken his wife Doris or the children. The clock was ticking and he had no time to lose. First things first. He stooped to pull an enamel pan from underneath the icebox. Being careful not to slosh melted ice on the floor, he emptied the pan in the sink and quickly scooted it back underneath with his boot. Glover then went about his daily routine gathering items, as he'd done the morning before, as he would do the next morning.

Rumors are flying like a bunch of blind bats blastin' loose from hell, he thought while putting lunch fixin's on the countertop. A troubling feeling crept around his insides. *I hope it's a rumor. Has to be. Ever'body says there'll be layoffs tomorrow. Makes no sense. There's plenty of work*, he reasoned.

He'd set out a bowl of butterbeans, a jar of Hellmann's mayonnaise, and a Pyrex bowl filled with deviled ham, mustard, sweet pickle relish, and diced onions that he had mixed the night before. Opening the oven door with one hand, he grabbed a loaf of Merita bread from the makeshift breadbox with the other, careful to close the oven door so it wouldn't snap shut and wake the children.

God forbid I wake up Amanda. She'll cry loud 'nuff to wake the dead, he reminded himself.

1

Glover plugged in Pasquali, the percolator. Whether an Alabama-thing or just peculiar to the Daniels household, they often gave names to inanimate objects they considered a part of the family. He'd filled the pot with water and scooped dark coffee grounds into its perforated basket the night before. The gleaming chrome percolator hissed like a cornered snake, and then mellowed into a hushed hum as its coils heated to fiery red. Finally, Pasquali happily hiccupped as boiling water rhythmically dripped through the grounds.

Opening the cellophane sack, Glover leaned over and sniffed. There was still a whiff of freshly baked bread, even if it was a couple of days old. His rough, calloused fingers grasped four slices of soft white bread. For a moment, he toyed with the idea of making toast.

"Nah, no time, an' I better leave the bread for the kids," he muttered in a soft Southern drawl, while twisting the top of the bag before returning it to its nesting place inside the cold oven.

His world was Marianne, Molly, and Amanda, his children, his babies, his girls. The love of his life, his sweetheart Doris, came to mind, mustering a warm, smiley feeling within.

The hardest part will be tellin' Doris and th' girls that I lost my job. They'll be disappointed, an' I hate that. His heart ached at the very thought.

Focusing on the task at hand, he laid the bread slices side by side atop a worn, red linoleum countertop and removed the lid from the butterbean bowl. He stared at large white limas, comfortably snuggled in congealed bean juice, like sleeping babies. For a split second, he hesitated to disturb them; then he reached for a tablespoon and dipped heaping spoonfuls of the jelled beans onto one slice of bread. Carefully, he slathered

2

mayonnaise on the other slice and flipped it over to cover the bean-laden bottom layer. After a tap or two with the palm of his hand to even the spread (but not enough to squeeze it past its borders) he placed the sandwich slap dab in the middle of a well-worn square of waxed paper.

Glover tried to get a week out of each square, but the creases from being folded and unfolded had worn away the wax and left tiny tears. Even so, it would do for this day, so he folded the wrinkled paper around the sandwich as neatly as a nurse making a hospital bed.

Compounding worry from rumors that there would be layoffs at the pipe foundry was news that Doris had recently announced.

"We're expectin' baby number five in February," she'd whispered in Glover's ear, when she could no longer attribute morning sickness to a mysterious illness that had nothing to do with a developing fetus.

"Are you glad?" she asked hesitantly.

"You know I am!" he said as he clutched her close to him and twirled around. She started to say something else, but he kissed her words away.

He and Doris had married in 1932, when he was twenty and she was seventeen. He'd hit the jackpot. She was everything that he had hoped to find in a life mate, and after seventeen years of marriage, she still made him feel like the luckiest man alive.

I hope it's a boy this time. I wouldn't take a million dollars for any one of my three girls, an' a boy won't replace our precious son. Still, I hope it's a boy, he thought.

In 1941, he'd buried his only son, who had been killed by lightning. Memories of seven-year-old Jackson, rain trickling down his freckled face, were like knives twisting in Glover's

3

flesh. It seemed like yesterday when a sudden summer storm had unleashed cataclysmic bursts of lightning. Jackson Daniels had scurried to the front porch, the door slamming behind him. He suddenly remembered he'd left his toy trucks parked beneath the tree. He dashed out to get his toys when lightning struck the giant oak. In that same moment, Glover opened the door to see his only son thrown ten feet across the muddy yard, instantly lifeless.

With time and a great deal of effort, Glover had hidden memories of that devastating tragedy in a secluded corner of his mind, safely out of reach from conscious thought. Remembering was more than he could manage.

Focusing on the task at hand, Glover moved on to the deviled ham. With a butter knife piled high, he smeared the mixture on one slice of bread and folded it in half. Repeating this process, deviled ham sandwich number two came together. He folded crinkled waxed paper around the sandwiches, and then stacked them inside his lunchbox.

Using his index finger, he scraped the bowl slick and clean of all traces of ham filling. Pungent mustard made his tongue tingle as he licked the yummy spread from his finger, then carefully, he placed the bowl in the sink, so as not to make a clinking sound and wake anyone. A generous slice of buttery pound cake rounded off the lunch menu for the day. He closed the lid and set the box near the door in plain sight, lest he forget it.

"Coffee. I need coffee," he said aloud, although the only one present to hear was he.

Strong coffee streamed from the percolator's spout into his mug. The wafting aroma was intoxicating. Glover slowly inhaled to savor every second, while placing leftover biscuits and crispy fried fatback on an ironstone plate.

Pulling up a ladder-back chair to their enamel-top table, he tilted a crock pitcher full of sorghum, generously drizzling syrup over everything on the plate. From a dark, sticky puddle he speared a chunk of biscuit, put it in his mouth, and savored the taste of buttery sweetness. Chasing it down with a few bites of bacon, he glanced at the clock on the stove. Where had time gone? It was later than he thought. Quickly scarfing down the rest of his breakfast, he gulped the last swallow of coffee then cleared away the dishes.

While jabbing his brawny arms into the sleeves of a worn-smooth corduroy jacket, Glover glanced around the kitchen to be sure he had not forgotten anything. Placing his gray felt fedora on his head − adjusting it forward over his right eyebrow and slightly downward until it felt just right − he picked up his lunch box and stepped outside, quietly closing the door behind him.

They never locked the door. As a matter of fact, neither he nor Doris knew where they had put the key − they knew that they had one, but it had been a *blue moon* since they'd last seen it.

As regular as clockwork, Mitchell Chestnut, the iceman, would be making his rounds. After knocking softly, if no one answered, Mitch would go on in and tiptoe about the kitchen, mindful of not waking anyone. Once he'd settled a new block of ice in the upper compartment of the icebox, he'd leave quietly as he'd come. At the end of the week he'd fish money Glover had left to pay for that week's ice out of an amber glass catchall bowl on the countertop.

A soft, gentle breeze caressed Glover's face, prompting him to take a deep breath of September's crisp morning air.

5

He wasn't a homely or unattractive man, but neither was he handsome in the truest sense. Heather blue eyes spoke of his Irish heritage; a charcoal shadow covered his jaw and cleft chin. Jet black hair, outlining ears that stuck out just a wee bit too much, was linked to family tales that somebody generations ago had married a Cherokee Indian, although nobody knew if this supposed relative was a man or a woman. Unlike his brothers that towered past six feet in height, Glover wasn't a tall man. Once, his mother had described his five-foot, nine-inch frame as "stocky." Stocky or not, every inch of his body was solid muscle.

Hurrying across the porch, his steel-toed boots slapped weather-beaten plank steps on the way to the yard. Force of habit reminded him to step over the next-to-last step, the loose one.

It was too early in the month for the air to be nippy, but it had at least lost the heat and humidity of August. Glover reached to pull his hat down a little snugger before he began the walk from his house on Cherry Street to the foundry on 12th Street. There was no way to accurately gauge the distance; two miles was his best guess.

Glover had walked to the foundry so many times that conscious thought was no longer needed to make his way. His feet just seemed to know to follow worn paths that cut through neighboring yards, down the back alley, and out to the main city street.

Streetlights cast a soft glow that emitted a sense of safety, although there was little if any danger on residential streets in Gadsden, AL, in 1949. In fact, Glover and Doris were not the only ones who never locked their doors, day or night. It was an era when deals were finalized with a handshake because a man's word was as good as gold. Dishonesty was not tolerated, privacy was respected; and a man would fight to keep his

6

reputation untarnished.

Glover walked briskly, swinging the lunchbox in his right hand, whistling softly beneath his breath. Although he knew a million songs, more often than not he whistled the tune to "Stardust". The walk seemed shorter if he whistled or sang – he wasn't much of a singer, but he was a born whistler. Seemed like whistling took his thoughts to kinder places – places where smiles were born.

Occasionally, a light shone from a window in an otherwise dark house, prompting him to wonder if a mother was tending her baby, or maybe the breadwinner of that household was getting ready to leave for work.

He reckoned that the sun would overtake the dingy blue-gray of an early morning sky just about the time that he crossed the railroad tracks. From there he could see the foundry's smokestacks.

Another year was creeping toward an end as the decade of the 40's morphed into the 50's. Glover kept up a steady stride and thoughts of the past kept time with his rhythmic pace. He had survived the destitute years of the Great Depression and entered the 1940s with hope for a better future, at the time unaware that a power-crazed maniac named Hitler had plans to conquer the world.

One by one he had confronted painful memories from the sparse years of the 30's, allowing them to strengthen him rather than beat him down. Far too many times he had rummaged in the cupboards knowing there was no food, but searching empty shelves anyway in hopes that he had overlooked even a handful of spilled flour, a few coffee beans, a stray can of soup.

Countless days of looking for work, any work, and the disappointment and despair from repeated rejection had instilled in him a genuine appreciation for his job at the pipe foundry. Glover's yearly income of almost $2,400 was more money than he had even dreamed of earning.

With each brisk step, his lunchbox swung like a clock's pendulum, while memories of WWII played like celluloid film feeding through a projector at the picture show. There were pleasant scenes from his years of Army service at Ft. Robinson, Nebraska, in the Quartermaster K-9 Corps, a special unit where he worked with animals. He enjoyed that more than when he worked with men.

After the war, he came home looking for a fresh start with a renewed determination and firm goals – to focus on family life, new beginnings, and better days. Finding work at the foundry made those goals seem within reach.

Just as he crossed the graveled parking lot to the pipe shop, first light broke overhead, ushering in a new day. Another chance to prove to himself and the world that he was a man, a breadwinner, strong and capable, willing to fearlessly meet the challenges of each day. He opened the paint-chipped metal door, ready to earn his pay.

Straight to the timekeeper's desk he headed. The timekeeper (a short, jolly man in his fifties that everyone called Junior) recorded Glover's arrival time as they exchanged pleasantries and caught up on the latest baseball scores.

"Who's it gonna be?" asked Junior.

"Looks like the Yankees an' the Dodgers," replied Glover. "We'll know soon. My bet's on the Dodgers to win."

Be that as it may, who would play in the World Series was not foremost on Glover's mind, although he had five dollars in the baseball pool.

He was uneasy. Three days ago, his helper Robard

Jacobs (a tall tan man with biceps like cannon balls) asked if he'd heard there would be layoffs at the end of the week.

"One day at a time is my motto," Glover said. "It's 'bout all I can do to handle the bunk that comes up each day. Don't do any good to pile on anythin' extra. It'll all work out, Rob. You lived long 'nuff to know you do whatcha gotta do."

Squelching his concerns for the time being, he placed his lunchbox in its usual place on the usual shelf, carefully balancing his hat on top. It was his one and only hat – a man's hat was a very personal thing.

He hung his jacket on a nail below the shelf while wiggling his finger in his ears. Noise from industrial fans competed with the racket of the furnace. Just minutes before, Glover's thoughts had been shrouded in silence, occasionally interrupted by birds with sweet, melodious song. In contrast, the foundry was a cornucopia of eurythmic sounds, reverberating off an expansive tin roof, so that the men had to yell to be heard.

"How's it goin', Ed? Mornin', Jesse." Glover greeted the night shift workers heading home to catch some shut-eye, as the 6 a.m. shift was just getting started.

Working in an iron foundry was not a job for every Tom, Dick, and Harry – and definitely not for the lazy or effete. The foundry was like a dry sauna from the heat-radiating coke furnace where pig iron, a product derived from the reduction of iron ore in a blast furnace, was melted. Molten iron was poured into molds that cooled and solidified to form castings – in this case, pipe. In summer, the heat was nearly unbearable. Glover nibbled salt tablets to replace sodium lost as sweat seeped from every pore in his body. Hoping to escape the brunt of the heat, the men often came as early as three in the morning and left shortly after midday.

9

An ironworker held a dangerous job, although, so far, Glover had escaped injury. Not everyone had been so fortunate – a summer ago his buddy had been killed as a result of a massive spill. Afterward, morale had hit an all-time low at the plant, and some had quit to find jobs that offered less risk. The commonality of butting heads with hard times had united the men in an unspoken brotherly band, as the loss of one affected all.

Glover hardly minded the noise or the dust or the heat. To him, his aching muscles, his strained back, his tired and sweaty feet inside heavy steel-toed boots, were badges of accomplishment. He didn't take lightly his good fortune in being able to provide for his family – to be healthy and strong.

Glover raised the lid to the hammer bin. Scanning the jumbled maze of mallets, ball peen, and sledge hammers, he searched for his favorite. It fit his hand perfectly, had good balance and weight, and was marked with a small notch near the end of the handle that he had carved with his pocketknife. It was first come, first served. Every now and then his favorite hammer was selected by one of the other men, and this was one of those times.

"Dadgummit," he muttered under his breath. Disappointed, he picked up several hammers, swinging them to get the feel and finally choosing one that would do. He'd considered hiding his favorite hammer so he'd always have it, but somehow that didn't seem right. He was a rule keeper and not inclined toward underhandedness. Next-best hammer in hand, he went about the tiring task of setting molds for the afternoon pour-off.

Glover's stomach was the nearest thing to a watch that he owned. As breakfast wore thin, gastric rumblings signaled the approaching nine o'clock hour. At nine sharp a whistle shrilled above the noise of the foundry, officially declaring break-time, a welcomed twenty-minute rest period.

He took his lunchbox off the shelf, settled his fedora on his head, and walked outside to search for a spot underneath shady, sprawling oaks, where others squatted on the ground or leaned against a tree. Chain-smoker Jerry Jelks drew deep on a cigarette between frequent gut-wrenching coughs. Most of the men unwrapped something sandwiched, baked, boiled, or fried from their lunch boxes.

"I heared it's a sure thang," grumbled Homer Rigsby. Homer had eight children, and his 90-year-old mother lived with them. Altogether, he had eleven reasons to worry about losing his job.

Talk was rampant about possible layoffs. Everyone had an opinion or prediction, none based on reliable information as far as Glover could determine.

"I dread to thank what'll happen if I lose this job," said Lamar Wilkerson. "'Fore I got this job, we like t've starved t' death."

"You ain't tellin' me nothin' I don't know," said Clarence Watson, as he stepped behind a bush to spit a chew of tobaccy. "We gotta boy that can quit school an' git work at the lumber yard. They's wantin' somebody young, but I hate for him t' miss out finishin' school. He's only got one more year. He'll be first in our family to grad-jate high school."

Glover glanced across the way to where six colored men had gathered to smoke, eat, or pass the morning break talking and telling jokes. They worked alongside the white men, but they didn't openly socialize with them. Race was a touchy issue; and ignorant, fear-driven men, who deemed it safer to quietly wade into the stream of racism, rather than think and follow the true convictions of their hearts, kept both white and black people in their "rightful" places. Every man knew that the ultimate price of breaking "the rules" could be a personal encounter with the Ku Klux Klan.

Founded a year after the Civil War by six Confederate veterans from Pulaski, Tennessee, the KKK denounced Negroes, immigrants, Catholics, Jews, and organized labor. The Klan used violence to invoke fear in both blacks and whites. Neither being ostracized by one's peers to the extent of life-threatening danger to self and family nor looking out the window into the dark of night to see a wooden cross wrapped in gasoline-soaked burlap and set ablaze was a risk that many were willing to take.

Hosea Osborne was the only one Glover recognized among the men. They had become acquainted when Hosea moved his family to a small house on a dead-end street that ran not far behind Glover's house. They were good neighbors – Glover sharing vegetables from his garden with the Osborne family, Hosea helping Glover cap an abandoned well at the back of the Cherry Street property.

Ever so cautiously, Glover lived out his convictions that people are people. It was just that simple to him. Nothing complicated, nothing based on anything other than the fact that regardless of physical differences underneath all skin ran red blood. That was the common denominator as he saw it. People are people, his mother had taught him, and if a man earned respect from others, then give honor to whom honor is due.

Hosea worked at the foundry as a stoker, shoveling coal into the mouth of an insatiable furnace. Glover felt sure that Hosea's job was secure. There would be a fire in the furnace as long as pig iron was melted, and somebody would have to feed that gluttonous inferno.

The responsibility of feeding and sheltering families, most with several children, was on the men's shoulders. They − and they alone − were the breadwinners. If they didn't work, kids didn't eat, and bills went unpaid.

Keen-sighted beyond his years, Glover tried to think on other things than the possibility of a layoff looming over their heads, but his fellow worker's words tumbled in his mind like circus acrobats doing somersaults.

He'd financed a Philco floor model radio that not only had AM/FM but also housed a two-speed phonograph. There were two payments remaining. Surely they wouldn't repossess the radio with only two payments left! Come to think of it, he was fixin' to make a payment, so there'd only be one payment left. He could scrape that up somehow, if push came to shove.

Glover smiled inwardly as he thought of himself each night after supper, settled in his navy blue chair with a matching footstool to read the *Gadsden Times*. Doris sat across from him in her gooseneck rocker that had belonged to her mother, and before that, her grandmother. Sprawled about the well-worn rug, squeaky-clean and sweet-smelling, were the children, bathed and dressed for bed. Sounds from the Philco filled the room with magic moments of laughter, suspense, and best of all, *The Grand Ole Opry* every Saturday night.

Two short, shrill toots of the whistle signaled that break-time was half over. Glover listened to Oscar Hill, a gaunt-looking man with nicotine-stained fingers curled around a cigarette, elaborate on how he would lose his home and everything he owned if there was a layoff. Jobs were scarce, especially ones paying union wages.

Suddenly and with certainty, Glover called a halt to his

13

renegade thoughts!

What was it that the Bible said about an unguarded mind being like a city with weak walls? He could never remember exactly how it went, but he had the gist of it.

He decided then and there that he would not allow rumors or gossip to cloud his thinking. He would not be a victim of fear or angst. Nobody knew if there would be layoffs, much less whether such would target him. *One day at a time,* he thought. *There are enough challenges for today, an' tomorrow will take care of itself. Enough of this!*

Glover opened the lunchbox and gazed at the bounty nestled inside. Usually he ate one single-slice sandwich for morning break, but today was different. All this talk had unnerved him. He needed more than deviled ham could offer.

He slowly unwrapped the butterbean sandwich, giving himself time to change his mind. But, no, the soft, plump sandwich called out to him.

Taking a deep breath, he raised it to his mouth and sank his teeth into the tender bread and beans. He closed his eyes to fully capture the intermingled flavors of bacon grease and Vidalia onions used for seasoning, and to thoroughly contemplate how life is better between two slices of bread.

Aroused taste buds relished the pleasure of each bite; his anxiety lessened, and his nerves began to settle. With each mouthful filling his stomach, his spirit rebounded to its usual positive disposition. Full and refreshed, he neatly folded the waxed paper, closed his lunchbox, and headed back to the foundry, contentedly whistling "Stardust". All was well, and life was good.

He caught Hosea's eye and tipped his hat. Hosea nodded his head and quickly followed the other stokers.

14

*

A rowdy rooster, from somewhere in the distance, officially announced the beginning of a new day. "Same thing, different day" could have been his message. But, in the opinion of some, this was the best day in every week. It was Friday. And today, truth or rumor would come to light when the paychecks were handed out.

After emptying the icebox drip pan, Glover set a jar of mayonnaise, a fried pork chop, and a potato pancake, left from last night's supper, on the countertop. It was four in the morning; he needed to leave the house by five. Absentmindedly, he jabbed Pasquali's plug into the wall socket. The usual hissing and humming ensued. Removing half a loaf of Merita from the oven, Glover laid two slices side by side on the counter top, then spread both generously with mayonnaise. Carefully, he trimmed meat from the chop's bone and piled it on one slice of bread. Before adding the potato pancake and topping the whole kit-n-caboodle with the remaining slice of bread, he gnawed the bone like a hungry pup. Who can adequately explain the sheer pleasure and pure, unadulterated satisfaction that comes from gnawing a bone? When there was not a single trace of meat left, he just as thoroughly licked his fingers and placed the bare bone on a saucer to be added to the day's table scraps.

"This is for you, Briscoe," he said as he plunked the bone on the plate. The speckled hound dog in the backyard would devour the bone before the day ended.

Glover loved Fridays. Not only was it payday, but also he looked forward to being off work on Saturday and Sunday. Reaching for a notepad lying on the counter, he checked his list

15

of things that needed to be done:
1. nail down loose board on front step
2. pull up tomato and pole bean stakes
3. clean garden tools/store for winter
4. gather seeds from dried okra
5. pull corn stalks

He would ask a neighbor to turn the dried stalks under with his tractor. Glover's garden spot, out behind the car-less garage, was about twenty-four feet wide by forty feet long. In exchange for plowing, Glover would supply the neighbor with fresh vegetables throughout the summer. (The neighbor grew feed-corn that he traded for beef to someone who raised cattle.) More often than not, services were the common medium of exchange, rather than money.

Laying the list aside, Glover said, "All the talk of lay-offs at the foundry will come home to roost today," quietly talking to himself. He often did that. When a situation called for it, he even answered his own questions.

Maybe the chatter that had buzzed around all week, like a worker bee gathering pollen, was just rumor. Or maybe it was truth. He would find out which today. It had been his experience that truth is such a powerful force that it is seldom denied for long. On more than one occasion he'd seen Truth come to light in spite of Rumor's best efforts to hide it.

On Friday mornings, Glover always fried two eggs, over medium, and two slices of bacon, extra crispy. There were leftover biscuits for sopping the runny egg yolks or topping with blackberry jam made from berries that Doris and the kids had picked. It was his version of a payday celebration. He didn't get many *"attaboy"* compliments – not that he needed to be praised for carrying out his responsibilities. This was his way of rewarding himself. It was his secret. He knew that it was silly; if anyone ever found out, he'd be embarrassed beyond recovery. Glover Daniels enjoyed Friday breakfasts with a generous measure of satisfaction and just a smidgen of guilt.

The time required to fry bacon and eggs caused him to run late. Grabbing his lunch box, he hurried out the door, nearly colliding with Garret Carter, a twenty-year employee of Barkley's Dairy. Elsie the Cow peered from above the shirt pocket of his white uniform, as Garret set a metal carrier cradling four glass bottles of milk outside the door. In exchange, he took four empty bottles, placed there by Molly the night before.

"Mornin', Garret," greeted Glover as he dodged the familiar deliveryman.

"Good morning, Glover. I'm leaving a quart of chocolate milk for the girls to try. Complimentary. Let me know if they like it," he said as he stepped aside. Obviously, Glover was in a hurry.

More often than not, Glover took the milk inside; but today there was no time.

"Garret, if you would put the milk in the icebox, I'd be much obliged," he said. Running down the steps into the darkness, he headed along the familiar route to the foundry. He was never late and could barely tolerate people who felt no obligation to be on time. Glover regarded tardiness as a sign of irresponsibility.

His feet flew, and his thoughts kept time, as he mapped out the day. He'd go straight to the furniture store downtown as soon as he got his paycheck, regardless of whether there was a pink slip along with it or not. It wasn't far − a hop, skip, and a jump − from the foundry to Broad Street where Sterchi's Furniture was on the corner across the street from one of two movie theaters in town.

Broad Street buzzed with activity seven days a week. Put a penny in a sidewalk scale, and a person could get weight and fortune. J.C.Penney, Sears & Roebuck, and W.T. Grant were the largest stores. Snelgrove's Drug Store was usually packed at lunchtime every day, but one could always go to the lunch counter at F.W. Woolworth 5&10, where a three-decker ham-and-cheese cost 50 cents. Any one of the barbers at the barbershop, located on the ground floor of the ten-story Hotel Reich, could give a hot towel/straight razor shave and a haircut for 35 cents. And, women far and wide knew that Fancy Smith at Complete Coiffures pinned a French twist that would last a week, sometimes longer.

Kids were fascinated with the shoe-sizing fluoroscope at the Buster Brown Shoe Store. Once they inserted a foot, they could see bones stuffed inside a shoe. Alabama Power Company and Trofe Dairy, as well as dress shops and general merchandise stores, filled in along the busy street.

At night, under a canopy of glowing English-style streetlights, neon signs above shop doors or shining through storefront windows illuminated the darkness with soft shades of color.

Up and down the street, penny parking meters, lined up like guards at Buckingham Palace, marked angular parking spaces. Fords, Chevrolets, Plymouths, Buicks, and Hudsons made up most of the traffic on the bustling street; but the favorite family car was the 1946 Woody station wagon. Although the price of a new car was more than half a year's salary, Glover longed for his own transportation. "I'm gonna look for a used car soon as I can see a way," he'd said numerous times.

Glover would cash his check at the furniture store and

make a payment on the Philco. Then he'd walk to Kanelo's Fish Market to buy red snapper for their supper. Perch was a better buy at thirty-five cents a pound, but the thick filets of snapper at fifty-six cents a pound would be tastier and go further. Layoff or no layoff, he would treat his family to a fish fry.

Softly whistling "Stardust", Glover crossed the railroad tracks, as daylight broke the eastern sky. He couldn't sing worth a flip, but he could whistle with the best of them. Doris's favorite song played over and over in his head while he thought of her sitting in front of the phonograph – with her eyes closed and a silly, dreamy expression on her face – listening to Bing Crosby croon the lyrics to "Stardust".

Closing the heavy shop door behind him, Glover headed for the timekeeper. God forbid that anyone forget to check in and not get paid for that day. Glover had completed the sixth grade, but many of the men did not read or write, thus the need for a timekeeper. The minimum wage was forty cents per hour, but most made more, even the helpers. This was due to representation by the ironworkers union that demanded fair pay and tolerable working conditions.

A sense of apprehension filled the air. Today they would know who no longer had a job, if in fact there was a layoff. With solemn attitudes the men went about their duties. Glover tried not to let the mood engage him. He knew for a fact that a cheerful person among the sad is as irritating as a drunk among the sober. Therefore, he kept his optimism to himself and went about his business.

Morning hours moved along at the pace of a stubborn mule, followed by lunch, a gloomy occasion as the men dished up dread with their sandwiches and cake. Early afternoon came and went, and soon it was time for the pour-off.

19

A massive bull ladle, attached to a trolley along a monorail hanging from the ceiling, dangled over molds waiting to be filled. Iron was fluid at 2500 degrees Fahrenheit and ready for transfer from the furnace to the bull ladle. The heat of the iron at the time of pouring had an important effect on the properties of the castings. Fiery and glowing, the red liquid looked like flow from an active volcano.

As the overhead ladle was pulled along its track, workers filled the molds. In some instances, a two-man ladle, resembling a longhorn steer's head, was used. When the situation called for it, the ironworker used a one-man ladle with a handle three or more feet long to distance himself from spills or splashes. Powerful hands and brawny arms maneuvered the melted pig iron over the molds. Correct pouring procedures were critical – the dos and don'ts clearly mastered by skilled ironworker Glover Daniels. Speed with which the iron was fed into the molds would determine the characteristics of the castings. Rapid pouring could rupture the core; slow pouring could affect the desired surface hardness.

Having filled the final mold, Glover tended to one last check of the day's work. Satisfied that all was well, he retrieved his lunchbox, slapped his hat on his head, and made his way to the paymaster's office.

It was as plain as daylight that the paymaster was not an ironworker. Raymond Dexter Wright was tall and thin, and his skin looked as if he'd been bleached. Slender, uncalloused hands revealed that his work instrument was a number two pencil, not a hammer or ladle. Dressed in a starched white shirt and gray slacks with razor sharp creases, Raymond's black hair was parted down the middle and plastered so that not a strand was out of place. No, he was not an ironworker, but he was an important person in the whole of things. He couldn't pour iron; the ironworkers couldn't tally figures or keep books. They needed each other, and there was a mutual respect that united them.

"Y'all get on up here. Crowd in close so ever'body can hear." With paychecks in hand, the paymaster shouted for the men to gather around for an announcement from Jerry Edgar Wallis, the foreman.

Nervously, the men shifted from foot to foot as they waited for stragglers to bring up the rear.

When everyone was present, Jay Ed, as he was better known, hopped up on a 55-gallon drum to address the group. Many of the men, with expressions of dread and worry clouding their faces, stared at the dirt floor, just waiting for the ax to fall.

Speaking loudly over the noise of the fans, Jay Ed said, "I've got some news. There's some changes comin'."

He pushed his thick bifocals up on his nose and scratched his left ear. Jay Ed couldn't see past a foot in front of him, with or without glasses. The men at the back of the gathering were little more than a blur.

"These changes won't affect everybody. We've lost one of our biggest pipe customers, and 'til we're able to fill that void, the company's had to come up with a Plan B."

Pausing to reach inside his back pocket and pull out a crumpled white handkerchief, he wiped his nose. The crowd stood motionless while the squint-eyed man wadded the handkerchief and stuffed it back in his pocket. He adjusted his glasses, cleared his throat, and finally continued as the anxious group looked on.

"After a lot of consideration, they've decided to try a new product. They've got an order for 2000 pot-bellied stoves."

Total silence ensued while the men grasped what Jay Ed

21

had told them. Momentarily, a murmured sigh of relief spread among the surprised workers like a wave washing over a sandy beach.

Jay Ed's deep bass voice drew their attention once again to the matter at hand as he bellowed, "I need forty volunteers to train to work on this project. The pay is ten cents an hour more. Could be some overtime. I'm not sayin' there will be. I'm not sayin' there won't be. It'll take a while to get familiar with the new molds. Anybody ready for a change o' pace?"

Glory Hallelujah!!

As the veil of dread lifted, each man shook hands with someone near him. Lamar Wilkerson pumped Homer Rigsby's hand and pounded him on the shoulder. The men laughed; some were teary-eyed. All were filled with gratitude that they'd dodged a phantom bullet.

Glad to have something to discuss other than the impending doom of layoffs, a buzz rose from the crowd as each man weighed the pros and cons of signing up for this new venture.

Interrupting the men, Jay Ed spoke again. "I only got forty slots to fill!" shouted the foreman. "If you're up to this and sure you wanta do it, holler out your name. Raymond'll sign y'all up rite on the spot."

"Castleberry!"

"Tanner!"

"Wesley!"

"Ford!"

"Howard!"

Several men spoke loudly and clearly, as the paymaster wrote their names on a sign up sheet.

Glover was comfortable in his duties, but comfortable or

not, he wasn't inclined to make sudden changes. With new business out of the way, the paymaster handed out the checks, in lieu of pink slips.

"Daniels," called Raymond Wright. Glover stepped forward to receive his pay, and then like a homing pigeon, he headed for the furniture store downtown. From there he proceeded to the fish market, then fifteen blocks or so down Fifth Street toward the old frame house on Cherry Street.

Glover knew when he'd enter the kitchen, with the fish tightly wrapped in brown paper tied with cotton string, that he would find preparations for a fish supper well underway. Homegrown potatoes, cut into French fries, would be floating in a bath of cold water to keep them from turning brown. Hushpuppy batter would be chilling in the refrigerator, while shredded cabbage and carrots marinated in a mayonnaise, sugar and vinegar dressing. Doris would have a mixture of coarse-ground corn meal and flour, generously seasoned with salt and pepper, ready to coat the fish filets. Filled with lard, iron skillets he'd made at the foundry would be sitting on the stove, ready to cook the fish and fries to a golden, crispy brown.

Had he thought about it in time, he would have walked past the movie theater to see what was playing. But Glover had fish on his mind, and he knew that there were those at home listening for the squeaky floorboards on the front porch to signal his arrival.

*

Autumn breezes flirted playfully with orange, scarlet, and canary yellow leaves. Some banded with the gentle wind and tumbled through crisp, cool air before settling on the ground. Others clung stubbornly to the tree's branches, fighting a losing

23

battle.

Sunrise came later as the days grew shorter. It was dark when Glover left home and dark when he arrived at the foundry. Only in the afternoon, on the way home, did he get to enjoy painted leaves in all their glory. He recalled how he'd watched these same leaves bud last spring. By midsummer they'd become oases, blocking the sun's glare.

Another autumn faded into winter. Glover walked the familiar path to the foundry, regardless of rain or shine. On stormy days, his boots and pants legs got soaking wet sticking out from underneath his knee-length rain slicker. No harm. The heat of the foundry soon drank them dry.

When patches of ice spotted the sidewalk, and winter's wind blew cold, Glover hunkered down inside his wool overcoat. Furry earmuffs, the band tight on his head stretching from ear to ear underneath his hat, made it easier to brave the elements on his way to and from work.

The months flew by as quickly as the leaves had blown from the trees. Another Christmas came and went. Another decade ended.

After two World Wars and the Great Depression, Americans were filled with hungry hopes, yearning for a time of peace and prosperity. Time, and only time, would reveal whether the 1950s would be the decade of deliverance.

Along with his fellow countrymen, Glover Daniels was filled with great expectations as a new decade dawned.

Chapter Two
Getting to Know Doris

An Arctic wind, wailing like a banshee caught in a bear trap, stung his cheeks when Glover Daniels stepped outside the foundry. January lived up to its reputation as the coldest month of the year with below-freezing temperatures throughout the day. He pulled his fedora down around his ears to anchor it from sailing away, jammed his hands into the pockets of his overcoat, and geared down for the long haul, setting his bearings toward home. Icy gravel crunched beneath his boots as he hurried across the parking lot.

Beep, beep, beep.

Glover glanced over his shoulder to see a car pulling up alongside of him.

"Need a ride?" inquired the driver.

No need to ask twice. The offer was received with a flood of appreciation. Without a moment's hesitation, Glover jumped upon the running board and into the passenger seat. With a hearty slam of the door, he welcomed refuge from the wind.

Glover recognized the driver, a co-worker, who was a core setter at the foundry. Although they didn't work in the same area, they often talked at union meetings, sometimes played cards afterward, and were known to occasionally share a swig of moonshine when it was passed around. Glover had never been introduced to the man but had heard others call him Buddy.

"Hey, Buddy." Glover shook Buddy's extended hand. "It's colder'n a well-digger's butt out there."

"You ain't jist whistlin' Dixie." Buddy reached over and dialed the heater to high.

A steady flow of warm air blasted from the 1940 Ford sedan's heater, as the little black car rolled to the edge of the parking lot. Looking both ways, Buddy shifted into first gear and eased into the traffic.

"Whar' to?" Buddy inquired.

Glover pointed as he gave directions to Cherry Street and watched closely. His chauffeur shifted into second and then third gear. The classic sedan became the focus of conversation as it glided along frosty streets, its motor purring like a contented kitten.

Buddy explained, "This baby's a humdinger. The engine's a 85 HP Flathead V-8."

Bragging like a proud papa, Buddy pointed out the hydraulic brakes and an extra seven inches in the span of the seats that set it apart from previous models.

Its well-pleased owner swerved to miss a pothole.

"I 'herited this li'l darlin' from my wife's grandpap. He passed on last month. Pappy was her only owner an' he babied her like a new calf."

"Well, to tell the truth," said Glover, "I've never owned a car. But Lord knows I want to. I'm gettin' somethin' just soon as I can see a way."

He pondered whether to tell Buddy about one small stumbling block; not only had he not owned a car, he'd never driven one. He thought that he probably could drive from having watched others. Dozens of times in his mind, he'd pushed the clutch to the floor and applied the brakes, bringing the imaginary car to a smooth stop. He'd practiced mentally easing the clutch out while gently pressing on the gas pedal, applying equal pressure on both. There were only three gears – how hard could it be? No two ways about it, in his mind he could drive a car – on a road, maybe not.

Before he realized it, his thoughts had become words and he blurted out, "I haven't act'ally driven a car. I think that I could. I know that I could, but so far, I just haven't had a chance. We've never known too many people that own cars."

Well, things were about to change. Not only did Buddy give him a ride home, he also offered to give driving lessons.

It was a done deal. The first sunny Saturday they'd go to the old airport where Glover could learn to drive on a deserted runway. In the meantime, he would get a learner's permit and a handbook to study for the driver's license test. Glover was as happy as a Christmas elf.

The hour that it usually took to get home from work was accomplished in less than half the time and in considerably more comfortable circumstances. As the shiny black car, generously adorned with chrome, pulled to the curb in front of his house, Glover again said "much obliged" and hopped out. Bone-chilling wind prompted him to scurry inside the warm house.

The smell of simmering vegetable soup and freshly baked cornbread escaped as Glover opened the front door.

In the heat of late July and early August, vegetables that were gathered from the garden were destined to become soup mix that would bring a hint of summer to a cold, winter day. Tomatoes were allowed to ripen until they were too ripe to slice and serve, but not so ripe that they were spoiled. With the sharpest knife, corn was methodically cut and scraped from the cob, green beans snapped, and purple hull peas shelled. All were combined in the largest stockpot that they owned and cooked until tender but not done, then ladled into sterilized quart-sized Mason jars. After a water bath in the canner, the boiling hot jars were set aside to cool until the lids sealed with a click. They were stored in the pantry where they sat like prized trophies to await winter's arrival. When potatoes, onions, and carrots were added to the mix, along with a generous chunk of fatback, a steaming pot of vegetable soup fit for a king fed the family.

"Daddy! Daddy! Daddy!"

Before he'd taken off his overcoat, Glover was greeted by the delighted squeals of his three-year-old, Amanda. Blonde curls bouncing and sky-blue eyes sparkling, she ran toward him with outstretched arms. Glover scooped her up to be smothered with teeny, wet kisses. Ten-year-old Marianne and eight-year-old Molly followed the commotion to embrace their father and welcome him home.

This is what life is all about, he thought. This was why he worked and planned and somehow made a way when there seemed to be none. These children, totally dependent on him, drew the best out of him. They made him reach higher and try harder. Their innocent trust in him hid his many shortcomings and motivated him to dream big dreams.

The moment that Doris appeared in the doorway, a solemn expression clouding her pretty face, Glover knew that something was wrong.

As he leaned to kiss her, he nuzzled his stubby beard against her ear lobe and whispered, "What's the matter?"

Without a word, Doris reached into her apron pocket, pulled out a letter, and inconspicuously handed it to him as she told the girls to put the butter dish and cornbread on the table. Glover scanned the handwritten page.

The letter was from Doris's sister Avis, telling that their mother was gravely ill. The seventy-year-old woman had suffered from a series of bouts with pulmonary problems for the past year. Phthisis had weakened her immune system causing her

28

body to fall prey to an outbreak of shingles. The doctor had admitted her to the hospital for a treatment of intravenous injections of sodium ascorbate; large doses of vitamin C were the usual approach to combating shingles in 1950. Avis suggested that Doris come as soon as possible just in case, God forbid, things took a turn for the worse.

It was sixty miles from Gadsden to Talladega, Doris's hometown. Usually the trip took little effort; but not this time, as she was about six weeks away from birthing a baby. Also, the winter weather could make traveling more difficult. The older girls were in school, and then there was the money for train tickets to consider. Glover would mull these things over and come up with a plan; and they would talk about it after the children were in bed.

The steaming soup was a confetti of colors in crock bowls — yellow corn, orange carrots, white onions and potatoes, green beans and brown peas floated in a rich, red tomato broth.

All heads bowed; Marianne said the blessing. "God is great. God is good. Let us thank Him for this food."

In unison, each joined in with a final, "Amen."

Glover fished the fatback from the soup tureen and sliced it thinly. "Too much fat will make you sick," he said as he placed a bit in each bowl. He always served fat with the same warning, but it was so tasty all were willing to take the risk.

"Y'all leave room for rice puddin' with cinnamon raisin sauce," Doris said as she filled the girl's glasses with milk.

By bedtime he would have a plan. He was the leader and decision maker in this family. Glover Daniels never failed them.

After the dishes were washed, dried, and put away, and the children were dressed for bed, Glover clapped his hands and said, "Let's count the money in the bank."

29

Doing this on a weekly basis not only kept a tally of cash on hand, but it also taught the girls to count money and make change. This bank was actually a mustache cup that sat behind an empty sorghum syrup can on the top shelf of the kitchen pantry.

Off-white with gold trim, the porcelain cup had belonged to Doris's grandfather. Photographs of the old man showed why he needed a cup with a clever sieve-like insert that was designed to keep hair over the upper lip away from contents in the cup. Grandfather sported a handlebar mustache, looking to span twelve or more inches, and obviously plastered in place with a generous amount of mustache wax. The cup had served Grandfather well, and now it had an even loftier calling. It was a perfect place to bank spare change and bills set aside for rainy days.

Stretching on his tiptoes, Glover reached behind the syrup can to fetch the cup. The girls were anxious to dump the contents on the kitchen table and then sort the coins and paper money.

Marianne counted bills while Molly counted quarters, dimes, and nickels. And with Doris's help, Amanda counted pennies. The sum total was $18.74. Glover removed a five-dollar bill and put it in his billfold. Tomorrow he would go by the L & N Depot and buy tickets for the trip and check the time schedule. Change left over would go to Doris, in case she needed money while she was away.

Bedtime was eight o'clock sharp on schooldays.

"Sleep tight. Don't let the bedbugs bite," teased Doris as the girls climbed into their beds. Glover kissed freshly scrubbed cheeks and tucked the children under layers of handmade quilts; then he turned the gas heater down on low for the night. A chill quickly settled throughout the old house. First one up each morning, which was usually Glover, turned the heater on high to chase away the cold.

A round wind-up alarm clock sitting on the bedside table ticked redundantly, as Glover felt the goose down and feather mattress settle beneath him.

"How sweet it is," he said as a wave of relaxation swept over his body. He pulled a mountain of quilts up to his chin and snuggled close to his wife, in the spot warmed by Doris before she had moved over to her side.

Staring at the ceiling of the dimly lit room, Glover spoke in a hushed tone. "I'll get train tickets on the 4:15 for Friday. Y'all take a taxi to the train station, an' I'll meet y'all there at four." It was unspoken but clearly understood that Amanda would accompany her mother.

"Marianne and Molly'll be home by the time you get back," Doris replied. "You keep them on Saturday, then take them to Bessie Pearl's on Sunday mornin' in time for Sunday school."

Neighbor and good friend, Bessie Pearl Pennycutt would care for them and see that they got to school on Monday, Tuesday, and Wednesday. Bessie, a widow and retired schoolteacher, lived two doors down from them.

Doris continued, "I'll make arrangements with Bessie Pearl tomorrow, an' I'll go to Troncali's to use their phone an' call Avis an' tell her what time we'll get there so somebody can meet us at the train station. It'll be dark by the time we get there."

Marie Troncali, the neighborhood grocer's wife, gladly shared her telephone, as it was one of few in the neighborhood. The telephone operator would tell Doris the cost of the call, and

Doris would pay Mrs. Troncali.

"Catch an earlier train back on Wednesday an' take a cab from the depot." Glover patted her belly and kissed her cheek.

"'Night." she turned over and bunched the pillow under her head.

"I'm missin' you already." He snuggled close to her backside and closed his eyes.

Every minute of the next two days would be spent packing and tying up loose ends. Nearly eight months of pregnancy slowed Doris down, requiring more effort to accomplish the simplest things.

She was worried about her mother and wanted to see her. Doris needed to go home.

*

A few travelers milled about the L & N Depot on First Avenue. As the local hub for one of the nation's premier railroads, the Louisville and Nashville, the old Spanish Colonial style train station had been a stalwart for the town. The L & N had played a vital role in the growth of industry and commerce. It was a popular means of transportation when going long distances, especially for those who typically depended on their feet to get from one place to another. Started in 1850 in Kentucky with less than 300 miles of track, the L & N had grown to a 6,000-mile system that spanned 13 states. It had survived the Civil war and economic depression, while operating both freight and passenger trains.

Glover spotted Doris when he opened the door to the waiting room at the station. She was wearing her calf-length, black wool coat, which no longer buttoned due to her expanding waistline. A rust-colored felt cloche covered her ears from the cold. Amanda looked like a doll dressed in her burgundy coat with matching leggings; curly blonde curls straying from underneath her bonnet. Her tiny hands were stuffed into a white furry muff that looked like a giant marshmallow hanging from a ribbon draped around her neck.

No sooner had Glover given them each a hug, they heard the whistle of engine Number 85 approaching the station. Moving to the outside platform, they spotted the powerful iron horse edging closer on trembling rails. The majestic cortege puffed into the station and slowly rolled to a screeching halt. The conductor hopped down, carrying a step stool and positioned it under the door to the passenger car, as if he had done this a million times before. Number 85 straddled the track making hoarse, rhythmic, throbbing sounds, like a breathless runner gasping for air.

Passengers said their farewells, luggage was loaded, and any business that needed to be conducted by the engineer, conductor, porters, or terminal employees took place.

At last, with all passengers seated, the step stool was placed inside. Number 85 was ready for the fifty-nine mile trip from Gadsden to Talladega, a trip that would take a little less than three hours. The conductor stood in the doorway with one last call – "AAALLLLL AAABBOARDDDDD!!!!" Upon hearing the all clear signal, the engineer revved the mighty engine to a thunderous roar, interspersing several ear-piercing whistle blasts.

Massive iron wheels groaned as they strained to set the train in motion, until slowly it began to roll forward. Squeals of metal grinding against metal signaled that the train was gradually gaining speed, rolling toward the next stop.

33

Hands buried deep in his pockets, Glover shivered from the cold, although he had on a heavy sweater under his coat. He stood on the depot platform until the red caboose was almost out of sight, struggling with the feeling that part of him was moving farther and farther down the tracks. When the train was out of sight, he pulled his collar up around his neck and headed home.

Leaning into the wind, Glover's thought of Doris' jade-green eyes that sparkled as if they were connected to a source of life from somewhere deep within her soul. He loved the way her light-brown hair glistened red when the sun shone on it. It looked neat and ladylike when she wore it pinned up in a French twist; his heart fluttered when he thought of how her hair looked unpinned and hanging loose around her shoulders. Like the women in her family, she was tall − at least 5'8" − just an inch shorter than Glover. If he had to name his favorite thing about her − although he could think of several things to choose from − it would be her bubbly, contagious laugh.

Soft-spoken,well-mannered, a lover of music and books, Doris was his Southern lady. Their first years together were lean years, but they'd struggled through and stuck together. In spite of marrying young, they'd grown up and grown strong together.

Glover opened the front door at home to find the girls with their homework scattered on the floor near the gas heater. A blue flame flickered to adequately warm a radius of a few feet; beyond that the room was chilly. The house was old. Probably fifty years old, maybe more. Wainscot framed the rooms halfway up the walls; from there faded wallpaper climbed to ten-foot ceilings. The floors, same as the wainscot, were dark-stained oak. Doris had insisted on a sofa with blonde bamboo arms covered in a print of bold red roses on a white background. It was on sale at Sterchi's Furniture, and although the sofa matched

34

not one other thing in the entire house, she fell in love with it. In Glover's opinion, the sofa should have been on sale; or better yet, somebody should have been standing at the door trying to give it away!

Like candlelight in the night, Doris's sofa stood out amongst the dark wood, Duncan Phyfe coffee table, and her antique gooseneck rocker. To appease Glover, they had purchased him an upholstered chair with a matching footstool. That quieted his protest of the bamboo sofa, for a while anyway. Doris counted on him liking it after he'd gotten used to it. That was yet to happen.

While waiting for Glover, the girls had set the table with Doris's everyday dishes. For quite some time, she had collected *Autumn Leaves,* offered by the Jewel Tea salesman, who delivered household items weekly. Although she would never tell Glover, she sometimes bought cleaning products or baking soda that she didn't really need just to get coupons. When she'd saved enough coupons, she redeemed them for a plate or cup or some piece to add to her set. Jewel Tea also offered a pattern called *Fiesta* – heavy, colorful stoneware – but she chose *Autumn Leaves* because the fall of the year was her favorite season.

Doris had left a tuna noodle casserole that was ready to pop into the oven. Marianne and Molly had cooked it and made a fruit salad from canned pears. A few biscuits, warmed-up, and iced tea completed a tasty meal that they all dug into. When the dishes were washed and dried, Glover fed Briscoe while Marianne turned down the beds. The kids didn't have to be told what to do; they just went about their chores. They'd been trained well by a mother who wanted her daughters to grow to be strong, confident women and capable homemakers. Glover was so proud of both of them.

Doris always cleaned the house from top to bottom on Saturday mornings. Marianne and Molly helped with the mopping and heavier cleaning. Amanda was in charge of dusting.

When everything was spic-and-span, the two older girls received their weekly allowance of a quarter each. Amanda only got a nickel – the larger the job, the greater the compensation. As soon as the chores were finished, the older girls made a beeline from Cherry Street, fifteen blocks into town, straight to the movie theater.

The long walk to the theater did not faze them, and they never complained. They knew walking was just part of getting someplace, and it was totally safe for children to be out and about on their own.

The Saturday festivities at the picture show often worked into a full day's event. Showing on the silver screen would be a double feature movie, a cowboy serial, several cartoons, and the Movietone news. The theater opened at 10 a.m. More often than not, the kids didn't start the walk back home until 4:00 in the afternoon. Abbott and Costello, the Three Stooges, Hopalong Cassidy, Roy Rogers and Dale Evans, Red Rider, or the Bob Hope and Bing Crosby road movies could be seen for ten cents, the cost of a movie ticket. With a quarter to spend, that left fifteen cents to buy a drink and two nickel candy bars or a drink and one candy bar and one popcorn. The movies ran again after the first go-round; if the moviegoer wanted to see them a second time there was no additional charge. That was a typical Saturday, but tomorrow would be different with Doris out of town.

Bedtime on Friday nights was extended to 8:30 because there was no school the next day. As this Friday came to a close, three members of the Daniels family huddled near the gas heater to listen to the radio. Glover adjusted his specs as he unfolded the newspaper. Truth be told, they weren't actually *his* eyeglasses. Doris's aunt Celeste had lost them during a visit several years ago. When they'd turned up, long after she'd returned home, Glover decided to try them out. He couldn't see diddly-squat when he looked across the room, but the words jumped off the newspaper when he looked down through the thick lenses.

The sisters sat on the rug with their Shirley Temple dolls and played "beauty shop." Glover knew that before the little hand of the clock was on eight and the big hand was on six, there would be curlers in his hair. Per the girl's instructions, he would pretend to be under the hair dryer while reading his newspaper.

Of these things he was certain. He'd been to this beauty shop on other Friday nights.

*

Not only was there no house cleaning on Saturday morning until Doris returned, but Marianne and Molly were also in for another treat. They would not have to walk to town to the movie. Buddy was coming to give Glover his first driving lesson while the girls were at the picture show. Their daddy gave them each a quarter and told them to get ready to travel in Buddy's car. Both children were excited since car rides were few and far between.

Warmly dressed and antsy to get to the picture show by ten, the girls took turns watching out the front window for Buddy.

"He's here! He's here!" they shouted as the black sedan

37

pulled to the curb. Glover ushered the exuberant kids out the door, down the steps, and into the car with its heater blasting away.

A few minutes later, they let the girls out in front of the Princess Theater, where the sidewalk was crawling with excited children lining up to buy tickets. Marianne and Molly hurried to the end of the line.

Buddy pulled back into heavy morning traffic, heading the snazzy black car toward the outskirts of town. It was a toss-up as to whether Glover was more nervous or excited. Maybe driving was harder than he thought it would be. What if he caused some irreparable damage to Buddy's car? It didn't take long before the what-ifs were about to get the best of him, as what-ifs are prone to do.

Calming down, Glover reasoned with himself. *There are thousands of drivers on the roads these days. They all learned from scratch. If they can, I can.* Bolstered confidence was building as they neared the turnoff from the paved road to a dirt cut-through that led to the end of a deserted runway.

Abandoned, when several years ago a new airport was built on the other side of town, the runway now served as the perfect place for novice drivers.

The car rolled to a stop in the center of the asphalt strip. Buddy slid across the seat to the passenger side, and Glover ran around and got into the driver's seat. Grasping the wheel with both hands to get the feel of it, he took a deep breath, relaxed, and focused on the task at hand.

"Take 'er easy, fr'end. Git your mirror turned jist rite so ya can see what's behind you."

After adjusting the rear view mirror, Glover turned the ignition key. The car leaped forward with such a jerk that his

38

fedora tilted on his head.

"Man, ya gave me whiplash!" joked Buddy as he regained his composure, after nearly bumping his head on the windshield. He remembered his first time behind the wheel. He all but burned the clutch out of an old Chevy that his daddy had won in a poker game.

First things first. Glover pushed the clutch to the floor and *then* turned the ignition key. The engine sprang to life and idled smoothly. Now, to shift into first gear. He wasn't exactly sure where that was, so he grasped the knob on the end of the gearshift and proceeded to move it this way and that.

Buddy watched. "It's better fer you t' find firs' gear without me tellin' you. It takes a time or two t' get the hang of it, but ya will. Now, don't make this hard. It ain't brain surgery." Twenty-eight-year-old, blonde-haired, brown-eyed Buddy, with dimples the size of jumbo jellybeans, was grinning from ear to ear.

When Glover was satisfied that the gearshift was where it was supposed to be, he eased up on the clutch and down on the gas pedal. The car lunged forward in a series of jumps and leaps, like a toad with his toes on fire. Once again the motor stalled, and the car rolled to a standstill.

This was harder than he'd thought. No two ways about it. It was definitely easier to drive in his imagination than it was in reality.

"This ain't genius stuff. Thank 'bout all the drivers on the road. They all had a first lesson, ya know. Now, le's do this, man. Ya good 'nuff to pour arn in yur sleep, so I know ya can drive."

Don't count your chickens before they hatch came to Glover's mind, but he didn't say it.

39

At Buddy's insistence, he once again held the clutch to the floorboard with his boot and started the car. Finally! After two or three tries, Glover managed to steer the vehicle along smoothly.

"Man, ya got it now. I told 'ya. We cruisin' 'long, livin' the life of Riley." Buddy clapped his hands like a child. Ever adventurous, he loved a challenge, and he loved to win. He never once intended to leave until Glover was driving like a pro.

Turn signals were given by an outstretched arm pointed in the direction of the turn. Glover wanted to practice turn signals, but when he rolled the window down, frosty air invaded the toasty warm car like Teddy's Rough Riders charging up San Juan Hill.

Buddy hollered, "Whoa, iceman! Throw some glass in that hole," as he reached over to turn the heater up. "Ya can practice yur turn signals later while yur sittin' on the john."

Before they realized it, nearly two hours had flown by. Glover's confidence was catching up with his ability. In fact, he was convinced that he was a driver. He wouldn't place any bets that he could pass a driving test, but he could definitely drive on a deserted runway. No two ways about it.

"Call me butter, baby, 'cause I'm on a roll!" Glover shouted and slapped the steering wheel.

Another lesson was scheduled for the following Saturday, weather permitting. With Buddy once again behind the steering wheel, they headed to Cherry Street.

Glover figured, with gas at 18 cents a gallon, a dollar would generously compensate for the fuel that he'd used; but Buddy strongly protested.

"Don't hurt my feelin's, man. Ya don't pay me for nothin'. Fr'ends don't pay each other; they he'p each other out. I might need your he'p someday."

Little did Glover know that day was rapidly approaching.

When dropped off at his doorstep, Glover was on cloud nine from sweet victory. Bidding his brave instructor good-bye, he made a beeline for the kitchen and Pasquali. He needed coffee.

After such an eventful morning, Glover planned to settle into the impression his body had sculptured in the upholstery of his navy blue chair, prop his feet on the matching footstool, and sip coffee while listening to *Bobby Benson and the B-Bar-B* on the Philco.

*

Just in case anyone had forgotten what day of the week it was, townsfolk woke up to church bells tolling "don't be late for church." The temperature had risen into the middle thirties, and the weatherman had promised a break from cold winds. Sunny, clear skies with gentle breezes and temperatures reaching forty-two degrees before the day's end were predicted.

Dressed in his wool suit, a birthday present last year, Glover whistled as he briskly walked to church to meet Bessie and the girls after Sunday school. Glover was not much of a Sunday school person; although more often than not, he made it to the 11 a.m. preaching service each week.

Admiring the toes of his polished wing-tip shoes, he climbed the marble steps of the First Baptist Church and leaned against a majestic Doric column to wait for his children.

He'd had a heck of a time getting tiny, silver cuff links through the French cuffs of his white dress shirt. Then it had taken him ten minutes to decide whether he should wear his gray tie or the blue striped one. Doris would have popped in those cuff links in an instant and selected the blue tie without a second thought. Glover needed his wife at every turn and missed her so much that it hurt. Had she been gone two days or two weeks? It seemed to him like every bit of two weeks.

Brushing tiny flecks of lint off his pants leg, he smiled as he remembered that he'd hoped to get a new hat for his birthday. Doris thought that he needed a new suit more than a hat and had paid the outrageous sum of $28.90 for the double-breasted, pinstriped, charcoal gray suit. More than once he'd thought how he could've bought a sack of new hats for a lot less money. But, the new suit did make him feel a little like Spencer Tracy in the movie *Woman of the Year*.

A buzzer signaled that Sunday school was over, and dismissed attendees poured out of every door like water rushing through holes in a rowboat.

"Daddy, Daddy." Glover turned to see his daughters climbing the steps to meet him. He had dressed them in matching, long-sleeved wool sailor suits and navy leggings. Each girl had a gigantic red hair bow pinned on top of her curly head.

Molly's bow was cocked at a curious angle. It had slightly dislodged when the class had sung, "If you're happy and you know it, jump up and down," and totally dislodged when they'd sung, "If you're happy and you know it, shake your head." Glover adjusted the bow, and the threesome ambled into the sanctuary and found an empty pew near the back.

Following a stirring organ repertoire, the robed choir rose to sing; their beautifully blended voices belting out the "Doxology". Phineas Plyler, minister of music, instructed the congregation to turn in the hymnal to page three-fifty-four. He led as everyone joined in favorite hymns "What A Friend We Have in Jesus," followed by "Love Lifted Me."

Peering through his horn-rimmed eyeglasses, Brother Plyler read announcements before Pastor Willcott stepped to the pulpit to deliver a message. A middle-aged man with thinning hair and a kind face, the pastor told a hokey joke to grab the attention of his listeners; then he read from the book of Jonah in his King James Version. Several times during the sermon, Glover found himself thinking of the pot roast − with carrots, onions, and potatoes cooked around it − that would be on Bessie's dining table shortly past noon. She'd told him what they were having when she'd invited him to dinner.

A twinge of guilt prompted him to discipline his wandering thoughts and plug into the ongoing sermon, which wasn't hard to do. The story of disobedient Jonah, who was thrown overboard a ship and then swallowed by a big fish, could only be told so many ways. Fish. That made Glover think of food, and his wandering thoughts were back to the pot roast. There could be an apple pie. Bessie Pearl Pennycutt was known for her extraordinary, melt-in-your-mouth, slap-your-grandma apple pies. Last fall, Doris had helped core and slice apples. Once dried, they were put on standby for winter pie baking.

As the word "pie" came to mind, he heard the word "die" coming from the pulpit. Having not heard the context surrounding the word, he assumed that Jonah thought that he was going to die, as one might be prone to think while sitting inside a whale. That brought to mind his ill mother-in-law. Glover had always thought of her as a peculiar old woman. He didn't necessarily dislike her. On the other hand, he had the distinct impression that she had never liked him. It seemed apparent to him that she was partial to two of her children and less favorable

43

to the other two. Maybe he was wrong. Right or wrong, Glover didn't want her to die. Be that as it may, he knew that the combination of her age and her ailments did not add up to a bright outcome. He wished her peace no matter what.

As the choir stood to sing the closing hymn, Glover gently shook the girls who had drifted off to sleep shortly after the sermon began. Spotting Bessie Pearl in the second row of the choir, he nodded as she motioned to the right, indicating where she had parked her car.

He made a deal with himself. If she'd baked an apple pie, he would stop after two slices, whether he wanted more or not.

*

At twilight Glover walked along the sidewalk from Bessie Pearl's house to his own, enjoying how the streetlights bathed the neighborhood in a warm glow. The temperature was rapidly dropping and he made a mental note to leave the faucets dripping so that the pipes wouldn't freeze. When he'd gone back to Bessie's to eat a roast beef sandwich for supper and to tell the girls good-night, she'd sent him home with a piece of apple pie to take for lunch the next day. Glover knew that slice of pie didn't have a chance of making it into a lunchbox.

Just as he was about to climb the steps to the porch, he heard a car pull to the curb behind him. To his surprise, the familiar black Ford sedan rolled to a stop, and Buddy quickly got out, slammed the door, and double-timed it up the walkway.

"What's happened?" asked Glover, as they went into the house.

Buddy was as jittery as kids at a slumber party in a haunted house. His brown eyes were round like saucers, and he

44

kept nervously jerking his head to the right to fling a strand of greased hair that kept falling in his eyes.

"Hey, man, I need a he'pin' hand." Buddy jiggled the change in his left pants pocket. "I gotta problem. A big problem. Ah, ya know I wouldn't bother ya, Glover – ah, if this wadn't real important," he stammered and started again. "I hate t' bother ya, but I's just hopin' you'll he'p me out."

"Ya see – ah, I been makin' home brew on the side t' make a few extra bucks. This is jist temporary." He held up his right hand orchestrating each word. "An' I jist got done with a batch, ya see. Ah – well – ah, my brother-in-law got word through his brother-in-law, who knows a feller that works in the sheriff's department, that the Feds are sniffin' 'round 'ere, an' I jist got t' thankin' that the best thang I can do is t' git the stuff outta my place an' hide it somewhere. I know that yur wife an' kids are gone, an' man, I wouldn't askya if it wadn't a 'mergency. Believe me. I wouldn't. Glover ya know I wouldn't, but – ah, do ya have somewheres over here that I can hide it for jist a few days? I'm talkin' jist a day or two." Buddy was talking so fast that it was all that Glover could do to follow him.

Warning bells and whistles went off in Glover's head when he heard Buddy's cockamamie scheme. Glover was always quick to help anyone in need, but this time the favor that was being asked of him was way beyond anything that he'd ever been called upon to do.

Never had Buddy expected that such a dilemma would stem from 25-quart jars of home brew that he'd cooked up! He'd been so engrossed in working on his recipe and hiding the stuff until it fermented that getting caught was low on his list of priorities. Suddenly, what he'd given little thought to had become an urgent issue. Riddled with fear that he was about to be discovered, the novice brewer was forced to move his wares to a safer place – and in a hurry.

As Glover mulled over the dos and don'ts of this situation, he knew that not only was making the foul concoction illegal, but also they lived in a dry county that forbade the sale of alcoholic beverages.

"Oh, no! Not for all the tea in China," said Glover.

"This is a temp'rary sit'ation, man. All the brew'll be sol' on Tuesdee nite after the union meetin'," pleaded Buddy. "I got it promised."

He had hoped that turning to a friend and confidante would provide a solution, but it seemed to be provoking a lengthy debate instead.

"Whoa! Hold your horses! I really don't know what I can do," protested Glover. "Buddy, I'd like to help, but I just don't know 'bout this."

"Fr'end, I'm desp'rate, an' I don't know where else t' turn." Buddy was scared, and it showed. He had a young wife(no children yet), and leaving her to spend time in a federal penitentiary was something that he would rather not do.

Glover's thoughts were racing in his head a mile a minute. If Doris knew, she would be afraid because of the illegal aspects of the situation. There was always the chance that the authorities might know that the brew had been moved and trace it to him. Glover wanted no part of this but hesitated to come right out and say so. He wanted to be a friend. He was appreciative of the driving lesson and the rides home from work, and he liked this fellow a lot; but risky business was more than he wanted.

Be that as it may, Human Reasoning reared its brainy head and whispered that it was only for a short time, and Doris

46

would never know. If she ever confronted him, he could come up with something from that vast plain between the truth and a bald faced lie.

Glover's resistance weakened: he began to lean toward the idea of helping hide the brew.

"I can't think of anywhere we can hide it here that it won't be found. We can look, but there aren't any good hidin' places that come t' mind." Glover reluctantly turned toward the kitchen.

They went throughout the house looking for somewhere the brew would not be discovered should there be a search. Just as he'd seemed to exhaust all possibilities, Glover remembered a loose section of wainscot in the girls' bedroom. By this time he'd given up all resistance; and although he didn't feel good about it, he'd decided to help Buddy.

"Come to think of it, I do know one place that might work."

They examined the wall. Sure enough, a four-foot span of tongue-and-groove beadboard could easily be removed and the jars stored inside. It was on an outside wall, but surely insulation would protect the brew from the cold.

After a few trips to and from the Ford sedan, clutching the Mason jars in brown paper bags, they had all 25 jars neatly stacked inside the wall. A couple of taps with the hammer, and the boards were reattached. Sweat was trickling down Glover's back like he'd plowed the back forty, caused more from tension than being overheated.

"I'll come by after work on Tuesdee and git th' stash. Nobody'll ever know. Don't worry. Hey, man, ya don't know how much I 'preciate this." Buddy, obviously relieved, shook Glover's hand like he was jacking up a two-ton truck.

47

Glover slept restlessly that night, wondering why he had ever gotten snookered into such a scheme. He hated it when his back was against the wall, and he was pressured to go against his better judgment. He just wanted the brew out of his house. Tuesday could not come soon enough.

On Monday, a thick blanket of frost covered the ground as another cold front moved into the area, plummeting temperatures into single digits. Marianne and Molly stayed at Bessie Pearl's since schools were closed due to the weather. Glover leaned into brisk wind, bracing himself against the cold as he made his way along slippery sidewalks to the foundry. Opaque puffs of vapor hung in the frosty air when he exhaled. Playfully, he blew smoke rings, and huffed and puffed like a locomotive – all the time being careful not to inhale too deeply and fill his lungs with a blast of frigid air.

On this day, no one at the foundry was complaining about heat from the furnace. At least they'd had a short break from the harsh weather with a warmer day on Sunday. Alabama weather – one of the great mysteries of life! Especially in January.

After work Glover headed to Bill's Barbeque, hoping that Bill was open for business. Glover was happy as a rescued pup when greeted by a brightly glowing neon sign in the front window that read OPEN – COME IN. Nearly frozen, he clapped his gloves together to warm his hands and hastened his gait. Stepping inside, he was welcomed by pleasant warmth and strands of Eddy Arnold yodeling the "Cattle Call" from a peacock-colored jukebox. Glover's stomach growled when he sniffed aromas coming from the coffee pot and hash browns sizzling on the grill. It wasn't home, but beggars can't be choosy.

"Hey, Glover. What can I do you in for?" joked Bill

Bailer, who looked more like an accountant than a cook.

"How 'bout a barbeque, hash browns, and a bowl o' chili? Throw a spoonful o' slaw on the barbeque, if you don't mind." Glover pulled his leather gloves off and straddled a round stool at the counter. The usually busy cafe was nearly deserted. A young couple huddled in a back booth; a man sat at a table near the jukebox shouting requests to a redheaded woman dropping nickels in the slot.

"You batching it?" Bill flipped a pile of hash browns and two sizzling burger patties, grabbed the coffee pot, and poured Glover a cup all in one fell swoop.

"Yeah, just for a few days. Doris's mama's sick an' she's gone to Talladega."

"Hope it's nothin' serious. Enjoy a little break though. There's a poker game over at Wayne Dill's tonite. Consider yerself invited. His wife's outta town too."

"Thanks anyway. My girls are with my neighbor. I need to check on them," Glover replied as Bill set a steaming bowl of reddish-brown chili in front of him, along with a bottle of hot sauce and a basket of saltine crackers.

The very last thing that Glover wanted to do was to play poker. All he really wanted was to walk in the front door of his house and see his wife. He wanted the home brew off his premises and for things to be normal again.

Little did he know that all too soon his life would be anything *but* normal.

*

Tuesday morning Glover awoke to a whiff of something that smelled like vomit. Springing upright in bed, he wrinkled his nose and pinched his nostrils together.

49

It didn't take a Philadelphia lawyer to figure out the source of the foul odor. Tossing quilts aside, Glover leaped from his warm bed with the speed of a fireman on call.

"No. Oh, no, no, no!" he whined.

His bare feet felt like they were submerged in an icy pond as he, dressed in boxers and a tee shirt, hopped across the hardwood floor. He hurried to the gas heater in the living room to turn it up, only to discover that there was no flame. The heater sat cold, inoperative, and useless.

Glover checked the pilot light. It was out. The safety switch for some unknown reason had shut the unit off sometime during the night. *Thanks for nothing!* He thought.

Striking a match, he turned the lever to activate the gas flow and lit the pilot light. Slowly he turned the handle that regulated the flame. Poof! The gas ignited. A welcomed mixture of red, white, and blue flames danced along the heater's grate like Rockettes at Radio City Music Hall.

Sniffing like a bloodhound, Glover followed his nose to the girls' bedroom.

"No! No! No!" He shook his head sideways as he spotted mousy-brown liquid seeping from underneath the baseboard. A sudden shiver sent him racing back to the bedroom. Poking his feet into the legs of his corduroys, he jerked them up, plucked his flannel shirt off the doorknob, and then sat on the side of the bed pulling on two pair of socks. Returning to the scene of the crime with hammer in hand, he pried the beadboard loose.

Kneeling down to survey the damage, he discovered that all but seven Mason jars (of which he promptly poured the contents down the bathtub drain) had frozen and burst during the night. Most of the foul-smelling brew spilled on the floor when he removed the wainscot. Amid the residual brew were scattered shards of glass and small chunks of ice.

Glover fetched a tall metal trashcan from the kitchen and carefully filled it with broken glass. The overpowering stench intensified when he dipped a cotton string mop into the home brew and wrung it out over a galvanized mop bucket. There was no hot water because the gas water heater had also shut off. *When it rains, it pours.* Glover struck a match to the pilot light, only to wait until the tank heated.

Working quickly, he filled the mop bucket and with red, tingling hands blistered from frigid water, he emptied the stinking contents into the bathtub. Finally, after what seemed like eons, the mess was gone. Although he'd bleached the mop and trash can, the stench of brew still filled the house.

Glover knew that there is a reason why homebrew stinks – Lord knows he'd seen his daddy make enough of it. In addition to the four basic components, bootleggers often added ingredients that were eye pleasing, such as soap to make suds on the brew, or rubbing alcohol for an added kick. Yeast, a basic ingredient, had a very distinct odor whether it was in bread or a quart of "gut rot." No telling what Buddy had put in the putrid stuff, since this was his first batch.

"The Lord works in mysterious ways," Glover said to himself. "Only He knows how many have been saved from stomach crud and Montezuma's Revenge." He nearly always tried to see the good in things.

Intense cold kept Glover from opening the windows to air the place out, and he figured that it would be just his luck that some neighbor passing by would get a whiff and summon the sheriff.

Swinging cabinet doors open and then slamming them

51

shut, he searched the cupboards for Arm & Hammer baking soda. Doris used baking soda to absorb odors in the icebox: it stood to reason that it would attack the sickening stench. He generously sprinkled white powder from a yellow-papered box of soda inside the wall.

Salt. She used salt for everything, same as her mother had. She claimed it would heal wounds, remove stubborn stains, or pickle eggs. Doris even threw it over her shoulder for good luck, not that she was superstitious. He didn't know if it would help at all, but it was worth a try. Glover emptied a box of Morton's table salt on top of the baking soda.

Perfume might help. He'd gotten a bottle of *Evening In Paris,* Doris's favorite perfume and planned to surprise her when the baby came. He waffled on this step. A dollar was more than plenty to pay for perfume just to mask the stink of homebrew. *Oh well, desperate times call for desperate measures. I'll get her another one.*

As he unwrapped the gift, he mumbled to himself, "I coulda saved the three cents I paid t' get this wrapped."

He wadded white tissue paper into a ball and stuffed it in the empty baking soda box. Removing a cobalt-blue bottle from its baby-blue satin lined box, Glover wiggled the ornate silver stopper loose. Vigorously shaking the bottle, he sprinkled droplets of perfume along the baseboard and inside the wall, until every drop he could shake out was soaked into the baking soda and salt.

A somewhat pleasant, somewhat icky odor filled the room.

He'd done all that he knew to do. A few taps of the hammer fit the tongue-and-groove boards snugly in place, sealing the odd potion inside the wall. A quick swipe with a damp rag got the last traces of spill.

Cleaning the disgusting mess had taken so long that he had no time left to make breakfast or pack his lunch. At least, he'd had enough forethought – sometime between mopping and cleaning – to plug in Pasquali. Glover filled the largest mug that he could find to the brim with coffee and hurried out the door, sipping and sloshing as he bounced down the steps and to the path through the neighbor's backyard.

When he reached the deserted main street, he moved from the sidewalk to the centerline, hoping to avoid icy patches. Not wanting to carry an empty cup all the way to the foundry, he lifted a pile of frosty leaves and shoved it underneath, while reaching overhead to snap a sizable branch from a tree. The branch marked the pile so that he could find the cup on his way home.

It was cold. It was pitch-black dark. And Glover Daniels was both hungry and tired. He consoled himself by thinking that surely things could only get better. "Think good thoughts," he repeated to himself.

Going about his duties at the foundry, Glover impatiently counted the minutes until morning break. At the sound of the whistle, like a bullet zipping from the barrel of a snub-nose Smith & Wesson .38 Special, he headed for the core setter's shop. He lost no time finding Buddy.

"You got a lot of moxie, Buddy! You an' your blasted brew are 'bout to get the best of me! I've been moppin' since before the sun come up an' I've got half a mind to mop up this floor with your ass!"

The story of the frozen brew mishap did not go over well with Buddy from the start, especially when Glover told that he had poured the seven unbroken quarts of brew down the drain.

53

"Are ya crazy, man! What the hell's wrong with you? Seven quarts o' good brew jist wasted. What were ya thankin'? Why didn't ya jist put 'em somewhere else? You coulda brought 'em with you an' left 'em in my car. Damn, Glover. You ain't got as much sense as I give you credit for," Buddy ranted. They'd stepped into the supply room so that no one could overhear.

"If anybody's crazy, that would be YOU! You need to straighten up and fly right! I hope you can find some way t' make 'xtra money that don't involve the law. An', by the smell of that poison, Lord only knows how many men are 'live 'cause them jars froze. Don't quit your day job, hot shot! I'm bettin' brew-makin' ain't 'xactly your callin'!" In a state of anger, Glover tended to talk with a country drawl, like he did when he was a boy.

"Ya got no right t' bad mouth my brew, much les' pour it out!" Buddy's face was as red as a certain reindeer's nose, and a blue vein pulsated on his temple like it was going to pop at any minute. "Don't knock it 'til ya tried it! I come t' you for he'p an' a lotta he'p you turned out t' be!"

Glover bit his lip and willed himself to calm down. What was done was done. No use beating a dead horse. He'd said too much already. So far, this had been somewhat less than an ideal day.

Heated words were getting them nowhere, and they both knew it. Buddy dropped his head and looked away.

"I'll talk to you later." Glover spun around and hurried out the door.

Glover knew that after the initial contention wore off, a round of *token* apologies − token because each thought that he was right − would be exchanged, and they'd let bygones be bygones. His mama raised him to say what he had to say and then let it go. She never allowed him to hold a grudge. Growing up with his aggravating brothers had given him plenty opportunities to practice what his mama had preached.

When Doris got back and it was clear as day that she had not detected any hint of the homebrew fiasco, *and then* Glover would consider the matter laid to rest. If Doris ever found out what had happened she would be so disappointed in him. The things that she didn't say when she was hurt or disappointed spoke louder than anything she said. He'd promised himself that never again would he get talked into such nonsense.

Glover was headed back to the foundry when the foreman, on a mission to deliver a telegram, spotted him. Jay Ed shouted for Glover to wait – the message was for him. Telegrams often brought bad news, and Glover's hand trembled as he opened it. The message read:

MOTHER DIED 2AM STOP COME STOP BRING GIRLS STOP

Jay Ed promptly excused him and told him to take as many days off as he needed. Grabbing his coat and hat, Glover ran most of the way home, forgetting to retrieve his coffee mug from the leaves.

A warm house greeted him, and he was pleasantly surprised that there were no unusual odors. At least something was going his way. Maybe things were looking up.

Not wasting a minute, he began a search for their beige Samsonite suitcase. It was nowhere to be found, until Glover knelt down on one knee and lifted the blue chenille bedspread. There it sat underneath their brass bed in the darkness, like a child playing hide-and-seek.

He packed clothes for himself and the girls and several things he thought Doris might need. Stretching to reach the mustache cup on the top shelf, he took a five and two one-dollar bills and slipped them into his billfold. The cup was down to two one-dollar bills and a handful of change – another thing to think about.

Glover left the Samsonite on the front porch and headed two doors down to Bessie Pearl's house. For the second day, due to inclement weather, the girls were out of school. After joyful greetings, he told them that they were going to join their mother.

"I'll drive you to the train station." Bessie wrapped a wool scarf around her neck and tucked the ends inside her coat. "It's too cold for y'all to walk."

Glover wished that he knew how to go about nominating her for sainthood, even though he wasn't a Catholic.

Tickets in hand, they settled in the depot waiting room. It was noon, and they hadn't eaten dinner; Glover hadn't eaten since the previous day.

"We have time for a sandwich, if I hurry," Glover said while mentally counting how many hamburgers he would need to buy. He figured he'd have one cut in two for the girls to share.

Bessie Pearl stayed with the children while he went across the tracks and down the street to Monroe's Hamburger Heaven. The little hamburger stand was packed with the midday crowd, making Glover antsy, because he knew that the train would arrive in less than half an hour. Fortunately, anticipated burger sales had prompted the cook to fry the meat ahead of time, which shortened each customer's wait.

Glover placed his order, and in no time a spry elderly woman, not a day less than eighty-five, wiped her hands on her apron and placed a sack of burgers on the counter. "What else can we get for you today?" A sweet smile brightened a face cracked by time.

Glover pointed to a bag of Lay's potato chips as he counted out money.

"Much obliged." He picked up the food and headed back to the station.

"Do not dawdle," he warned the children as he passed out the food. Both girls nodded yes as Bessie spread a napkin in each lap and piled chips on it. She unwrapped the hamburgers and they all dug in. Glover nearly swallowed his whole. Missing breakfast had left his stomach as empty as a pocket with a hole in it.

"This may be the best hamburger all-the-way I've ever eaten." Of course, a dirty sock simmered in swamp water would have been good by this time. He stuffed wadded waxed paper in the empty sack and started on his second burger.

Just as he'd eaten the last bite, they heard the whistle from an approaching train, prompting them to clean up in a hurry. Bidding fond farewells, Bessie buttoned Molly's coat and handed Marianne a pair of gloves. Glover patted his coat pocket for tickets, grabbed the Samsonite, and ushered the group outside to the platform.

From the train's window, Marianne and Molly waved and threw kisses to Bessie. She waved back and smiled at little flailing arms slinging invisible messages of love as the train pulled away from the station.

The nearly three-hour trip would seem longer, but Glover would put the time to good use as he gathered his thoughts. Since his feet had hit the floor at 3:45 a.m., he'd been going non-stop.

Like a mother's lullaby, the steady clickety-clack of the

train's wheels soon lulled the children to sleep; even Glover nodded off a time or two. Somewhere between dozing and reorganizing his thoughts, a plan emerged. Rather than taking a taxi from the station to his mother-in-law's house, he would use the phone at the depot to call and see if someone would come and get them.

His head felt like a giant woodpecker was frantically pecking on it. He needed to get himself together so that he could be strong for the family. Without a clue as to what he could say or do to make things better, he would at least be there. Together they would weather this storm as they had so many others.

*

White gladiolas, carnations, and roses filled an ample floral bouquet tied with black taffeta ribbon. A declaration of death and bereavement, it hung on the front door of Glover's mother-in-law's old three-story Victorian house.

She was at home, but not as anyone had ever seen her before. She lay in an ornate bronze casket that the funeral directors carefully slid out the back door of a shiny, black hearse onto a metal gurney, steadying it as they rolled it along the cracked sidewalk. Four men reverently lifted it up the porch steps and carried it into the front parlor.

Born in 1880 and deceased in 1950, Doris's mother rested in the Victorian parlor where for so many years she'd hosted numerous Sunday school meetings, wedding and baby showers, and frequent afternoon teas that began at four and lasted until supper at six. Every Christmas for as long as anyone could remember, she'd placed the tree in front of the window so that the lights could be seen by passersby. Once again the parlor was a busy gathering place, although for this occasion she was an honored guest in her own home rather than the hostess. Her coffin was placed along a wall with roses scattered on faded wallpaper peeling at a seam. The Duncan Phyfe camelback sofa that helped hide the loose paper had been moved to the back bedroom. Eight Queen Anne dining chairs had been placed around the room for visitors.

Nestled in plush, quilted white satin, she lay – her cheeks rouged, her round gold-rimmed glasses in place, her sightless eyes closed. She wore her best Sunday dress, the navy blue print with a Peter Pan collar that she'd crocheted and pinned in the center with a cameo broach. Thin, waist-length graying hair was braided and twisted into a bun at the base of her neck, as she'd always worn it. Her delicate facial features, wrinkled with age, were bathed in the peacefulness that death sometimes brings.

Doris said,"Mother'll be here two days an' two nights." She stood gazing at her lifeless mother, consoled by Glover with his arm around his wife's shoulder. "Deacon Berryhill an' Deacon Morehouse'll stay throughout the night. Everybody has been so anxious to help.

"Would you like to come an' say good-bye to Big Mama?" Doris motioned for Marianne and Molly to come and see their grandmother one last time. No, actually they wouldn't. Neither child had seen death and they were slightly frightened as well as a little confused. But both knew from seeing so many tears that there was a loss greater than either of them could comprehend. Amanda was not permitted to view her grandmother: three-year-olds were far too young to be exposed to death up close.

A lump gathered in Doris's throat. She saw that the

children were not ready for such good-byes, so Glover took them outside. *What will I ever do without my mama?* Doris held an ache inside, knowing if she did not control it, she would be crying her eyes out again.

A steady stream of family, friends, neighbors, and acquaintances came to pay their respects and sign a guest book placed on a three-legged half-table near the front door.

Neighbor Opal Bates had elected herself to manage kitchen traffic and see that the food was just so-so. Two long tables were loaded with every kind of casserole, vegetable, meat, or dessert that one could think to cook up in a hurry and would go a long way.

"Glover, can you run over next door and then down to Hazel Hunt's house and get them to empty their ice trays?" Opal asked while thrusting an enamel dishpan toward him. *Ice cubes. What a nice convenience for those fortunate enough to have an electric refrigerator!* It was a full-time job to replenish the cubes that were piled in a dishpan on the sink's drain board so that everyone could have a glass of iced tea − even the ones that didn't take time to eat.

"Knock, knock," whispered Patsy Borden as she eased past folks standing around the kitchen. She carried a platter of fried chicken from Sunday school members and handed it to Opal. Hardly a visitor came without a platter of food, a cake, or a casserole.

All mourners were escorted to the kitchen and encouraged to fill a plate. If they weren't hungry at the time, they'd fix a to-go plate to have later. It was common knowledge that Southern people were incapable of burying anyone without putting on a spread with enough food to feed every person left alive − even if they lived in other states and would not be attending the funeral. Food served as a common denominator – a soother, a comforter, something good in the midst of sorrow.

Agnes Beltram, pianist at the church since time began, came every day and played hymns on an antique English piano in the parlor. Although the piano needed tuning, her arthritic fingers tickled the keys as if they were fingers that had never grown old.

> To the old rugged cross I will ever be true;
> Its shame and reproach gladly bear;
> Then He'll call me someday to my home far away,
> Where His glory forever I'll share.

Some sang along; others just listened. Many, with tear-stained faces, bowed their heads as in prayer.

The piano, laden with blooming plants, looked like a mini-greenhouse. Visitors admired each one and read the attached card to see who'd sent it. This filled the time – one hardly knows what to say or do in times of grief. Floral sprays filled in throughout the rooms, releasing a sweet fragrance to challenge the stench of death.

Someone from the funeral home had placed signs at each end of the street that stated: **Funeral Zone. Drive Slowly.** Those passing by dropped their speed to a crawl to show respect for the grieving family and friends.

The children, wearing 'boggans with pom-poms bobbing from the caps crown, played on the grand old house's wrap-around porch, making good use of an oak swing. They played Simon Says in the driveway or hopscotch on the sidewalk, which ran from the porch to the garage behind the house. Occasionally, an adult came outside to shush them and remind them to be respectful of the dead. Not being sure just what that meant, they obediently quieted for a while.

Glover helped with the dishes, made iced tea and coffee, entertained the children, and ran interference whenever there was a problem. He was concerned for Doris and kept a close eye on her. His heart ached for her loss, and he wished that he could do something to make things better for her. But, he knew that the pain caused by the death of a loved one must run its course.

The funeral was held in the little white wooden church at Spring Hill, a few miles outside of town. Not far down a country dirt road, the building sat nestled in a secluded meadow surrounded by hundred-year-old oak trees, their bare branches stretching heavenward. The cross atop the lofty white steeple stood salient against a blue cloudless sky.

The burial was in the adjoining cemetery, where the history of generations of family members was etched on tombstones. A newly dug grave, flanked by a bounty of floral displays and tearful mourners, marked another fallen leaf from the family tree. Perhaps, it was the beginning, not the end. One hopes for a better life in a better place.

After the funeral, Glover and his family stayed over another night, and the next morning his brother-in-law, Edward Earl, drove them home.

As they sped along, Glover gave an account of his recent driving lesson.

"We'll visit for a weekend and give you another drivin' lesson," offered Edward Earl. "Practice your turn signals in the meantime," he teased, referring to the remark that Glover had said Buddy made.

A gathering for all who wanted to attend would be held in a week at the offices of McCutcheon, Esbenshade & Heck,

Attorneys at Law, for the reading of Mae Ellen Westbrook's Last Will and Testament.

Neither Doris nor her older sister Mary would be able to attend. Avis or her brother Owen who lived in Talladega would write of any news pertaining to them. Doris knew her mother had money in a savings account, but she had no idea how much. Miserly habits were among her mother's well-known traits. Earning money as an expert seamstress and dressmaker, she had supported her children after the death of her husband. Even after the children were married, she continued to run a thriving alterations business. For a number of years, her living expenses had been minimal, so there was a possibility that she had saved a substantial amount. Also, the house and personal property would be distributed, but none of her children knew her intentions.

*

Back on an even keel, Glover settled into his daily routine in the weeks following the funeral. Thank God, the weather had warmed up to above freezing, the children were back in school, and things at work were running smoothly.

"I love having you back home." Glover pulled Doris from a sitting position. To say that she was somewhat limited in her activities was an understatement. Bless her heart, the poor woman could not see her feet nor get out of a chair without struggling like she was in quicksand. Was it his imagination or had Doris put on a lot of weight lately? It was close to her delivery date and maybe the weight gain was normal. However, he didn't remember her having gained as much with their other babies.

"Auntie will be here soon." Doris waddled toward the

doorway. Glover's aunt was to arrive over the upcoming weekend to stay until the baby was born – and as long afterward as she was needed. Unmarried, Auntie was the Florence Nightingale of the family, and every time there was a new addition, she could be counted on to help. Her uncanny way with babies was phenomenal, and new mothers welcomed her for as long as she would stay. Not only did she lighten a new mother's load, but she also was a congenial, most pleasant houseguest. Glover hoped her visit would be for at least two months, since babies were not taken outside the house for the first six weeks other than a visit to the doctor. They were fragile and a great deal of effort was extended to shelter them from disease. Care was taken to screen all visitors for coughs or colds, as pneumonia was the second cause of infant deaths in 1950. The primary cause of death was dehydration caused from diarrhea, and many babies died simply because lost fluids were not replaced.

For the first six months the new baby would sleep in Glover and Doris's room.

"There's hardly enough room to cuss a cat in, but we'll have to make do." Doris had studied the room from every angle. The truth of the matter was that there was only one way that the furniture would fit. Their full-size bed was butted up against the only wall without a door or window. To make the bed she had to scoot it out from the wall, sit in the middle, and try to smooth the covers on the backside. That had become impossible in the last few months, and Marianne had been appointed temporary bed-cover-smoother.

"We can pull the bassinet next to our bed at night an' roll it in other rooms durin' the day." Doris looked around the room one more time, hoping against hope that a perfect plan to squeeze three pieces of furniture into a closet-sized room, with walking-around space left over, would pop into in her mind.

The tiny white wicker bassinet, that had nestled each of their babies, now sported a new yellow gingham liner and quilt that Doris had sewn and fit into the oval basket on legs.

Glover had dug his old canvas army cot out of the storage bin in the garage to set up in the girls' bedroom. Auntie would sleep in the double bed with Molly. Marianne would sleep on the cot. Amanda slept just outside Glover and Doris's bedroom on a small daybed built by Doris's dad when Doris was a little girl.

"We're runnin' out o' space. This is like the ol' lady livin' in a shoe. We've got to get a bigger house." Glover stated what everyone in the family already knew. He wanted to move to a roomier place, but their budget didn't allow more than the $35 a month that they paid for rent. Try as he may, Glover could not see any way that a bigger house was in their immediate future.

A note had arrived in the mail telling them that the reading of the will had been postponed for an additional week due to Mae Ellen's lawyer being away on business. A few days after the newly appointed time had come and gone, another letter from Avis arrived. When Doris handed it to him, Glover opened the envelope and read the handwritten page:

Dear folks,

We now know what Mother wants done with her money and belongings. Her wishes are complicated and I can't explain them in a letter. All three of us would like to come to visit on Sunday, if that is convenient for you. Also, we can bring Auntie so that she won't have to ride the train.

I'll bring a baked ham and potato salad, so please don't go to any trouble. We all need to sit down and have a long talk

65

about Mother's will. You'll find that what she's done is typically Mother.

> *Will arrive around 10am.*
> *Love,*
> *Avis*

Chapter Three
Rub-A-Dub-Dub

The kitchen windows fogged as steam rose from three large stockpots and a super-sized pot used for canning, all filled with boiling water.

Shaped like a rotund gentlemen with long, thin legs, a wringer-washer waited on an enclosed porch just off the kitchen.

Glover had already filled the washer's tub once and washed the dirty laundry. That water had been emptied, and the machine was ready to be filled again for the rinse cycle. Carrying the pots one by one, strong-armed Glover dumped steaming water into the machine effortlessly. Albeit, when Doris did the laundry she did a pretty good job of hoisting the pots. The trick being to fill them less than half full – twice as many trips, but half as heavy. He added cold water to hot until he was satisfied that the temperature was just right. Then he set the agitator in motion with a push of the start button.

Rhythmic, swishing sounds made by splashing water prompted Glover to whistle a happy tune. It never took much to set him off 'til he was whistling like an English teakettle.

Contrary to most households, Saturday (when Glover was home) had replaced Mondays for doing laundry; Tuesdays were set aside each week to do the ironing. Usually, come hell or high water, Doris washed on Monday and ironed on Tuesday. No one was sure who'd set this ritual in motion, but every household that the Daniels family knew anything about washed on Monday and ironed on Tuesday – winter, spring, summer, or fall. For the time being, due to Doris's need of bed rest, washday had been temporarily changed.

While the clothes rinsed, Glover went about the business

of getting as much done as he could toward tomorrow's expected company.

"As best I can figure, there'll be 15 for dinner," he said as he counted on his fingers.

That number included the five in his family, his two sisters-in-law Avis and Mary and their husbands Edward Earl and Frank, his brother-in-law Owen, Owen's wife Amy, at least three of their kids. And Auntie.

"Just in case they bring anybody else, I'll plan on 18."

He decided to get a head start and set up the children's table in the corner of the kitchen. It was a family custom at large gatherings to feed the children first while the women dished up food and poured drinks for the adults.

It was somewhat of a milestone when a child was old enough to be promoted from the children's table to a place at the regular dinner table. The time for this was usually determined by age and by how much a child whined that they didn't want to sit with the "babies" any longer. Until then, those that were members of the little folks' table wasted no time cleaning their plates, so they could go outside or to one of the bedrooms to play while the grownups ate. The older children were responsible for the younger ones; it was a general consensus of opinion that children learned responsibility *by doing*.

In keeping with the parenting trends of the day, neither Doris, Avis, Mary, nor Amy tolerated tattling. They'd agreed that when there were disagreements among their children, they would let the kids work it out themselves. After all, each parent had preached the Golden Rule – *Do unto others, as you would have them do unto you* – since the kids were toddlers, and the same principle was taught at school. If nothing else, this method maintained sanity and kept the adults out of minor squabbles.

Swollen feet and ankles and high blood pressure required Doris to keep her feet elevated and do as little as possible. Dr. Davis would make a house call sometime late in the afternoon before heading home for the day. Saturday morning's patients were seen in the office, but afternoons were reserved to visit the contagious, the critically ill, those without transportation, and in some cases, expectant mothers that were near their due date.

Just as Glover finished gathering chairs for the children's table, the washer shut off, having completed the rinse cycle.

"Marianne! Molly!" he shouted for the girls to come and bring wire coat hangers. He swung the wringer across the washer tub and flipped the switch that started the rollers turning. Grasping a long-handled wooden spoon, he fished the clothes from the water and guided each piece through the wringer. The rollers squeezed the soppy clothes as flat as a flitter, the extracted water flowing back into the tub. Catching the squished items as they came out on the backside, he tossed them into an enameled pan. An experienced laundress – or launderer in this case – knew that the wringer not only squeezed clothes, but also anything caught in its grasp. Fingers, hands, arms, and even hair could become entangled in the rollers and cause serious injuries.

Marianne and Molly hung the larger pieces on the hangers.

"Drape the towels over the side of the bathtub," instructed Glover. "Y'all know where to hang things. Just don't hang anythin' heavier than a dishtowel on the kitchen chairs. We don't need peelin' paint to deal with."

There was no use hanging anything on the backyard clothesline during the winter. Items froze and defrosted several times, taking the better part of a week to finally dry – and then

69

every piece smelled like wet puppies. Laundry only took a day or two to dry inside the house.

"Glover," called Doris. "You'll need to check the wet clothes tomorrow mornin' b'fore the company gets here."

"I will," said Glover. "Me or the girls'll hang what's still wet on the back porch." They would dry more slowly there, but at least the house wouldn't be cluttered with drying laundry.

"And check the socks. I know that Molly has one pair that needs to be darned!" yelled Doris. She was tired of socks with holes in the toes ending up back in the underwear drawer rather than the darning basket. She liked to stitch a hole up before it was stretched to kingdom come. In her opinion, there was no reason that a pair of socks, when properly mended, couldn't be worn until threadbare.

When the last shirt squeezed through the rollers, Glover pushed the washer to the back door and flipped on the pump, quickly hooking the drain hose over the rim of a five-gallon bucket. Sudsy water flowed like draft beer as the pump made loud, retching, gasping sounds. Each time the bucket filled, Glover carried it down the back stairs and emptied it away from the house – no need to take a chance on water puddling and freezing near the doorstep. Had it been summer, he'd have taken the rinse water to the garden and watered plants – if the water weren't too soapy. When the pump made slurping sounds like someone sucking the last drops of soda through a straw, he turned it off and pushed the machine back to its resting place. Thank goodness it would be a week before they repeated this ritual.

Chapter Four
Bank of Integrity

Tiptoeing to the bedroom door, Glover peeked in to see if Doris was sleeping. Propped up on pillows, she thoughtfully scribbled a list on notebook paper with a yellow pencil. Amanda, with a coloring book opened on her lap, was working tediously to stay within the lines while shading Minnie Mouse's hair bow bright red. Looking up, Doris smiled and patted the bed, coaxing him to sit with them.

"I've planned for tomorrow." She pointed to her notes. "I've made a list for Marianne and Molly. They need to look over the iced tea goblets for water spots. Lord knows I'll be embarrassed to death if Avis sees even one spot on an ice tea goblet. She'd rather see a hair in her food than a spot on a glass. An' get the Sunday dishes out of the cupboard an' set the table. Let Amanda set the children's table and make sure she does it right. Forks on the left. Tea needs to be made. You sweeten it. Marianne puts too much sugar. Better make two gallons. The gallon jars are under the sink. Also, have the girls check first thing in the mornin' to be sure there are enough napkins ironed. Use those off-white linen ones with our monogram. What're we fixin' for our part of the dinner?"

"How 'bout if I open three quarts o' green beans, stuff a coupla dozen eggs, an' make a peach cobbler for dessert?" asked Glover. While visiting relatives in Georgia last summer, they'd brought home two bushels of peaches along with a toe sack of sweet onions and a bushel of butter peas. Accompanied by an old crock churn that Doris planned to use as a planter, these items rode in the baggage car of the train. Shortly after returning home, the peaches were peeled, sliced, covered with simple syrup, and canned for cobbler making.

"Suits me. If there's two dozen eggs, you'd better cook all o' them. You know Frank eats stuffed eggs like he's eatin' peanuts. An' don't put too much mustard, okay? You put too much mustard." *Lord, the aggravation of having to let somebody else do what you did better.*

"First thing in the mornin', I'll bake a cobbler an' cook the beans an' eggs while the girls go 'bout their chores. You rest. I don't want you worryin' 'bout anythin'. Just relax an' have fun with your sisters an' brother. We're gonna have a great time." He kissed her forehead and patted her expanded tummy.

He hoped that his sister-in-law didn't bring a dinky ham. He hesitated to look a gift horse in the mouth, but she was far too frugal for his taste.

"It'll be just like her to bring a ham not big enough to fill a hollow tooth," he mumbled while thinking, *Surely Avis knows that it'll take a fifteen pounder for this crowd.*

As long as the ham was big enough, with side dishes and desserts they would bring, he knew there'd be enough food. If he had any money to bet, he'd place it on Mary bringing a pan of cornbread dressing. Didn't matter what meat was on the table. Didn't matter if there wasn't a turkey within a hundred miles, Mary brought dressing regardless of what anybody might say. Actually, there needed to be food for two meals. After dinner they'd cover the leftovers with a clean tablecloth and leave them sitting on the table, ready for the company to eat supper before heading home.

First things first. It was dinnertime for this day, so they set out the leftover fried chicken from last night. Chicken and dumplings from two days ago were still good, and there was bologna and pimento cheese, if anyone had rather have a sandwich.

He opened a jar of pickled beets, because Doris craved them. The woman had eaten enough beets in the last eight months to feed the eastern half of the United States. Glover chuckled to himself at a sudden mental image – a bright beet-colored baby.

Once they'd eaten, the leftover leftovers were put away, and the dishes washed.

Before settling in his navy blue chair, Glover selected WVOK, a Birmingham station that featured country music played by Joe Rumore, and turned the volume on low. Unfolding the newspaper, he thumbed through pages until he found the sports section, folded the pages back, and read the headlines. The older girls played with their dolls in their bedroom while Doris and Amanda took a nap.

A little before four o'clock, Glover heard a car pull up in front of the house. Pulling back the curtains and peeking out the window, he saw Dr. Davis coming up the sidewalk swinging his black bag and looking very doctor-like in a dark brown overcoat – with a smart looking fedora to match. Glover hurried to the bedroom.

"Doris. The doctor's here. Do you need anythin'?"

After she assured him that she didn't, Glover hurried down the hall and swung the front door open.

"Come in, come in." Glover took the doctor's hat and coat, deposited them on the coat tree, and motioned for Dr. Davis to follow as he led the way to the back bedroom. "Doris an' the girls have a tasty little gift for you an' your family. Doris did the supervisin' an' the kids cooked up some fried apple pies."

"Sounds mighty good." Dr. Davis made a mental note to

73

not hurry out and forget them.

Earlier, Marianne had squeezed in a straight-back chair from the kitchen near the bed, so that Dr. Davis would have somewhere to sit.

"Well, how's my favorite new mother?" The doctor patted Doris on the foot, as she lay propped with pillows. There was little use of lying down, as comfort was nowhere to be found. She struggled to get up, but he waved for her to stay put.

"Well, how's my little mother feelin?" Without waiting for an answer he took a stethoscope from the black bag and plugged it into his ears. Raising Doris's maternity smock, he placed the chest piece on her abdomen and listened intently. After several minutes of listening, he checked her feet and ankles.

"Well, well," he muttered while wrapping a blood pressure cuff around her arm. He seemed deep in thought as he squeezed the rubber bulb. Glover asked if the doctor would like a cup of coffee, but he didn't answer, as if he'd not heard a word. Noting her blood pressure reading, Dr. Davis sat down in the chair.

Sensing the tightness of the small space, Doris made a suggestion, "Why don't we move into the livin' room where we'll be more comfortable?"

The doctor led the way and headed straight for the navy blue chair with the matching stool and sat down.

"It's just a chair, an' not ever'body knows it belongs to me," muttered the chair's owner as he turned toward the gooseneck rocker. The thought occurred to Glover that maybe he should letter a sign sayin' OFF LIMITS – PRIVATE PROPERTY and lay it in the seat.

Rather than having to struggle to get out of a chair, Doris

squatted and then plopped on the sofa, where it was easier for her to get up. Albeit, the news that was about to be delivered would make who sat where unimportant.

Looking over his wire-rimmed glasses, Dr. Davis chose his words thoughtfully. "I've detected two heartbeats." He leaned forward, propping his elbows on his knees and weaving his fingers in the "here's the steeple" position. He then rested his chin on the steeple.

"The same thing occurred a few months ago. I wasn't sure. It isn't always a clear-cut thing. There are many reasons why a second heartbeat is hard to detect, and I didn't want to sound a false alarm. Bein' as there were no other signs that norm'lly indicate multiple births, I didn't say anythin'. But now, I think that we'd better seriously consider the possibility of twins. With Doris's recent weight gain and now hearin' what sounds like two hearts beatin', I want you to be prepared, just in case you give birth to twins."

He paused in case either Doris or Glover wanted to ask a question. It seemed the cat had gotten both tongues.

"My other concern is Doris's blood pressure and the swellin' in her feet and ankles. These are symptoms of toxemia or preeclampsia. It's a condition that can be potentially dangerous to both mother and baby."

Still, both listeners were as silent as a snowy night.

"Let's not panic. But better safe than sorry. I want you to go to the hospital on Monday mornin' for lab work. Once I know the results of the test, we can more closely monitor the situation. In the meantime, keep your feet up and rest."

Abruptly, Doris cleared her throat and began to chat like she'd not heard a word the doctor had said, while Glover could not put a complete thought together, much less carry on a

75

conversation.

She even remembered to get the brown paper bag of fried apple pies. After sticking the bag under his nose and taking a deep sniff of the syrupy sweet odor of cooked apples and cinnamon, the doctor asked her to come into his office on Monday morning after lab work. Blindly minding their manners, they escorted him out the door with many thanks.

At a total loss for words, they just stared at one another for the better part of a minute.

Finally, Doris broke the silence and said, "I'm goin' to lie down."

Heading for the kitchen, Glover could only manage four words. "Coffee. I need coffee." He didn't know whether to laugh or cry. He needed to clear his mind and think this through.

With a steaming cup filled to the brim, Glover made his way to the living room, sipping while being careful not to slosh the hot drink. He eased into his chair. As he leaned back, resting his feet on the stool, his thoughts gathered like clouds on a stormy day. The doctor had seemed more than a little concerned about Doris. Was it caution or serious concern? Glover would not allow himself to think of any harm coming to Doris. He could not and would not even consider it.

He needed to organize his frenzied thoughts by starting with the things that he knew for sure.

First of all, he knew that babies were a blessing, and from that standpoint he was thrilled. From a realistic standpoint, the family was cramped inside this small house, and adding two babies to the mix would make things more uncomfortable than ever. These two things he knew for sure.

Next, he added the things that were unclear. Where would they put two babies? How could they take care of two infants? How were they going to pay for all of this?

Glover blew on the hot coffee and slowly sipped, gazing over the rim aimlessly into space. They were all about due a cheerful, exciting surprise, and two babies would certainly accomplish that. He didn't like surprises to begin with, but if it had to be, why not a cheerful, exciting surprise?

He thought of all the challenges that he'd met head on during his life and how they'd made him stronger. He knew that he was geared to fight, not run. More than once he'd proven to himself that the tougher the challenge, the keener his determination. He thought of his precious girls; a million dollars would not buy one of his children. In his heart, he knew for a fact that whether there were two babies or ten, he would love them and provide for them. Anyway, it wasn't like they had a choice.

Conclusion: if there were two babies, then there were two. That had already been decided. It was a done deal.

Relief replaced surprised shock and gently budded into glad acceptance.

Doris! Oh, sweet Doris! Glover sprang from his chair, almost knocking the empty coffee cup off the side table as he headed toward the bedroom.

There sat his very pregnant wife in the chair that was intended for the doctor, her eyes filled with tears as she stared at the wall. She knew Glover like the back of her hand, and she knew that he was thinking the *two-baby* news through. She had patiently waited, knowing that he would soon tell her the words that she needed to hear.

Taking two steps into the tiny room, he pulled her up into his strong arms. Glover held her like there was no tomorrow, tenderly smoothing her hair and whispering in her

77

ear, "I'm so excited that there may be two babies."

He kissed her tear-stained face and coaxed a smile from her with a smile of his own.

"We're in this t'gether. We'll make it work." He nuzzled her neck with tender kisses.

Trusting him completely, Doris relaxed in his arms. She loved how his mind worked – how he always had to have time to think things through. Confident that no matter what the future held for them they would be fine, she clung to him and thanked God that he'd given her this rock of a man to be her lifetime partner.

They decided not to say anything to anyone since they were not sure themselves that they were having twins.

The girls thought that the Stork was bringing the baby. They would really be surprised if it brought two.

*

From outside Glover heard the sound he'd been waiting for.

Toot! Toot!

He looked over the Sunday newspaper page at the clock atop the bookshelf faithfully going about its business of keeping time. A quarter til ten. He knew it! Avis was never late; she'd probably been giving everyone his or her marching orders since the crack of dawn. Throwing the newspaper beside his chair, he rushed to the front porch with Marianne, Molly, and Amanda close on his shirttail shouting, "They're here! They're here!" Bringing up the rear, Doris, who was drying her hands on a checkered kitchen towel, waddled like a penguin and tried to keep up. They all clamored down the steps to where a 1946 Ford

78

Woody station wagon, with every door standing wide open, was parked at the curb.

Glover never tired of looking at this fabulous, fascinating automobile. The combination of chrome, light and dark polished wood (neatly crafted along the sides and back), and shiny black metal fenders and roof was almost more than he could take in. The crowning touch was a spare tire, suspended beneath the window on the lower part of the back door. The car had three full passenger seats and could easily seat nine − that is, if everyone wanted plenty of room to sit comfortably. Not the case on this trip. The rule was first come, first served. Those unfortunate enough to not get a seat were left to sit in someone's lap. Thirteen people piled out of the Woody and scrambled for standing room on frostbitten brown grass at the curbside.

Covered dishes and casseroles in boxes or brown paper bags were stashed in every available space inside the car. The only room left for Auntie's two beat-up brown leather suitcases, older than Auntie and most everyone else in the family, were behind the rear seat.

"Hey, Auntie." Glover gave her a peck on the cheek as he reached for the satchels. "What I love 'bout these bags is knowin' that Noah carried one in each hand when he got on the ark."

There was much laughter and chatter as the cramped riders stretched and greeted their welcoming kin. Following a rash of hugs and kisses, food containers were passed around for everyone to carry. Auntie had balanced a three-layered caramel cake in a covered carrier, on her lap all the way.

Sliding her pocketbook over her arm, she said, "I'll put this little darlin' on the kitchen counter my own self. I wouldn't trust it to another livin' soul." She headed up the walkway

79

steadying the cake in outstretched arms, her black, leather purse swinging to and fro.

Once inside the children's bedroom, the visitors peeled off layers of warm clothing, piling it on the bed.

Glover loved these get-togethers and he especially loved these people. His family was so unlike Doris's. His two brothers and two sisters, who had inherited short tempers from the Irish side of his family, were all borderline hell-raisers. Seldom did the siblings get together that a disagreement or fight didn't break out. Fortunately, Glover had inherited a temperament akin to his mother and her English ancestors. She'd been a gentle, loving woman who favored Glover because he was the youngest of five children and more like her than the others. His father resented their closeness and often teased him, calling him Mama's Boy or Sissy Girl. Not only had Grady Daniels mistreated Glover's mother, but he'd also raised his older sons to drink and fight.

Although Glover cared about his brothers and sisters, he seldom spent much time with any of them. The oldest sister Annie Sue lived in California, and his older brother Henry lived in Florida. He'd not seen Sue in five or six years, but Henry came to visit every now and then. His other sister Nora and his baby brother Howard lived in Gadsden, not far from Cherry Street. He saw them occasionally, usually when they needed him to get Howard out of jail.

Doris's older sisters Avis and Mary, although five years apart in age, looked enough alike to be twins. Mary, the older of the two, wore bright red lipstick and a blue felt beret to cover her curly brown hair. Avis was as plain as a brass doorknob. This seemed to serve to her advantage. Simplicity combined with a double measure of sweetness resulted in a winsome lady, admired by both family and friends. Both women brought an air of happiness and love that was apparent as they milled about the kitchen chattering like silly schoolgirls while they put the meal together. Tall, big-boned, blonde Amy was more like a sister than a sister-in-law, and smart as a whip to boot. Amy Westbrook had a dry wit known to crack up the most sober-sided.

"Y'all remember my cousin Sadie? Well, I went to her wedding last Saturday." Amy stirred the potato salad then licked the spoon like it was a popsicle. "It was very emotional. Even the cake was in tiers," she solemnly stated.

Doris grabbed her abdomen and shook with laughter. Avis grinned and rolled her eyes. Mary coughed to stifle a snigger. Auntie chuckled politely. Queen of deadpan humor, Amy remained poker-faced as she raked green beans from a pot into a bowl.

Despite a throbbing headache, a good laugh helped Doris to join the playful conversation. She was determined to enjoy girl-talk while she could, knowing that soon enough she'd be babbling like a baby to a baby. Maybe even two babies. She was itching like a good case of poison ivy to tell everyone that she might deliver twins, but she and Glover had agreed to keep it secret – so she would not tell.

Marianne, Molly, Amanda, and their cousins – Anna, Charlotte, and Lillie – sat in a circle on the bedroom rug. They were playing with one of the cheapest and most fascinating toys of childhood – paper dolls.

The men gathered in the living room to catch up on the latest news. Three things were **never** discussed in mixed company: politics, religion, or sex. With only men present, any subject was open for discussion. Avis's husband Edward Earl, and Doris's brother Owen were ironworkers. Mary's husband

Frank was a district representative for the ironworkers union. When the four men got together, there was always a lot to talk about.

They'd discuss not only job-related issues, but also the matter of the potentially explosive conditions along the 38th parallel in Korea. The United States and Russia had developed an international power struggle that had been labeled the Cold War. Different beliefs and ideologies – capitalism and communism – vied for dominance. The men would voice their opinion as to whether President Harry S. Truman was handling things according to their preferences. All of the men in this family were rock solid patriots, each having served in various branches of the military.

However, the subject of what was in Mae Ellen Westbrook's Last Will and Testament was delayed until after dinner. Business was never discussed in front of children or where they might overhear – they were allowed to be children and not burdened with things too lofty for innocent minds. When the kids had eaten and then gone out to play, the adults would discuss the business that they'd come to talk about.

The clock chimed twelve times just as Avis summoned the men to come to the table. After being fed and sent outside to play, the children had discovered a pile of cardboard boxes in the back alley where new neighbors had discarded them. Imaginations whirled as ideas for a playhouse using the boxes evolved. With creative strokes from broken crayolas stored in a rusty coffee can, boxes became chairs, a sofa, a bed, a stove.

The temperature hovered around fifty-five degrees. While some played "house," others took turns riding Marianne's blue and white J.C. Higgins (Sears Roebuck) bike up and down the sidewalk – the walkway was as straight as an arrow, just right for pedaling fast from one end of the block to the other. Glover had attached poker cards with clothespins to the front bicycle wheel spokes. The faster the wheel turned, the faster the cards fluttered, making a frap-frap-frapping sound. A child's vivid imagination turned that sound into a powerful, revved-up engine. Unfortunately, more time was spent retrieving the catapulted cards and reattaching them than listening to the noise they made.

All the grownups found a place at the dining table, anxious for Glover, the head of the household, to serve slices from Avis's sixteen-pound ham. The others passed around the potato salad, cole slaw, green beans, and carrot and raisin salad. Amy had prepared a congealed salad with lemon Jell-O, crushed pineapple, cottage cheese, and chopped pecans. Although she'd packed it in chipped ice for the trip it was a bit runny, but for the most part still held its shape. Glover noticed that Frank had four stuffed eggs on his plate and mounds of an absolutely delicious corn casserole. (Not that Glover had appointed himself food monitor – he just *happened* to notice.) Predictably, Mary brought cornbread dressing, explaining as she always did that dressing goes with anything. She also knew that there would not be one bite left: she could hold her own with the best of them and had cornered the market on cornbread dressing. And besides, breaking the turkey/dressing tradition was a power play – a woman breaking new ground.

The dinner was a delightful smorgasbord, embellished with priceless fun and fellowship. They sat around a claw-foot, oval table, talking and enjoying their time together. Frank always had a new joke to tell. Everyone politely laughed, but wondered if Frank had somehow missed out on joke telling in the third grade and was trying to make up for lost time.

83

Afterwards, Amy and Mary cleared away the empty dishes and stacked them in the sink. Amy piled all the iced tea glasses in a dishpan of sudsy water to soak per Doris's instructions. "Y'all wash my good glasses separate so they don't get chipped," she'd said.

"Those were Glover's mama's crystal glasses," Auntie held a goblet up and rang it with a gentle flick of her thumb and index finger.

The room filled with the aroma of perking coffee, as the percolator's clear glass dome bubbled. When the perking stopped, china cups for the ladies and mugs for the men were filled. Auntie cut the caramel cake into generous wedges, and Avis dished peach cobbler into white porcelain lotus bowls. There was a choice, of course, but almost everyone had some of both.

"Just give me a sliver o' cake. I'm cuttin' back," said Mary. Avis shot a glance across the table at Doris, who was biting her lip to keep from laughing. They knew that Mary would have no less than five slivers − equal to an average slice of cake or more − before it was all over. Although she billed herself as a freethinker, on occasion one might be led to wonder if she were playing with a full deck.

A couple of the men discreetly fumbled to loosen their belts as Glover poured another round of coffee. It was time to get down to matters at hand. Doris asked about the reading of her mother's will and the outcome.

Owen spoke first. "Mother left $12,000 in a savings account and, of course, the house and its contents. Her wishes were that I, being her only son, and Avis, who took care of her the last years of her life, split the money equally. The house she left to Avis."

84

Stunned silence filled the room as Doris and Mary realized they were not even mentioned in the will.

Soft-spoken Owen continued, "The only reasonable explanation that I can offer as to why two children were not included is that Mother intended to make a point."

It was more or less common knowledge that Mae Ellen Westbrook had resented the husbands that Doris and Mary had chosen. Not because she necessarily disliked Glover or Frank, but she thought that both girls could have done better. She felt that they had married beneath themselves, and the fact that the daughters had disobeyed and gone against her wishes had left a bitter taste.

But, the real bone in her craw was that Mae Ellen had been a teetotaler of the highest order, and both Glover and Frank were social drinkers. It was a well-known fact Glover's father had bootlegged moonshine – until the feds totally destroyed his whiskey stills – and sent the old man off to Atlanta to spend three years in the federal penitentiary. Little good that did! It was rumored that he sold moonshine from his deathbed. Mae Ellen was never able to come to terms with such shenanigans.

The jolly mood the cheerful group of diners had known quickly turned to heaviness and hurt feelings. It was a harsh reality that their mother would treat any of her children so callously.

"This is the conclusion that I've reached." Owen cleared his throat. "I feel that not only human reasoning, but perhaps divinely inspired insight, can help us see past the words on the pages of a will. We all loved Mother and knew her so well. Why would any of us be surprised that it was her intention to make *her* point? You know as well as I do that she *always* had to have the last word." Heads wagged up and down as the group acknowledged their agreement.

Indeed, she'd had the last word once more, this time from her grave. Mae Ellen Westbrook had adequately expressed her feelings in a manner that spoke louder than any words.

Owen continued, "Doris, you and Mary know that Mother loved each one of us. She had no favorites. Y'all also know that Mother was as strong-willed as a deaf mule. But I think we'd all agree that she was a wise woman and well aware that she'd raised us to be decent and honest. She knew each of us so well that she felt she could predict what we'd do. You know she had that annoying way of being right most of the time." Again heads wagged, acknowledging that Owen had hit the nail on the head.

Widowed, Mae Ellen had been a single mother for a family of five. Conquering her share of challenges, she'd guided and nurtured her offspring into adulthood and lived long enough to see them practice the principles that she'd taught. They'd earned her trust, and she'd believed that they would do what was right in any unfair situation. She felt, so to speak, that she could bank on their integrity.

"Avis and I have discussed this theory up one side and down the other. The more we've talked over the matter, the more clearly it seems that having her final say was what Mother intended. It's typical, textbook Mother. Y'all know that's the truth if it was ever told."

Owen took two small black books from his shirt pocket.

"Avis and I believe this is what Mother wanted, and she knew darn well that we'd do it." Reaching across the table, Owen handed a bank book to each of his disinherited sisters.

Balancing the book on her baby bump, Doris opened it, looked inside, and without a word passed it along to Glover.

86

He'd never deposited money in a bank. As a matter of fact, he'd only been inside a bank once or twice – people without money don't need the services of a bank. Slowly, he opened the little book to see that both his and his wife's names were written on the inside page. Then he turned to the next page, where he read the figures in the balance column. Glover fixed his eyes on the numbers, trying to believe the unbelievable. The amount was $4,000.

Avis interrupted the stunned silence to say, "I inherited the house and I feel that I shouldn't take any of the money. We wanted the $12,000 to be equally divided between Owen, Doris, and Mary. Owen and I told Mother's lawyer to transfer the money into individual savings accounts."

There were tears, lots of tears. There were hugs, and thanks, and much, much love. Auntie was an observer at this meeting, and she could not have been prouder of these people that meant everything to her. Being blood-kin only to Glover, she still felt like everyone there was part of her. From the beginning they'd treated her with love and respect and had taken her in as one of their own. She'd be taking care of her nephew's new baby very soon. Auntie's goal was to live long enough to see this next generation carry on the principles for which these decent, hard-working people stood.

Glover couldn't quite wrap his mind around what had just happened. This windfall had stirred a mixture of feelings. He was somewhat confused, slightly bothered because this new situation smacked of sure change. But mostly, he felt like jumping up on the table and doing an Irish jig.

It was going to take a great deal of thought and planning to know how to make the most of this good fortune. He hoped that the responsibility of making sound decisions regarding how the money would be best spent wouldn't simply replace any weight that had been lifted. It would take time to think this through. For now, he would pigeonhole the matter on the back burner of serious considerations, and let it simmer for a while.

The rest of the afternoon was filled with activity. Edward Earl, Glover, Avis, and Mary piled in the Woody and headed to the old airport for Glover's driving lesson. Owen, Amy, and Frank walked with the children to a nearby school playground. Doris motioned for Auntie to pile pillows on Glover's side of the bed and make herself comfortable, while she plumped up the pillows on her side. The two women stretched out to rest and make plans for their new arrival. Doris was itching to tell Auntie that her job might include an extra infant, and although she came close to breaking her promise to Glover, she couldn't. They'd agreed to keep the possibility of twins a secret.

Everyone reconvened for supper at 5 p.m. Peeling back the tablecloth covering the leftovers from dinner, they made ham sandwiches from scraps of Avis's ham. Glover licked his finger and pressed the last crumbs of caramel cake to his fingertip, promptly popping it into his mouth. Frank scraped the remaining spoonfuls of cobbler from the dish, licking the spoon like a lollipop, then scraping one more time to get any left behind. "Why don't you just lick the bowl?" laughed Doris.

"B'lieve I will." And he proceeded to lick the dish clean, his thick, curly brown hair bobbing with every lick.

"Frank!" exclaimed Mary as everyone laughed and cheered him on. "Lord knows he'll do anythin'. Mama's probably rollin' over in her grave. She hated ill manners at the table. "'Member that Thanksgiving that the Georgia cousins came? Somebody asked Carl Junior if he wanted more beans, and he said he was full as a tick. Right at the dinner table! The image of a blood filled tick killed everybody's appetite. I was 'fraid Mama was gonna come over that table after him."

"Ugh! I remember that," answered Doris. "Mother got up an' left the table. Never said another word to Little Carl the rest of the day." The more they remembered the stunned look on their mother's face as she glared at the teenage boy, the more they laughed. She had been raised in the Old South where manners were everything. For her, folks who were uncouth, loud, rude, or caused a commotion in public were ill bred, and she was not inclined to excuse their bad behavior.

It had been a wonderful day, filled with the kind of love and laughter that binds families together forever.

The mountain of coats and hats on the girls' bed shrunk as the travelers dressed warmly with the dropping temperature in mind. With Auntie staying, they had one less rider on the return trip. Fond farewells filled the air as twelve sojourners loaded in the Woody. Embarking on a two-hour drive, they headed for home, sixty miles south.

*

Swallowed in darkness, Glover lay in bed, staring toward the ceiling. His whole body felt like it was plugged into a wall socket. Questions were vying for attention like first graders frantically waving their hands, hoping the teacher would call on them. Where was he to start? So much had happened over the weekend. For consideration there was the doctor's visit, Doris's health, the question of one or two babies, the little black bankbook, the matter of their cramped living quarters, and comments from Frank about the questionable fate of the iron

89

industry.

One thing at a time, he thought; *slow down and take one thing at a time.* His analytical mind began to categorize the subjects for consideration and prioritize them. First things first. Doris needed to have this baby or babies, as the case may be, and get her blood pressure under control. He knew that the solution to this dilemma would begin tomorrow when she went for tests and then to see Dr. Davis. Glover thought it best if he missed a day of work and went with her. *Auntie could go, but I really need to be the one to go with Doris. If I'm at work, I'll just worry. I may as well go with her.* It was settled. He would go with Doris. He placed a mental check mark next to Doris's name and moved on to the next item needing a thorough mulling over.

Actually, he could kill two birds with one stone on this one. As to the matter of their need for a larger house, they now had the money to look for a place of their own. He would contact his friend, realtor Marvin Stoddard, who would help him find property that met their needs and was within their budget. Two more issues could be checked off his imaginary list – the subjects of cramped living quarters and how to spend the money. Glover had no idea what houses cost, but he thought that there would be plenty of money in the newly acquired savings account. On one hand, four thousand dollars was a small fortune to him. On the other hand, the amount seemed like just a number. He'd never seen four thousand of anything, so it was impossible for him to fully comprehend. For all he knew, there might even be enough money for a car too.

His thoughts moved on to Frank's comments about the fate of the iron industry. Working as a union representative, Frank was privy to information unavailable to the ironworkers. "Based upon changin' times in industry, especially the prospects of imported iron, I predict that in a few years, the foundries will close," he'd said.

This item placed last in the triage of his thoughts, as Glover decided to put the possibility of losing his job on hold. He would invest more thought into this later, but for now there were more pressing needs. Frank had said that it would be a few years, if indeed the foundries closed at all.

Confident that he'd properly assessed the issues at hand, Glover began to relax. Soon he closed his eyes and rolled on his side toward Doris. She slept soundly, snoring lightly. Glover followed suit as the coquettish *Queen of Dream Catchers* gently seduced him into her lair of sweet sleep.

*

Bessie Pearl opened the front door, which was never locked day or night. Sticking her head inside, she let loose with a "YooooooHooooo" that could rattle the pictures hanging on the walls. Molly came running, with Amanda close behind. Hugs and kisses greeted the early morning visitor as the children led the way to the kitchen. "Come, sit," said Auntie as she pulled a ladder-back chair from underneath the table while pouring Bessie a cup of coffee.

Glover came to investigate the commotion and joined in the replay of weekend events, also giving an outline of the plans for the day.

"Doris has to go to the hospital for lab work an' then on to Dr. Davis's office," he explained.

Bessie offered to drop the girls at school and take Glover and Doris to the hospital.

"I'll wait for y'all while they do the lab work and then

drive you to see the doctor. I have plans for the afternoon, but Glover can call a taxi cab to bring y'all home," she concluded.

Her plans changed when Bessie looked up from her coffee cup and saw Doris waddling through the doorway. Doris's hands and face were swollen, and her feet and ankles had almost doubled in size since yesterday. Without seeming alarmed, Bessie suggested that they leave right away and drop the children off a few minutes early. "If we are first at the lab, you'll finish and be first at the doctor's office. Maybe you won't have to wait long to see Dr. Davis," she said slowly, hoping to disguise her concern.

Bessie could spot trouble a mile away, and she had a strong inclination that Doris was in a heap o' trouble.

Glover helped Doris down the front stairs, out to Bessie's car, and into the front seat. He and the girls slid into the back seat, and off they went to their designated destinations.

While Doris waited in the hospital lab, Bessie found a pay phone and called her friend Frances to cancel their plans for the afternoon. "I want to stay with Glover and Doris to hear what the doctor says," she confided.

Bessie Pearl took a deep breath. She felt an uneasiness churning deep inside her, and she didn't like it. Not even a little bit.

*

Although Glover found the prevailing odor of iodoform, commonly used as an antiseptic, icky and unpleasant, he did like the order and neatness of hospitals. He loved how the nurses strutted about with starched-stiff-as-cardboard white hats, looking as flirty as a cockatoo's head feathers. Spotless white uniforms, white stockings, and white shoes painted a picture of high-class healthcare professionals. Not only did nurses make a strong statement with their uniforms, but they were also no-nonsense wardens of the hospital's rules – and they had the authority to enforce them. Glover had a lot of respect for both nurses and doctors. Committed to the Hippocratic Oath, they gave their time and devotion to healing others for little pay.

Dr. Davis, seeing increased edema since he'd visited Doris on Saturday, lost no time instructing her to go from his office directly to the hospital. In spite of the urgency of the hour, they'd taken a short detour by Cherry Street so that they could update Auntie on the turn of events and get Doris's suitcase. She'd packed enough gowns and bed jackets to last five days, the usual time a new mother stayed in the hospital.

In 1950 there were no specialists, and there were few female doctors. The doctor was jack-of-all specialties, and more often than not, a master of none. Doctors relied on reference books and the help of colleagues when unfamiliar situations arose.

Dr. Gordon Herbert Davis, 54, married with three children, had followed in his father's and his grandfather's footsteps.

Patients didn't always have the money to pay for Dr. Davis's services, so they paid him with whatever they had to offer. As a result, the doctor's pantry was full of canned vegetables and his freezer was packed with prime beef and pork chops. Horace Fletcher had replaced an old shed in the doctor's backyard with a garage. "I ain't got no cash on hand," he'd said, "but I do have wood from a house I tore down. I can build a garage fit for a Cadillac." Dr. Davis didn't own a Cadillac, but he was quite happy to have shelter for his big black Buick.

Doris's lab tests verified toxemia, a condition that sometimes occurs by sudden onset in late pregnancy, often occurring when there are multiple births. Toxemia, also known as preeclampsia, causes the breakdown of red blood cells and affects liver function and how the blood clots. Dr. Davis knew that serious complications could result if the condition was not treated properly and quickly. Doris could suffer from renal or liver failure. Full-blown eclampsia could result in convulsions and even coma. He felt much better knowing that she was under 24/7 supervision in the hospital, and he'd issued orders that would start the wheels turning toward resolving some of her issues. The sooner the baby (or babies) was delivered the sooner Doris would be out of the woods and on the road to recovery.

After getting Doris settled in a temporary ward, Glover assured her that they would be back for visiting hours from seven til eight-thirty in the evening. Children under fourteen were not allowed to visit. The girls would be disappointed, but rules were rules – and they applied to everyone.

Trying to concentrate on the sports page of the *Gadsden Times*, Glover restlessly counted the minutes until it was time to return to the hospital. There had not been a moment that Doris hadn't been on his mind. He needed to see her, to talk to her, to hear her voice. In an effort to stay busy throughout the afternoon, Glover decided to walk to the foundry and tell the foreman what was happening, just in case he needed to be off work.

After supper, Glover impatiently watched from the front window for Bessie's car. Finally, she pulled to the curb and tooted the horn at a quarter 'til seven. They drove to the hospital and waited in the lobby, where Glover's eyes remained glued to the round wall clock. The instant that the big hand moved to the number twelve, Glover jumped up and a bit too loudly said let's go.

Following directions given by an elderly candy striper, they located Doris. Pushing a heavy wooden door open, they saw four iron hospital beds in a sparsely furnished room – two beds occupied, two beds unoccupied. Glover, followed closely by Bessie, spoke to the other mother-to-be in a bed at the far side of the room and then hurried to the only bed curtained-off. Behind the draperies they found Doris, with the foot of her bed elevated as far as it would go. Her face was pale, puffy, and sagging at the seams. Although Glover was worried, he could see that she was being well cared for, and that brought a small measure of relief. After hugs, kisses, and inquiries as to how she was feeling, Bessie gave Doris the report sent by Auntie.

"All the girls send their love and want you to know that they miss their mommy." Doris had been in the hospital less than twelve hours, but to hear her children tell it, it seemed as if it had been a month.

Dr. Davis, making his nightly rounds, interrupted their reunion.

"My greatest concern is Doris's blood pressure. Much, much too high. She has begun to dilate. This is good news. I trust that by mornin' her blood pressure will be closer to normal," he said. "Then we'll see what we need to do next. There is a possibility of a Cesarean section if needed." He turned toward Glover with a *be prepared just in case* look, as he gently patted Doris's foot.

Having taken a mild sedative, Doris found it hard to keep her eyes open, even though she wanted to see and talk to Glover. He held her hand and reassured her that everything would be all right, knowing that he had absolutely nothing to base this prediction upon other than hope. Glover and Bessie

95

conversed as Doris dozed, nodding occasionally as she struggled to follow their conversation. Everyone knows that there is not much to talk about during a hospital visit once the conversation gets past "how are you feeling?" They just sat silently when they could think of no more to say; just being there made them feel better.

Throughout the day it had seemed that time had dragged along. Not any longer. Somehow time had gotten on the fast track, and visiting hours were over before anyone wanted them to be. The floor nurse stuck her head in the door, shooing visitors away.

Glover left the hospital with mixed feelings. He wanted to stay, but the doctor had assured him that sitting all night in the waiting room would accomplish little.

I must be patient, he reasoned. *Soon the baby will be here, Doris will be home, an' all will be well.*

*

Knock, knock, knock.

Glover's eyes flew open to stare through the darkness at the ceiling. Was he dreaming? He cocked his right ear to one side, as if that made hearing easier.

Nothing.

Then – knock, knock, knock.

Jumping out of bed and grabbing his pants, he glanced at the clock on the bedside table. It was 2:36 a.m.

Auntie, groggy and disheveled, stumbled into the hallway as Glover came out of the bedroom. Their questioning expressions told that neither had a clue as to who would be at the door at this early hour.

"Who's there?" queried Glover, as he reached for the doorknob.

"Mr. Daniels, this is Officer Phillip Isbell of the local police. May I please have a word with you?" replied the voice from the other side.

Glover opened the door, and Officer Isbell stepped inside. Apologizing for any alarm that he may have caused, he explained the nature of his unexpected visit.

"The hospital has requested that Mr. Daniels be notified of an emergency. I'm here to escort him to the hospital immediately," the officer politely stated.

Within minutes, Glover was dressed and instructing Auntie to contact Bessie Pearl at first light.

Officer Isbell's cruiser sped through the deserted streets. The Holy Name of Jesus Hospital was just across town, maybe two miles as the crow flies. An attendant was waiting at the entrance to the ER to take Glover upstairs to the maternity ward waiting room.

"What's goin' on?" frantically questioned Glover.

"I don't have any details, Mr. Daniels," replied the young man. "Dr. Davis'll be out to talk to you as soon as possible."

It was 2:48 a.m. according to the clock on the wall above a row of neatly lined, upholstered chairs.

Glover's head was spinning. It was as if time stood still.

It was as if time moved at the speed of an Olympic bobsled team.

Nothing made any sense. Panic pushed his buttons like an elevator operator.

What had happened? Was Doris all right? Had she delivered the baby? If something had happened that was serious

97

enough for him to be summoned by an escort, then it must be serious! *Oh, dear God... Oh, dear God... Oh, dear God* was all that he could think.

Wait.

I must be strong. I must stay calm. I must settle down. Oh, dear God... oh, dear God.

He paced nervously back and forth listening to his boots clicking on the polished tile floor. His hands wouldn't be still. He wrung them. He patted his hair. He jammed both hands deep into his pants pockets in an attempt to calm them as he continued to pace.

Just as he plopped down in a chair in a half-hearted attempt to further curb his jitters, the door opened, and Dr. Davis rushed in. Taking no time to exchange pleasantries, he pulled up a chair opposite Glover, and talking slowly, he told what had taken place in the past two hours.

"Doris's water broke around midnight. I was notified and was here in five minutes. Contractions began, although we'd taken steps to try to delay labor. We were hopin' to give more time for her blood pressure to normalize. Instead, it began to climb again. I felt that there was no need to wait any longer. I called for an OR team to prep for a C-section." He pushed his wire-rimmed glasses up on his nose as he carefully chose his words, hoping to make this easier for Glover.

"The good news is that you are the father of two baby boys. Other than small birth weight due to the toxemia, they appear to be healthy." A slight smile flashed across his face.

"The bad news is Doris has not fared as well." His eyes saddened. He glanced at his folded hands in his lap, took a deep breath, and continued. "She suffered a mild stroke that led to convulsions. Glover, I am so sorry to tell you that she is in a coma."

Glover felt a lump the size of a golf ball lodge in his throat. He swallowed hard and stared at the doctor, as he grappled with this astounding news. Doctor Davis quietly added, "Now, Glover, you know I'm believin' for the best; but to be quite honest with you, things could go either way. Maybe you should contact Doris's family and be prepared for whatever the outcome may be."

Chapter Five
New Beginnings

Tuesday, February 21, 1950, John Alton Daniels and James Edward Daniels took their first breath the moment each felt a sting on their tender, bare bottoms. Their cries sounded like the "Hallelujah Chorus" to an anxious doctor. The boys had beaten the odds and survived a precarious incubation period. Snatched from the warmth and darkness of their mother's womb and thrust into a cold, brightly lit hospital operating room was a necessary, yet abrupt, awakening. The shock was momentary. Each newborn was quickly passed to a waiting nurse who expertly cared for the fragile baby.

It was the beginning for the boys, but was it the end for their mother?

Doris Bernadette Westbrook Daniels lay in a delicate state of balance between life and death. She was in a place neither in this world nor completely out of it − a place of deep sleep where one cannot be awakened. She could not consciously hear, speak, feel, or move; her brain was functioning at its lowest stage of alertness.

Nurses bustled about, closely monitoring Doris around the clock, since maintaining breathing and vital signs within normal ranges were of the utmost importance. Dr. Davis visited the hospital at least three times a day to check on her. Everyone tending to Doris was doing all they knew to do. A Boston doctor, recently recognized for a paper he'd written on eclampsia in a renowned medical magazine, had been consulted; his expertise and willingness to help had greatly increased Doris's chances of recovery. All that was left to do was to make Doris as comfortable as possible and wait.

*

Avis and Mary were readying to bring the five-day-old babies, each weighing a little more than five pounds, home from the hospital. The boys had joined an exclusive group known as "Carnation babies," because they drank baby formula made by mixing canned Carnation evaporated milk, sterile water, and Karo syrup. This broke the long-standing family tradition of breast-feeding. These boys would be bottle-fed.

"I bought four dozen glass baby bottles, rubber nipples, bottle rings, a sterilizer, tongs, two cases of Carnation milk, and two bottles of light Karo syrup," said Avis, counting on her fingers.

After sifting through out-grown tricycles and playpens, chairs, trunks, and other assorted castoffs exiled to the attic of her garage, Mary had liberated and dusted a wicker bassinet for the welcomed – but unexpected – baby. "The other bassinet is ready. Slightly smashed-in on one side, but nevertheless ready."

"I got three dozen more diapers. That gives us six dozen. I think that'll do it," Auntie added. Doris had already laundered and neatly folded three dozen cloth diapers, and piled a handful of diaper pins on top of the stack.

Everyone was excited! Tomorrow Bessie Pearl would drive Avis and Mary to the hospital to bring the boys home.

*

Glover went to the hospital every afternoon straight from the foundry. Most days Buddy gladly gave him a ride and helped in any way he could. Co-workers had taken up a collection and given Glover forty dollars to help with expenses. The Women's Missionary League at the church had organized a prayer chain, and frequent prayer meetings were held in the tiny chapel adjacent to the church to pray for Doris's complete recovery. Pastor Willcott sat in the waiting room with Glover an hour or more each day. More often than not, he brought a box supper or a thermos of soup, knowing that Glover would miss dinner at home.

Visitors, one at a time, were allowed to sit with Doris for thirty-minute intervals five times each day. Glover left the foundry as soon as the pour-off was completed and usually made the 4:15 visitation. Afterward, he stayed at the hospital until 7:00, rather than go home and come back, to be admitted for thirty more minutes. Bessie, Avis, or someone from the church came at 7:45 to give Glover a ride home.

At straight-up-and-down 4:15 p.m., the doors to the ward opened, and Glover hurried inside. Upon reaching Doris's bedside, he held her hand and rubbed it gently across his cheek, his heart aching so badly that he was unable to hold back the tears. Although Dr. Davis had said that Doris couldn't hear him, he talked as if she were listening to every word. Even though it was a one-sided conversation, he told her how much he loved her and how much she meant to him. He talked about the baby boys – how beautiful they were, and how much they needed their mother. She would want to know about all the things that Avis and Mary were doing to get ready for the babies' homecoming, so he told her every detail. When he couldn't think of anything

102

else to say, he whistled. Doris loved to hear him whistle "Stardust." Hoagy Carmichael had no idea of the joy he'd given Doris when he'd penned this song. Glover whistled softly and slowly. He believed with all his heart that Doris would wake up, ready to go home. He had visualized that moment until it was as real to him as the nose on his face. So, lips pursed, he leaned close to her ear, and whistled her favorite tune.

A nurse peered around the door to remind him that visiting hours were coming to an end. Kissing Doris's cheek, he whispered, "I'll be back. Come back t' me, sweet angel."

After walking in the tranquil Memory Gardens on the east side of the hospital, praying with each step that he took, he sat down on a concrete bench. High in the treetops, the birds chirped and sang, carrying on a conversation that only the Lord could decipher. Not normally a smoker, Glover'd taken up smoking, giving smoking credit for calming his nerves – even though he knew better. He'd always disliked the bitter taste that tobacco left on his tongue, but for the present, it kept his hands busy and lessened the number of cups of coffee he tended to drink when he was stressed. Taking one final draw on a Lucky Strike, he tossed the butt on the grass and ground it with his boot. Heading back to the waiting room to track time until 7:00, he looked forward to Pastor Willcott joining him. Glover wasn't one to look a gift horse in the mouth; still he hoped the good parson would bring a thermos full of something hot and tasty.

*

Auntie was waiting on the front porch as Bessie pulled her Chevy to the curb. Passing Auntie, Amanda ran down the stairs to greet the newest additions to the Daniels family. Avis and Mary clutched the babies close to their breasts, hovering over them to protect them from the cool weather. Amanda wanted to see her brothers, but Auntie picked her up and carried her inside, cautioning that she should not get too close.

Soon the freshly diapered baby boys were sleeping soundly on Doris's bed. Leaning forward with her big blue eyes opened wide, Amanda stood on a step stool to inspect the tiny pair. Timidly, she slowly and quietly surveyed each infant from head to toe. Without a word, she turned her angelic little face toward Avis and grinned from ear to ear. Sparkling blue eyes and a beaming smile were her stamp of absolute approval.

"Amanda, your daddy has named the babies John Alton and James Edward. This one is John." She pointed to a baby, not really sure which was who.

"Well, what do you say we simplify that right now? Let's call them Jack and Jim Ed." Auntie looked at the identical twins.

"How are we ever goin' to tell them apart?" asked Mary.

Avis examined the hospital identification tags.

"Auntie, you got any red yarn in your knittin' bag?"

Auntie returned with a string of yarn and handed it to Avis. She tied the red string securely, but not too tightly, around Jack's teeny-tiny ankle.

"Now, Amanda, you'll know that the baby with the red string on his ankle is Jack. What is the other baby's name?"

"Jim Ed." Amanda clapped her hands. She felt as lucky as a leprechaun to have not one, but two, baby brothers

"Let's just be careful that we don't start calling him the red one," laughed Mary as she bent to gather the baby in her arms, already knowing that Frank would be the one to put that label on little Jack. She snuggled Jack close to her and kissed his pink cheek.

Meanwhile in the kitchen, Bessie Pearl's backside stuck out of the icebox while her head cooled as she counted baby bottles. Satisfied there were enough for the day and throughout the night, she stepped back, but not before grabbing a small cream pitcher. Coffee was perking. As soon as she'd had a cup, she was off to the telephone company.

For eight months, Bessie had been on a waiting list to get a telephone. She'd heard a rumor that party lines were down from ten customers per line to as few as six. Impatient, she had contrived a plan to pester Ma Bell until they gave her a telephone, if for no other reason than just to be rid of her. She would go about it with charm, as she saw no need to behave in an unladylike manner. It was her belief that one could be a pest without being tacky.

*

Glover Daniels was weary to the bone. He was operating on a fraction of his usual sleep hours. Whenever he was finally able to doze off, he would be awakened by someone stirring about the business of warming a bottle or comforting a baby. It seemed as if there was as much activity in the house throughout the night as during the day. He missed spending time with his little girls – when he would come home from the hospital each night, they'd be in bed. When he'd leave for work, they'd be sound asleep. Not only was he not sleeping enough, he also wasn't eating well. Every aspect of his life was topsy-turvy. He didn't know how he could go on this way much longer. Neither did he know what changes he could make that would improve the situation.

Avis and Mary could not stay indefinitely. They both
105

had families and responsibilities that they'd put on hold. Glover had to make some sort of arrangements for someone to help Auntie with the children on a permanent basis.

Bessie Pearl had suggested that Glover consider a young girl she'd taken under her wing recently. A month or so before, Bessie had hired LaVeeta Johnson, fifteen years old, as domestic help two mornings each week. Not because she necessarily had that much work for her to do, but because she knew LaVeeta to be a bright girl who needed all the support and encouragement that Bessie could give. She didn't know the details of LaVeeta's home life, but knew that it was not the kind of home where a young girl could bring her friends.

The summer that the little brown-skinned girl was twelve years old, Bessie had tutored her in math. A quick learner, she seemed to be distracted by personal problems that hindered her obvious thirst for learning. After LaVeeta dropped out of school, Bessie seldom saw her.

One afternoon, Bessie spotted her walking along the sidewalk swinging three fish dangling from a stringer. Pulling to the curb, Bessie beeped the horn and motioned for LaVeeta to come. Laying her fish in the grass, she ran to the driver's side of the car, smiling and excited to see Bessie.

"How did school go this last year? I trust that you were promoted to the next grade."

"No'm. I had to quit. My mama needs me at home. I work when I can to he'p out with grossrees." She looked away from Bessie as a frown swallowed the smile.

Bessie suspected that explanation was somewhat less than the truth, and it was. Fact of the matter was that life in Hester Johnson's house was hell, and LaVeeta had rather be anywhere other than there.

LaVeeta was afraid of her mother – and with good reason. She knew Hester's capabilities better than anyone. That knowledge had come on an early morning when LaVeeta was ten years old.

*

"LaVeeta, LaVeeta! Git in here!" Hester shouted from behind the closed bedroom door.

Groggy with sleep, the tiny little girl's bare feet hurried toward her mother's voice.

"Yessum," she said as she slowly opened the door.

A hand reached for the plaits on LaVeeta's head and jerked her inside the room.

Thrusting a cardboard, boot-size shoebox toward the trembling child, Hester whispered loudly, "Take dis somewhere an' leave it where nobody find it. Git rid o' it! Hide it! You hear me! Hide it!"

Eyes wide-opened and hands shaking, LaVeeta obediently took the box.

"What's wrong, Mama? What's in here?" she asked.

"Dat's for me t' know an' you to wonder. Don't look inside. If you do, I gonna beat you within a inch of yo' life. Now git! Don't come back here wid dat box!"

Hester wiped her bloodstained hands on the hem of her skirt.

It was almost daylight as LaVeeta made her way down rickety porch steps and into the grassless yard.

Where to go? What to do? At first she headed down the hill, approaching neighbor's houses. *No. No.* Then quickly she turned in the opposite direction toward a vacant lot nearby. The

107

grass was tall there, and the lot was littered with trash, discarded furniture, old tires, and rusty appliance parts. It was the only place that the stunned child could think of to hide the box.

Approaching the edge of the abandoned lot, she stooped to set the box carefully on the ground.

Mama gonna kill me if I look. She leaned close to the shoebox. *Lord only know what she up to. How can I jes leave it?* She sat very still mustering what little courage she could find. And then with a tiny finger, the frightened child carefully lifted one corner of the box.

Something inside moved.

Instantly, she closed the lid and kneeled down on the ground in the dim morning light, staring at the mystery box. Somehow summoning the courage to try again, she reached for a stick nearby. Using the stick to raise the lid little more than an inch, she leaned over and peered through the scant opening.

Although she could see something, she had no idea as to what it could be.

Inside the box, the bloody, discarded placenta still attached to a tiny newborn reminded LaVeeta of calf's liver. That was the only thing that came to her childish mind. She was familiar with calf's liver because they had it for supper far too often. She hated liver − the way that it looked, the way that it tasted − but she ate it anyway, lest she suffer the consequences of expressing her opinion. Why would her mother put liver in a box and tell her to hide it?

Lowering the lid, she suddenly stopped.

Something inside the box had moved.

She'd seen raw liver. She'd sliced and fried it for supper, but she'd never seen it move. How could this be?

On hands and knees, she raised the lid slightly higher,

focusing one eye close to the open corner of the box just as a teeny fist, hardly the size of a walnut, moved past the opening.

Quickly, she slammed the lid closed. Trembling from head to toe, LaVeeta felt her heart racing. Tears spilled from her dark-brown eyes. The terrified little girl just wanted to run and run and never stop.

She looked from side to side – over her shoulder – straight ahead – to reassure herself that she was alone. She noticed that daylight had crept in and the darkness was nearly gone. Soon, people would be out and about. And her mother would be expecting her to come home – without the box.

What to do? What to do?

She didn't know just what she would do, but she did know that she wasn't hiding, nor getting rid of the box as her mother had instructed. That was a big decision for a scared child, but perceiving the right and wrong of the situation, LaVeeta had made up her mind.

Maybe if somebody finds the box, they'll know what to do. That seemed to make more sense than anything else since her choices were few.

She knew that Charlie Boy Taylor and Rebel Waycross hunted rats with slingshots in this vacant lot early in the mornings. She knew because she'd seen them many times and gone the long way around because she was afraid of slingshots. Her brother LaMarcus had stung her legs with marble-size pebbles he'd flung from a slingshot, just to hear her cry.

LaVeeta considered the possibility that *if* the boys came this morning, and *if* they found the box, they might take it to someone who would know what needed to be done. But then again, they might shoot the box with rocks or even open it and harm the baby inside. She didn't have much time to think this

109

through.

"Charlie Boy an' Rebel are rough boys. They loud an' bossy, but they won't hurt nobody," she whispered to herself. Time was running out, and she had to do something and do it quickly.

Gently placing the closed shoebox on a mound of cropped grass, she cleared the cans and bottles nearby and threw them as far as she could. When satisfied that the box was in plain sight, she hid behind tall grass at the edge of the lot where she could see, but not be seen.

Hugging her knees, LaVeeta sat as still as the discarded toilet bowl on the ground near her.

Half an hour passed.

Second-guessing her plan, she was about to move the box to a more conspicuous spot when she heard voices a few feet away. Two barefoot twelve-year-old boys, dressed in tee shirts and blue jeans, appeared from behind the rusted carcass of an old icebox.

Peeping through weeds and willowy grass, she saw Charlie Boy and Rebel looking for rats — slingshots loaded, rubber bands pulled taut, ready to rapid-fire stones at an unsuspecting rodent.

"There's one! Git 'em! Git "em!" Charlie Boy yelled.

The boys aimed and let loose their carefully selected stones.

Ping! Ping!

The rat darted underneath a worn-out tire propped against what was left of an old washer.

"You blind? Missed 'em a mile," mocked Rebel.

"I didn't have a chance! You messed me up when you hollered! If you'd shut up, I mite hit somethin'."

The boys meandered around the junked lot, kicking cans and looking inside the tub of a dasher-less washer. A rat would have to be as deaf as a doorknob not to hear them.

"What's that?" Charlie Boy spied the shoebox.

"Ain't noticed that bein' here b'fore." Rebel stopped to look the situation over.

"Me neither," said Charlie Boy, cautiously walking toward the mound.

"Let's shoot it. It's just a cardboard box. We can put holes in it."

"Mite not be empty," observed Charlie Boy.

"Well, I ain't openin' it," declared Rebel.

"Scaredy cat! You scared o' everthang."

"Am not!" Rebel defended his honor. "If you're so brave, you look inside. Dare ya! Double-dog dare ya!"

For several minutes, the boys stood over the box, looking down, neither making any effort to open it. Then Charlie Boy, after digging in his pants pocket, pulled out his four-blade pocketknife.

Rebel wondered what good that would do if a snake, or mad dog, or some other vicious creature were trapped in the box – there could be *anything* in there!

With the longest knife blade extended, Charlie Boy gently pried the lid, ready to run in a split second.

His eyes grew round as saucers, and his face paled as if every drop of blood had drained from it.

"You look!" he instructed Rebel.

"What is it?" he asked.

"What da ya thank?"

There was no denying it. A tiny baby and a whole lot of something else filled the box.

"I'll stay here an' watch it," Charlie Boy said, barely above a whisper. "You go git he'p!"

Before he had uttered the last word, Rebel was hightailing it down a trail to get his mother.

LaVeeta didn't stick around to see what happened next. She knew that she'd done all that she could. On the way back home, she made up a tale to tell her mother. She only lied when it served to save her own skin.

As sure as she was of the nose on her face, she knew that Charlie Boy Taylor couldn't keep a secret if his life depended on it. She'd see him in a few days where they fished on the banks of the Coosa River. She could count on him to come over to her spot to get worms for bait, knowing that she'd dug enough for both of them. Smart little LaVeeta figured that she got the best end of a tradeoff − he baited her hook. If she closed her eyes and jabbed in the general direction of the creepy thing she could bait her own hook. But most of the time she would just wind the wiggling creature round and round the hook to keep from impaling it. More often than not, the worm would unwound once in the water and swim away.

When they'd meet again, LaVeeta would bet her last cent − if she'd had any money to bet − that Charlie Boy would be boiling over with news about the baby.

*

Vague, fragmented memories of a three-year-old are all that remained of LaVeeta's father. Since he'd moved on, several men had stayed with Hester − some for a few months, others overnight. LaVeeta had learned at a tender age that these men were all users and losers on their way to a better deal.

112

Presently, none of her mother's current escapades or her past abuses were LaVeeta's biggest problem. Her seventeen-year-old brother LaMarcus had become her greatest threat. When LaVeeta told Bessie Pearl that LaMarcus had come to her bed after the other family members were asleep and attempted to fondle her, Bessie immediately asked the young girl to move into her spare bedroom. Not wanting to treat LaVeeta as a charity case, Bessie offered housing in exchange for housework and companionship.

"If anyone asks, you are a live-in housekeeper and cook." Bessie wanted to cover all her bases, just in case some racist meddler tried to stir up trouble.

LaVeeta had jumped at the chance to escape and brought along a pillowcase stuffed with her clothes and personal belongings. Hester wasn't happy with LaVeeta's decision, but there was little that she could do about it. Bullying her own children was no challenge, but she tiptoed her way around white folks. There wasn't enough gold in Fort Knox to tempt her to lock horns with Bessie Pearl Pennycutt.

Smarter than the average bear, LaVeeta Johnson had seen an opportunity to rise above her raising and had not hesitated to latch on to it. The arrangement seemed to be working. The two women had mutual respect and enjoyed one another's company. Bessie helped LaVeeta with schoolwork to make up for all that she'd missed; LaVeeta kept the house spotless and ran errands. Bessie Pearl, who'd rather take a whipping than iron, had a closet stuffed with freshly ironed clothes – thanks to LaVeeta.

Glover had decided to take Bessie's recommendation and talk to LaVeeta about helping with the children once Avis and Mary had gone. It was a decision that he would never regret.

113

Day 8: *Patient stable. Condition unchanged.*

Before leaving the room, the morning nurse jotted a note on Doris's chart: *adjusted IV, turned patient on side.* The last thing they needed was for Doris to develop bedsores.

With each passing day, Dr. Davis was less hopeful that Doris would regain consciousness. Her vital signs were good and her blood pressure had returned to normal, but her reflexes and pupil size indicated no change. Doris was Dr. Davis's first eclampsia-induced comatose patient. He'd consulted with everyone whose advice he trusted, and the general consensus of opinion was that there was nothing more to do other than wait. Dr. Davis knew that the human body has an uncanny way of coaxing healing from somewhere within its mysterious reserves. When he'd done all that he knew to do, he must leave the rest to a Greater Power.

Doris had been comatose for eight days. If she didn't regain consciousness within two weeks of the onset, she probably would not regain consciousness at all.

*

A feathery tickle stirring inside Bessie Pearl left her antsy and as giddy as a schoolgirl after her first kiss. Someone from Southern Bell was scheduled to be at her house around 9 a.m. to install a new phone.

"Soon as he leaves, I'll call the hospital and leave my number in case anybody needs to get in touch with Glover."

Bessie felt that something more than the anticipation of

114

getting a telephone was causing a good case of the heebie-jeebies. Try as she may, she couldn't pinpoint the root of this unsettling feeling.

LaVeeta had gone to the Daniels' house to help Auntie bathe the babies while Avis, who'd borrowed Bessie's car, had taken Mary to the train station. Mary was going home for a few days to check on things. Upon Mary's return, Avis would take a three-day break and check on her family.

The telephone installer arrived at precisely 9 a.m., his leather tool belt latched around his hips. Tall, clean-cut, and friendly, he made short order of the procedure – the man could climb a telephone pole like a monkey! Wires were strung from the pole to the house, and in no time Bessie was writing down her new telephone number – ELmwood 5-3809. Although instructed by the installer, she already knew that only the first two letters of the exchange were dialed, and then the numbers.

Bessie Pearl was on a six-party line. Her ring was two rapid, short rings. If she heard any other combination of rings, she shouldn't answer – that call would be for one of the other five telephones on the same line. Ma Bell made no bones about it: she had high expectations of her customers, and improper telephone manners were not tolerated. Listening in on another party's conversation was not only tacky and ill-mannered, the eavesdropper risked losing telephone privileges. Ma Bell installed the phone, and Ma Bell could take it out. All parties were expected to be respectful of others' privacy and to keep their conversations brief, just in case someone else might be waiting to use the phone.

Admiring her basic black rotary-dial phone – even though it was as heavy as an iron frying pan – Bessie could hardly wait to put it in use. She called the hospital, a few friends, her sister in Atlanta, and her niece in Birmingham – in spite of the added expense of long-distance calls. As thrilling as it was to be the owner of a new Model 500 telephone, something more was teasing her subconscious. Try as she may, she could not put her finger on what. *Oh, well.......*

Happy as an elephant with a tub of peanuts now that she was part of Southern Bell's family, Bessie Pearl was off to take Amanda to the Gadsden Library for story time. (She was seriously considering calling home from the library just to hear her number ringing!) Then, it was home to spend the afternoon crocheting yellow and blue afghans for the new babies.

*

Glover had gotten home later than usual. Dr. Davis had left orders that he could visit for an hour, rather than the usual 30 minutes.

He'd sat beside Doris on the uncomfortably firm hospital bed, rhythmically rocking from side to side as he cradled her in his arms. The nurse would surely go berserk when she saw them, but he didn't care. Glover was near the end of his rope, and he just didn't care what anyone said or did. Strangely enough, the nurse, who usually watched like a hawk, was nowhere to be seen.

For the better part of an hour, Glover held Doris and whispered in her ear without a thought as to what he was saying.

"I can't make it without you. I don't want to live without you, sweetheart. Listen to me. Doris, listen to me. Your babies need you. I need you. We gonna raise these kids an' grow old t'gether. I can't make it without you, Doris. I won't make it. I don't want to go on without you." His voice broke with a sob,

116

and his body shook.

Taking a deep breath to calm himself, he realized that someone would come soon to tell him that visiting hour was over. Gently he pulled his arm from around Doris and slid off the bed. Turning to plump the pillow beneath her head, he smoothed her hair and gown, lingering as he stroked her arm. Then, lovingly, tenderly, he leaned and kissed her good-bye.

*

The front door opened, and momentarily the light switch just inside clicked on. A loudly whispered "Yooooohooooo," followed by a light tapping on the door, awakened Glover, Auntie, and Avis.

The three of them merged to an abrupt halt in the hallway. Glover stepped past the women, leading the way into the living room where they discovered that Bessie Pearl had come to deliver a message.

"The hospital called on my new phone to say that Glover should come as soon as he can get there."

Hurriedly Glover and Avis dressed, while tiptoeing to keep from waking the babies. Within minutes, they met Bessie at the curb. Avis stepped to the front of the car and held her wrist up to the headlights. According to her Timex, it was 1:05 a.m.

The three jumped inside, and the gray Chevy clung to the asphalt as Bessie gunned it. Moments later, skidding into the hospital parking lot, Glover took a deep breath, feeling as if he'd made a lap at the Indy 500.

Quickly leaving the car, Bessie, Avis, and Glover ran, heading to the second floor nurse's station. Although long-legged Glover had left the two women behind, they caught up with him

117

at the elevator.

Two nurses looked up as the three approached the nurse's station.

"What's happened? How's my wife?"

Before he'd finished asking the question, the short, older nurse sprang from her chair and hurried down the hall to fetch Dr. Davis.

"Dr. Davis is here. He'll talk to y'all. It'll just be a minute." The svelte, blonde nurse stood and looked in the direction that her starched-uniformed likeness had gone.

Plaid pajama top peeking from underneath his wrinkled sport coat, Dr. Davis stepped into the hallway. He took a few steps and hurriedly turned back toward the direction from which he'd come, motioning for the group to follow. Like ducklings, they fell in line – including the two nurses – keeping pace.

Entering Doris's room, the group formed a circle around the bed.

Glover gasped as he looked at the love of his life.

Glory Hallelujah! Doris's jade-green eyes were wide open.

Heart pounding a mile a minute, Glover leaned near, "Doris, Doris, I'm here." He stroked the back of her hand.

She stared blankly. A dull glare, not the usual sparkle, shone in her eyes. Doctor Davis waved his hand in front of her face. She blinked once.

"Doris, can you hear me?" inquired Dr. Davis, speaking slowly and leaning close to her ear. "Can you hear me, Doris?"

No response.

Glover touched her cheek. Slowly, she turned her head toward him. Her eyes did not reveal that she recognized her husband as she worked her way in stages to a hypnopompic state. From there she would eventually progress to full consciousness. It appeared, at last, that she was on her way back to him.

Suddenly, all the tension of eight days broke past the dam of self-control, and Glover began to weep. His shoulders shook, tears running down his face and dripping from his chin. He felt a touch on his hand. Through a veil of tears, he looked down to see that Doris's hand was outstretched and touching his. Turning to look at her, he saw a tiny tear rolling down her cheek.

Without a second's hesitation, he grabbed her and gathered her in his arms, holding her with the zeal of a man who'd recovered his most valued treasure from the clutches of a despicable thief.

Avis sobbed uncontrollably.

Bessie bawled like a baby.

Dr. Davis removed his glasses and mopped his eyes with his handkerchief.

Both nurses clung to one another, shedding tears of joy. They all gave new meaning to the phrase, "There wasn't a dry eye in the room." Tears soon turned to laughter and unmitigated relief.

Bessie Pearl realized what had been niggling around inside her spirit all day. It hadn't been all about the new telephone – it had been a premonition that this was resurrection day.

Glover gently lowered Doris to the pillow. His smiling look of love was greeted by an expression totally void of any recognition.

Dr. Davis spoke softly. "Confusion is to be expected, and continued recovery can be slow. But at least the recovery has begun."

Glover stayed the rest of the night, holding her hand and talking to her, in between catching a few winks of sleep in a bedside chair. Several times when Doris closed her eyes, he shook her and called her name just to see her eyes open again.

Avis would come at 5 a.m. so that Glover could go to the foundry, and Bessie would relieve Avis at noon. She would stay until Glover came again at four. Dr. Davis left orders that someone was to stay with Doris, and he suggested that they talk to her. A familiar voice could surely do no harm.

Chapter Six
Welcome to Campbell's Corner

An abundance of birdsong announced that spring had finally sprung. Grape-like clusters of lavender and white lilacs dripped from lush green vines, filling the morning air with a most delightful fragrance. Nearly all the red, white, and yellow tulips along the walkway were gone – all but a few stragglers remaining among the hostas, as they filled in. After a sound winter's sleep, the daylilies bordering the porch had awakened.

Janet Rose McKeever, lovingly known as Auntie, balanced her English bone china cup of Earl Grey as she pulled a weatherworn Boston rocker into a patch of sunshine. She'd had precious few minutes to sit on the front porch and sip hot tea. Such a break was comparable to a Florida vacation, as far as she was concerned. Rocking lazily, she sipped her tea and gazed serenely across the cup on this splendid rain-washed morning in early May!

Auntie's days were jam-packed with work from sunup to sundown. The three-month-old twins had grown like dandelions – seemed that Carnation formula had transformed the babies into chubby little butterballs. Baby talk had become a second language in the Daniels household as everyone babbled at the babies' round-cherub faces, hoping to coax toothless grins.

The boys weren't the only ones needing care – Doris also needed help dressing, eating, and bathing. For her, putting thoughts together and then verbalizing them was like fitting puzzle pieces.

121

Physically, Doris was gaining strength each day. Her blood pressure was normal, and other than one small seizure before being discharged from the hospital, she'd had no setbacks. Partial paralysis on her left side required that someone prop the babies with pillows when Doris gave them a bottle. Feeding them was easier than feeding herself, as she was learning that task again. Nevertheless, everyone could see that she was making progress daily, and no one doubted that her steadfast determination would lead to a complete recovery.

The aliveness of spring was exhilarating. This time of year always reminded Auntie of Miriam, her sister and Glover's mother. Gently bathing her tongue with tiny swigs of hot tea, Auntie reminisced of her childhood and memories of her older sister.

For Miriam, a lover of nature and beauty, spring had been her favorite season of the year. She'd died of tuberculosis when Glover was fifteen; he'd been a ray of sunshine in her life, perhaps the only ray toward the end. A marriage that had started well was doomed when alcohol became her husband's mistress. Liquor, his ladylove, turned him into a mean, loathsome drunk.

Unlike her sister, Janet had never married. She'd intended to marry her childhood sweetheart, but fate had interfered.

One of 16 million who lost their lives in World War I, Les Sherwood was killed in 1918. Les and Janet had been very much in love and planned to marry as soon as he returned from Western Europe. Janet's broken heart was slow to mend – she'd not gotten to say good-bye. Struggling to get her life back on track, she'd found purpose as a caregiver, a nanny, a protector of children.

As long as she was needed, Auntie would stay with

Glover and Doris. She dearly loved each of Glover's children. They required a lot of time and patience, and Auntie had plenty of both.

The rocking motion of the chair reminded her of the years ticking past. Without intending to do so, she'd fallen into that "middle-aged" category. Soon she would be fifty-five, too old to be young and too young to be old.

Was her life all she wanted it to be? It was.

Her tomorrows were wrapped up in her nieces and nephews. A flutter of excitement stirred, as she thought of the possibilities within Glover's girls' reach — opportunities that she'd only imagined.

Marianne and Molly wanted to be schoolteachers like paragon Bessie Pearl. And Bessie was determined the girls would go to college. She hoped they'd attend Jacksonville State Teacher's College, not far from Gadsden. Presently, tuition was $139.75 per quarter — Lord only knew how much it would be by the time the girls were ready for college!

Auntie smiled as she thought of Glover and Doris's daughters. Marianne had a mane of thick black hair, much like her father's. And Molly was a dead ringer for her mother, right down to a beautiful smile. As for just-turned-four-year-old Amanda, like Auntie, she had blonde tresses and a sweet disposition. With women being recognized as more than wives and mothers, the possibilities that the future held for these children were endless. Things were changing. More women were beginning to work outside the home; more were choosing to go to college.

The fifteen minutes or so that Auntie had sat and relaxed had been as refreshing as a catnap, and the innocence of a new day had been like a solace to her soul. Reluctantly, she slowed

123

the rocker to a stand still.

Time to get inside and get busy, she thought as she sipped her last drop of tea. Earl Grey had long since gone from hot to cold, like all tea and most "Earl Greys" are prone to do.

As Auntie headed toward the door, the squeaky boards on the porch floor sounded off like a gathering of rodents. She made a mental note to remind Glover to nail the loose boards down.

*

Glover headed across the parking lot from the foundry toward Stoddard's Real Estate on 3rd Avenue. Listening to the crunch of gravel beneath his boots, he stepped up his pace to get there on time. Marvin Stoddard was taking him to see property north of town. The school year would end soon and getting moved and settled before school started in the fall was a must.

As usual, there was a lot on Glover's mind. During the brisk walk to Stoddard's, he pondered the more pressing issues. He sometimes pondered what he would do if there were nothing to ponder. Time spent in deep thought, mentally fitting issues in proper order, gave him a sense of control.

If they moved from town, then he would need a car to get to and from work. Step one of being a car owner was a done deal – he'd gotten his driver's license. Bessie Pearl had taken him for the test over a month ago, and he'd passed. Having a driver's license in his hip pocket was like a ticket to independence. Now for step two – he had to buy a car.

Buddy had been looking at a 1948 Chevrolet that a man at the foundry wanted to sell. Buddy's Ford sedan would need to be sold – he hoped to get $125 for his car – before he could work a deal. Although, Glover knew that he should get a newer vehicle with less mileage, he wanted Buddy's car. *Practical Reasoning* said that this was foolish, but Glover couldn't get past the vision of himself behind the wheel, cruising along at 40 M.P.H., whistling "Stardust". Buddy was anxious for an answer as to whether Glover would buy the car or not. He was ready for something newer, and he didn't want the Chevy deal to get away. Glover was pretty sure that the answer was yes, although he wanted to give *Common Sense* a chance to talk him out of it.

Glover's life had changed so drastically that he could hardly make adjustments to one change before another came along. Although Doris's speech was hindered and her motor skills were compromised, she improved each day. Still, he knew that complete recovery would take time.

"Doris will regain much of the dexterity that she's lost. She'll carve a niche that suits her and her abilities," Dr. Davis had said, encouraging the family. "I feel that Doris will be fine, but it could take a while."

Glover was so grateful to have his precious wife home again. He was also thankful for Auntie, Bessie Pearl, and LaVeeta. Without them there was no way that he could take care of Doris and the children alone. On the other hand, with extra caretakers and two babies, the house had become more crowded than ever.

Friday morning celebratory breakfasts had fallen by the wayside for Glover. He was lucky if he could find a quiet moment to listen to the radio or sip a cup of coffee in his favorite chair. He sat with Doris every night, held her close, and talked to her as if she had never been to hell and back. She caressed him, and the look in her eyes said all that she was not able to verbalize. They had vowed their commitment to each other in sickness and in health − Glover had certainly lived up to his end of the bargain.

Just about everything had changed. And so be it.

If anyone could roll with the punches, that would be Glover Daniels. He was head of this family, and he would lead. A new house, a new car, or whatever it took to move forward and meet the needs of his household − that is what he would do. He'd met tough challenges all his life and he knew that changes, good or bad, could ultimately work for the overall betterment of those concerned.

Glover crossed the street and headed toward a brick house with a wooden sign planted in the yard that read **Stoddard Realty**, painted in large blue and green letters. Glover was eager to see what Marvin had to show him since he'd never owned property, nor had he expected that he would. This was a whole new ball game, and he was excited and ready to play ball.

"Glover, I think that I have some property that is just what you're lookin' for." Marvin shook hands, grabbed his truck keys off a pegboard on the wall, and guided Glover toward the driveway that ran alongside the building. Glover could always count on slim, graying Marvin to have an overflow of energy that seemed to splash on anyone near him.

Hopping into Marvin's gray Chevy pickup truck, they headed to a destination ten miles or so outside the city limits in the northern part of Etowah County. Along the way, they passed an elementary school and a few Mom and Pop businesses scattered here and there. As these faded in the rear view mirror, they kept on northward, the countryside becoming more sparsely populated as the pickup sped along.

Glover propped his elbow on the window ledge and allowed the wind to blow his brow cool as they passed patches of wooded areas thick with tall pines and oaks. As they rolled on, the landscape became kelly green fields of thriving, waist-high corn stalks basking in the bright sun. Dotting the cornfields were scarecrows – their job being to fool the crows into thinking that the farmer was in the field. Black as coal, the crows circled overhead looking for stray seed or worms stowing away inside the new sheaths. When the corn filled out, they'd greedily help themselves to a cob or two. Glover spotted a scarecrow with three crows perched on its shoulders and one sitting on the worn, felt hat atop its straw head. Pointing to the totem of straw and old clothes, Glover laughed and exclaimed, "Some watch dog that scarecrow turned out to be!"

"He's befriended them," replied Marvin, swerving onto the narrow shoulder of the road while peering out the side window. The cornfields soon gave way to cotton fields as the gray pickup whizzed along a curvy, two-lane blacktop. Neat rows of bushy green cotton plants stretched far as the eye could see. With ample rain, by late summer the fields would be covered with fluffy white cotton bursting from their bolls.

Turning off the main onto an asphalt road leading over railroad tracks, Marvin drove down a steep hill, leveling out to a long stretch of road that led to a residential area. A few brick (but mostly wooden) houses, infrequently spaced, adorned the roadside. Some had fruit orchards in side yards, chickens pecking in flowerbeds, and birdhouses made from hollow gourds to attract purple martins. Pointing out the window, Glover showed Marvin an apartment-like complex of two dozen or more gourds spaced along wooden strips nailed across a tall pole. The birdhouses dangled in the breeze like ornaments on a Christmas tree.

Glover liked the country-living feel but wondered if they

127

would be too far from town. Talk about changes! He had a ton of thinking to do.

Several miles down the winding road they came to a stop at a four-way intersection. Stancil's Grocery & General Merchandise, with both a gasoline and a kerosene pump out front, was on the right. Marvin turned to the left, leaving the pavement onto a dirt road that appeared to be well maintained. It had a light covering of fine gravel. But, gravel or no gravel, where there is dry dirt, there is dust waiting to be stirred-up. When the truck gained speed, a cloud of dust hovered behind the tailgate like an Arizona dust storm. Rounding a hairpin curve, Marvin slammed on the brakes and turned sharply to the right onto a long driveway. Glover looked over his shoulder out the back window of the cab. He watched a dust cloud blow past while Marvin dodged ruts cut deep into the dried clay. With no truck to chase, the dust dissipated into a pine thicket.

At the end of the driveway, nestled among mature hardwoods, sat a white, wooden house that had seen better days. As Glover got out of the truck, Marvin was giving a convincing sales pitch. "The house comes with five acres of land." The addition of land made the rundown house seem a bit more appealing.

Glover studied the wooded areas bordering the property. Large oaks, sweet gums, maples, cedars, and pines towered above thick undergrowth of privet, honeysuckle, and kudzu. *I bet there's a jackrabbit or two in there,* he thought.

Barely visible through the woods to the right of the house, Glover made out the lines of a roof and chimney on a two-story house. The sound of the neighbor's dogs had begun soon as the men slammed the truck doors.

Inside the empty dwelling, they discovered four spacious

bedrooms, living and dining rooms, a good-size galley-style kitchen, and one modern bathroom. Gazing out the bathroom window, Glover saw an outhouse at the end of a path leading from the back door. *Perfect for a chicken coop!* His mind raced, planning how the wooden outhouse could be converted into a nesting area for hens. Anyone else might have planned to tear the old building down; Glover saw something that could be put to good use.

There were no porches on the house. Glover didn't need to consult with Frank Lloyd Wright to determine that this wasn't good. Every Southerner worth his salt knew that a porch – a spot that would catch a cool breeze in the late afternoon – was a necessity in the summer. To say that summer in the South was hot and humid would be a vast understatement – the humidity was like an invisible blanket of smothering dampness, and the smoldering heat came close to melting concrete!

The frame house was balanced on pillars of concrete blocks, exposing the space underneath from front to back. Glover knew that cold wind rushing underneath in winter would make it impossible to heat the rooms, short of setting them on fire. That issue would need to be addressed before the first frost.

In the side yard, a 250-gallon propane gas tank, bordered by a bed of red and yellow canna lilies, sat on stacked fieldstones. It was a safe distance away from the house in case of leaks, but close enough that the gas man could refill the tank from his truck.

"No two ways 'bout it – the place needs a lot of work," Glover said shaking his head as if trying to shake some sense into it. He chose to see things not as they were, but as they could be. He envisioned a newly painted white house with decorative red shutters and cascading plants spilling from window boxes.

He saw a screened porch expanding the length of the house with brick underpinning all around. And with leftover brick, he could build a barbeque pit with a tall chimney in the backyard. The girls could have wiener roasts with their friends, and he could see himself, kicked-back, slowly cooking a side of pork on Labor Day. A whirlwind of ideas spun his imagination.

Marvin said that behind the house is an acre or more of cleared land just waitin' to be plowed an' planted. I could plant a garden larger than any I've ever grown. Not only would there be enough food for us, but there could even be enough to set up a small produce stand on the side of the road on weekends, he thought.

After looking inside the house, which appeared to be roomy enough and then some, Glover and Marvin walked the property past the clearing in back. Entering into a woodsy hush underneath a thick canopy of shade trees, they were pleasantly surprised to come upon a meandering creek. Small bream and minnows darted about in rippling water on its journey downstream.

"What a great place to raise boys!" Glover was getting more excited by the moment. "Well, girls too." But, he could see Jack and Jim Ed wading in the creek, scooping minnows in a bucket. This place had real possibilities. But, did he have enough money to buy it?

Back at the truck, Marvin, anxious to seal a deal, spread his paperwork on the hood of his truck.

"The asking price for the house and five acres of land is $4,000," he said. "However, being as you have cash, I think you can get it for $3,500. Maybe less. It's been listed for nine months, and so far, nobody wants to take on the repairs."

"I want to show the place to the family," Glover said,

looking back toward the house. And, although he didn't say so, he wanted to sleep on the pros and cons of the purchase before making a decision. Rushing into such a big transaction was not his way of doing things. If they could get the house for $3,500, that would leave enough to buy Buddy's car, and maybe a used electric refrigerator. They would not have rent payments anymore − that would free $35 a month that could go into a fixer-upper fund. He just needed time to think this through. Sipping a hot cup of coffee would make that easier.

"Let me know soon as you can. Although, we're not 'xactly overrun with buyers chomping at the bit to sign a contract." Marvin laughed as he gathered his papers.

On the return trip, Glover once again noticed the elementary school.

"Your girls will go to school there." Pointing at a large brick, two-story building with a flagpole near its entrance Marvin offered his opinion, "It's a good school."

"Does the bus come out where the house is?"

"You bet. Stops right at the end of the driveway."

This whole thing just kept getting better and better.

*

Glover opened one eye and squinted at the clock. It was 2:14 a.m. Lord, have mercy! Someone was tapping on the front door.

"Gettin' sleep 'round here is like pullin' hen's teeth," he muttered. He grabbed his pants off the doorknob and hopped toward the front door, teetering on one foot while blindly jabbing his other foot in the trouser leg.

Nearing the living room, Glover could hear LaVeeta

whispering (as loud as a whisper can be before it is no longer a whisper), "Mr. Glover. Mr. Glover."

Rubbing sleep from his eyes, Glover opened the door to find LaVeeta bathed in the glow of the streetlight. She was gasping for breath between sobs.

"Whoa, girl, whoa. Calm down. What the hell's goin' on?"

"I run from Miss Bessie's house 'cross the neighbor's back yard t' git he'p. My brother LaMarcus, he drunk an' bangin' on our front door. He tole me he gonna kill me if I don't let 'im in. Miss Bessie, she not wantin' to call the po-leece if you could handle the sit'ation." LaVeeta was talking so fast that Glover could hardly keep up, but he got enough to know that he needed to act in a hurry.

Quick as a flash, Glover was running shirtless and barefoot along the sidewalk. He leapt onto Bessie's front porch where LaMarcus was pounding on the door with his fists demanding that LaVeeta come home, and saying that his mama had sent him to get her.

Glover saw right off the bat that LaMarcus was too drunk to reason with him. He was swearing and raising such a commotion that Glover grabbed him by his shirt and flung him down the steps and into the yard. The fall knocked the wind out of him, sobering him a bit. At least, it shut him up. He sat up, shook his head, and staggered to his feet. Glover flew into him knocking him to the ground again.

By then, lights were on in houses on both sides of the street. Some of the neighbors peeped from behind curtained windows and some gathered on their front porches.

"Call the police, Bess!" Glover uttered through clenched teeth, while straddling LaMarcus and pinning his arms to the

132

ground.

Gadsden's finest were in Bessie's front yard within minutes. After being relieved of a switchblade tucked inside his boot, LaMarcus was arrested for public intoxication, disorderly conduct, and disturbing the peace. At least, he would be detained for the night. Tomorrow Glover would decide how to handle this, so that it never happened again.

Pandemonium under control, Glover hiked up his beltless trousers, and escorted Bessie and LaVeeta inside, closing the front door behind them.

"Y'all don't need to worry. Everthin's gonna be all right. Let me think on this an' we'll talk tomorrow. Now, y'all get settled down an' get to bed." Glover shook his tousled hair out of his eyes and looked down at his bare feet, noticing that his big toe was scraped and bleeding. Must have stubbed it when he took the porch steps two at a time. Pointing the wounded toe as far as it would stretch upward, he limped to the door while thinking, *I'll be in a world o' pain tomorrow when I cram that little darlin' in a steel-toed boot.*

After reassuring LaVeeta that this was not the end of the world, Bessie lay awake trying to figure how she was going to explain the fracas to the neighbors. Back home, Glover lay awake, after reassuring Doris that everything was all right. He was thinking how this needed to be nipped in the bud before it happened again, or even something worse took place. LaMarcus was young, strong, and apparently not the sharpest knife in the drawer. Neither LaVeeta nor Bessie could match his physical strength. Glover didn't trust him as far as he could pick him up and throw him – it seemed obvious the lad needed an attitude adjustment. And, a lasting adjustment at that!

The next morning, Glover left a note for Auntie to take

133

to Bessie as early as she could. The scrawled note read:

*Bessie, call the jail and find out what it will take to get
L. out and when they will let him go. Leave note at the foundry
with the timekeeper. Thanks. G.*

Bessie did as he asked and left Glover a note saying that
the fine was $18, and LaMarcus would be released when the fine
was paid. Tucked inside the envelope Glover found a ten, five,
and three one-dollar bills.

It was payback time. Buddy owed him one big-time, and
he was calling in the favor. During lunch break, Glover found
Buddy in the core setter's shop.

"Hey, Buddy. Need your help on a little matter. 'Member
that smart-ass LaMarcus Johnson?"

"Ain't he the one that stole Ol' Man Hawkins goat last
Fourth of July an' sol' it t' Benny Brakefield? All hell broke loose
when Benny barbequed Betty Hawkins's pet goat." Grinning,
Buddy untied the sleeves to his denim shirt that hung around his
waist like an apron turned backwards.

"One an' the same".

"What 'bout 'im? What's th' crazy fool done now?" He
slid his arms into the shirtsleeves and began to button the front.

"Tell you when we get outside." Glover held up his
lunchbox and turned toward the shop door. Buddy felt beneath
the workbench, pulled out a well-used brown sack, and followed
Glover.

Sitting on the tailgate of the nearest pickup truck, Glover
told of the previous night's ruckus.

"I can't take a chance on that good-for-nothing drunk
hurtin' Bessie Pearl or LaVeeta." Glover bit into a wedge of cold

cornbread, wiped the crumbs off his lips with the back of his hand, and chewed while he unscrewed the cup off his thermos.

"Darn tootin'. He needs t' be shut up tighter'n a henhouse door." Licking mayonnaise from the sides of a sliced tomato and Spam sandwich, Buddy shook his head in agreement. "If there's ever a mir'cle, it's that somebody hadn't killed that idiot 'fore now."

"Well, we aren't gonna kill him, but our ace in the hole is that he won't know that. Here's where our poker playin' skills come in. We'll make him think he's 'bout to meet his Maker. Way I see it, he needs to get his sorry ass out of 'Bama an' stay out! They'll let him out of jail soon as I pay the fine. You reckon we might be able to give him a ride to the bus station?"

Buddy chewed and continued to shake his head yes.

"We can work out the details on our way to town to get him." Glover poured buttermilk into the thermos cup. Dunking another piece of cornbread in the clabbered milk, he quickly put it in his mouth before it fell apart.

Buddy was ready and raring to go. It was a toss-up: the possibility of a good fight was almost as exciting as holding a winning hand in a card game. Not quite, but almost.

Mid-afternoon the two friends left the foundry and headed downtown to the city jail. Glover knew several of the cops in the local precinct from bailing his brother Howard out on a fairly regular basis.

"Hey, Floyd." He shook hands with a stout, balding policeman behind the front desk. "I'm doin' my good deed for the day. Need to get LaMarcus Johnson sprung."

"You know more drunks than I do, and I lock 'em up every day," Floyd joked as he slid a paper in front of Glover for him to sign.

"Eighteen dollars?" Glover pulled the cash out of his shirt pocket.

"Close 'nuff." Floyd took the money and pressed a rubber stamp first onto an inkpad and then onto the paper. "Follow me." A ring of keys jangled as Floyd pulled it from the top desk drawer.

To say that LaMarcus was surprised to see Glover and Buddy doesn't even begin to describe the look on the young boy's face. With that said, it took a bit of convincing to get him to go with them.

"You owe us for gittin' you out, you ungrat'ful nitwit. Come on, we'll take you home!" Buddy grabbed one elbow, and Glover latched onto the other as they steered him toward the door.

Once inside the car, Buddy drove in the opposite direction of LaMarcus's house to a secluded area near the deserted airport runway. LaMarcus was glad to be free. But, an anticipatory shiver ran up his spine when he realized that he'd simply moved from one type of incarceration to another. He remembered little about the disturbance that he'd caused the night before. Therefore, Glover painted a vivid picture to fill in any blank spots – especially the threats that LaMarcus had made to his sister and Bessie. By the time they turned off the main road, LaMarcus was pretty sure that if he came out of this alive, it would be his lucky day.

Buddy pulled the car into a stand of trees where they couldn't be seen by anyone passing by.

Glover opened the back door and pushed LaMarcus to the ground, sending the young man sprawling face-first into dusty red clay. Planting his number ten boot firmly between the scrambling captive's shoulder blades, Glover leaned over and through clenched teeth shouted, "You're a real smart ass. Big an' brave threatenin' women, but I don't hear any threats comin' from you now. Maybe my hearin's gone bad. No wait. I don't see your lips movin'!"

Buddy hurried around the car and joined the pair. "You ain't dealin' with no woman. I can guaran–damn-tee that you dealin' with somebody that can whup yo' ass!"

"And will!" added Glover.

The next few minutes were spent issuing a lesson in firm persuasion. A little roughhousing got LaMarcus's attention and then Glover began to work on giving him a new frame of mind.

"You're 'bout to make a change. A lastin' change." Taking a five-dollar bill from his pocket, Glover shoved it into the pocket of LaMarcus's torn blue shirt. "This is for bus fare. You takin' a trip. A long, long trip. And, when will you be comin' back? NEVVEERRRR!!! We're goin' to the bus station, an' you're gonna be on the next Greyhound that'll take you as far as five dollars'll buy."

"What you talkin' 'bout?" Fear shone from LaMarcus's brown eyes. "I can't go nowhere! I needs ta talk to my mama! She ain't gonna like this one bit, an' you gonna be the ones in jail."

"The hell you say!" Buddy screamed in his face.

LaMarcus knew that he'd made a bad move, and he decided that he'd better try a little damage repair.

"'Sides, Missur Bossman, I got a job I got ta go to in da mornin'." Perspiration streamed down the scared young man's dark brown forehead into his eyes, that were now the size of fried eggs – sunny-side up. He reached to wipe the sweat off his brow, but not in time to avoid a punch from Buddy that landed on his right cheek just below the eye, flinging his head to the side.

"You don't raise yo' hand 'ginst me, boy!" Buddy warned.

"I ain't doin' nothin' but keepin' the sweat outta my eyes." Reeling from the knuckle sandwich, LaMarcus covered his aching cheek with his hand.

"Well, Slick," said Glover, "fact o' the matter is, you know you got no job tomorrow. You ain't ever hit a lick at a snake in your life. You been cruisin' for a bruisin' ever since I've known anythin' 'bout you. An' the time has come."

"Maybe he'd like t' be hogtied an' drug behin' a pickup truck", Buddy sarcastically announced. "I'd be glad t' do the tyin' an' the draggin'."

Glover suddenly realized that he'd better wind this up before Buddy organized a lynching party.

The deal was sealed with a final threat. "If either of us ever lay eyes on you ag'in or hear of you bein' in Etowah County, YOU ARE A DEAD MAN!" Glover grabbed his shirt, lifted him off the ground, and drew him close enough that their noses touched.

"That applies if you git off that bus anywhere 'fore the state line, you useless lowlife. The bus driver's workin' for us, so you better not step yo' sorry rear-end off that Greyhound!" Buddy closed the conversation with his two cents worth.

Buddy and Glover were just doing what they thought was right. They'd been taught that drastic situations called for drastic measures. A real man was expected to protect women and children, and had not Glover taken matters into his own hands and set out to bring about a permanent solution, he could not have looked at his face in the mirror. Glover had no intention of seriously harming anyone, but being a seasoned poker player, he

138

talked a good bluff. Both he and Buddy knew that without strong motivation, LaMarcus Johnson was about as apt to do the right thing as a politician was likely to keep his promises.

A convinced and defeated LaMarcus was escorted to the bus station, where he reluctantly boarded a bus headed north. Glover and Buddy stood in the bay and watched the bus pull away from the terminal and out of sight.

"Reckon we won't never see 'im agin," Buddy concluded as they shook hands.

"I sure as hell hope not." They climbed into the Ford sedan and headed to the house for supper, each trusting that they would never be called upon to back up their threats.

*

LaVeeta had been as nervous as a one-legged tightrope walker since the night that LaMarcus had caused a ruckus, in spite of Glover's assurance that she had nothing to worry about. She knew LaMarcus. He was a loathsome varmint that had been nothing but trouble since he was nine or ten years old. Truth of the matter was, he'd never had a snowball's chance in hell from the day that he was born. When he was fourteen, he'd been held in the county jail for being drunk, stealing a tractor, and then wrecking it. He was a poor, pathetic soul − misery looking for a place to spread. LaVeeta was as scared of him as she was of her mother.

Now days, fear knocked less frequently at LaVeeta's door since she'd found a patch of peace by moving in with Bessie Pearl. She loved Bessie, idolized her as a teacher, and hoped that she could stay with her indefinitely. Working for Glover and Bessie gave her a small income so that she could put in on groceries and pay her way. That made her feel important, equal, a part of the family. The tiny brown girl had seen too much to live in a dream world – she knew that her skin was dark and that defined how others treated her. That awareness never left her. But, she felt something from the Daniels family and Bessie that she had not known from white folks before. Their heartfelt genuineness left no doubt in her mind that these people accepted her for who she was. Having known *lack* up close and personal all her life, she knew how to make a little go a long way. In the corner of the dresser drawer, underneath a cotton camisole, she stowed away most of her earnings in a worn leather coin purse. For the first time in her life, she had everything that she needed. And best of all she felt safe. Her nerves were settling down, and she could actually sleep at night without keeping one eye open.

Taking care of the twins was rewarding. In no way comparable to what she'd experienced taking care of her younger brothers and sister. LaVeeta's mother lived in a world of murky darkness, oozing from a depth of depravity that contaminated everyone she touched. Kind words left her mouth only when they served to disguise her divisive ways. She saw every child to whom she'd ever given birth as an ever-present reminder of something else in her life that she didn't want or need. Her reputation for stealing and lying had spread to those looking for domestic help. She'd been fired from half a dozen jobs whenever jewelry or other items had come up missing. When she could no longer get work, she'd depended on LaVeeta's marketable skills. Every minute that LaVeeta wasn't cleaning houses or babysitting kids and old folks, her mother had her cooking, cleaning, or caring for her siblings. Now that LaVeeta had moved to Bessie's, it was anybody's guess as to how Hester was paying the rent and buying food. Prostitution was a good possibility.

The people with whom LaVeeta now lived and worked never intimidated or scolded her. She *wanted* to please them. She *wanted* to do a good job. Confidence in her abilities was becoming real, and she was actually allowing herself to care about Bessie and the Daniels family. They'd given her the only real home that she'd ever known, but her greatest concern was that LaMarcus could take it all away.

If she never saw that deadbeat brother of hers again, that would still be too soon. But she worried about her younger siblings, especially thirteen-year-old Addie Maude.

Addie, stubborn and resentful from being belittled and mistreated by her mother, was still in school. But LaVeeta knew that soon she'd be made to stay home. Hester needed her to look after the two younger children − Hezekiah, six, and Anthony, four. It was a sure thing that Hester would not take care of them. As a matter of fact, most of the time she had no idea as to the boys' whereabouts. LaVeeta could only hope that someway, somehow, Addie would be able to escape a dark destiny riddled with physical and mental abuse. Survival would surely take up most of Addie's time and energy, and that left little room for dreams.

Perhaps there was a real chance that LaVeeta might realize her dreams, now that she was free from that wretched life. She wanted to go to college to become a teacher. Bessie said they would work toward that goal. To LaVeeta, it seemed like a far-fetched, impossible dream. To Bessie, it was as good as done.

*

141

Auntie placed the glass bottles one by one into a pan of boiling water and poked them with metal tongs, being certain that each was fully submerged. After a one-minute boil time, she fished the bottles out and set them topside up to air dry.

"Need any help?" asked Glover.

"I don't think so." Auntie stirred a batch of Carnation milk, boiled water, and a capful of Karo syrup in a large sterilized Pyrex pitcher.

"I have to stop an' think to 'member what the formula is," said Glover.

"It's easy." Using tongs, Auntie placed a sterilized nipple upside down in each bottle and then a cover and a ring to cap it.

"The milk and water are equal parts. The trick is adjustin' the Karo. A little more if there is any sign of constipation, less if not needed," she said, carefully removing the nipples and rings and then filling each bottle with five ounces of formula. When all eight bottles were filled, she dropped them into the wire rack inside the water-filled sterilizer. Placing the lid on the pot, Auntie glanced at the clock on the stove, noting the minute hand. After boiling one minute, she would lift the bottles out and set them on a clean towel to cool.

Sterilization was a crucial step in preventing the babies from getting thrush, a common yeast infection. Thrust rarely occurred after the first two months. But like most infants of the era, Jack's and Jim Ed's bottles would be sterilized until the twins were six months old, just in case.

"Come back later and you can help me put these in the icebox. Made a triple batch. Twenty-four bottles, eight at a time." She smiled with pride at another job well done.

"There is no way that we could manage without you." Glover put his arm around her shoulder and hugged her. "I mean it, Auntie. You mean the world to me."

"Thank you, Glover." She patted his hand. "We've only got a few more months to sterilize bottles. Soon Elsie the Cow will provide milk for the boys," she said with a laugh.

*

Western Union on Main Street closed at 4 p.m. Glover darted in the front door at 3:57 to lay claim to $125, wired from the bank in Talladega. Buddy had gotten the paymaster at the foundry, a notary public, to complete a bill of sale and the little black Ford sedan was officially Glover's as he handed Buddy the money. There on the bill of sale was Buddy's given name – Joe Harvey Higgins – but he would always be Buddy to Glover.

Glover inserted the key, cranked the engine, and listened to the melodic hum of an idling motor. He felt like Henry Ford himself had ordered this chariot – custom-made – just for him. Shifting into first gear, he eased the clutch out and pressed down on the gas pedal. As the car began to roll, he steered it toward home. Hallelujah! He had dreamed of this day but had not fully anticipated the feeling of freedom that came with owning a vehicle. Glover was so happy he felt that at any minute he might sprout wings and fly.

Doris, Auntie, and the kids were waiting for him, not only to ride in the *new* car, but also to go see the property that was for sale. Bessie and LaVeeta were anxious to see the house too – they would follow in Bessie's car.

Glover tooted the horn as the little sedan pulled up in front of the house on Cherry Street, where the excited family waited curbside. Amanda jumped up and down while clapping her hands when she saw her daddy behind the steering wheel.

After looking the vehicle over, as if they'd never laid eyes on it before, they loaded into the car and pulled away from the curb – Glover leading the way with Bessie close behind.

Right away – they hadn't reached the end of the block – all three girls were begging to give the little car a name.

"Daddy, let's call it Lulu," Molly suggested.

"I like that. What 'bout you, sweetheart?" He looked at Doris who nodded her head yes. No one offered a better name, and no one objected. So with a unanimous show of hands it was decided: the new car would henceforth be known as Lulu.

Glover hoped that he could find his way to the north Gadsden property. When he passed the elementary school, he felt a sigh of relief – he was sure that he was headed in the right direction. He pointed to the school, telling the girls that they'd be riding the school bus. That sealed the deal for Marianne and Molly. The prospect of riding a school bus superseded any fear of changing schools or living in a different house.

Doris sat in the front seat between Glover and Marianne, saying little as they rode along. Her mind was as sharp as it had ever been, and she fully understood all that Glover had told her about the house and land. Even so, it was difficult to express her thoughts, so she squeezed Glover's hand and returned his smile. An overpowering determination to regain her verbal and motor skills burned within her. Doris, although charming and feminine, was as tough as a ten-cent steak. Once she'd made up her mind, there was little that could dampen her determination.

Glover spotted the turnoff from the main highway.

"This is the turn – I think," Glover said. After going over the railroad tracks, he was certain that he was on the right road. "We're right. Look for some birdhouses made outta gourds."

"There!" he yelled at the same time that Amanda pointed

out the gourd village for purple martins.

Breezing past the birdhouses, they soon saw a crossroads up ahead.

"We turn here. Get ready for a dust storm."

Stopping at the intersection where Stancil's Country Store anchored the corner on the right, he turned left onto the dirt road. Lulu stirred up a little less dust than Marvin's pick-up truck had, but still, they rolled up the windows so that they could breathe. Bessie followed behind, dropping back several car lengths to give the dust time to dissipate so that she could see Glover ahead of her.

As Glover turned into the rutted driveway, he saw the white frame house suspended on pilings. Without his visionary glasses, it looked like a house that needed a front porch and a whole lot of repairs. Even so, it didn't take long for him to slip on his rose-colored shades, and he began to see a beautiful structure that would make a fine home for him and his family. With little or no effort, visionaries have an incredible ability to see potential when others miss it entirely.

"Y'all have to imagine how great it can be with a little fixin' up," he said as they piled out of the cars and headed inside. Glover stood back and looked from one person to another, anxious to read their reactions.

The girls ran from room to room, each placing dibs on a bedroom.

Doris, following the exuberant children, nodded her head in approval.

Auntie bounced a baby on each hip, a smile on her face.

Bessie winked at Glover and gave a thumbs-up.

LaVeeta didn't know whether to scratch her head or wind her watch. There was never a dull moment with these people.

"You have to see the garden spot an' the woods." Glover was extremely excited as he led the way to the back stoop and down the path toward the old outhouse.

Auntie put the boys down on a baby blanket that was spread on the empty living room floor. She'd stay with the babies while Glover led a tour of the grounds. As they walked to the clearing out back, he raised and spread his arms like Moses at the Red Sea. Everyone gathered around as he talked about rows of tomatoes, corn, beans, peas, squash, okra, and peppers that he would plant next spring. In the upcoming early fall, he could grow cabbage, lettuce, beets, and bush peas. He'd have to hire someone to plow the ground, but that wouldn't be a problem. Hey, maybe he would buy a used tractor if there were enough money left over.

One would have thought that there were fifty acres rather than five.

"Prob'ly have to hire migrant workers to help with the harvest," Bessie sarcastically commented in a friendly tone of voice. Glover just grinned.

Making noise and shuffling feet through a patch of tall grass to shoo off any snakes, they trekked past the garden plot to the creek placidly meandering through the woods. Playful delight ensued as footwear was hastily flung so that bare feet could bathe in cool, clear water. Toes wiggled in the soft muddy bottom of the creek bed sending fish scrambling for cover. Doris watched. She'd never learned to swim, and if the truth be told, she had no interest in activities that involved water in lakes, creeks, or pools. Spotting a boulder nearby, she sat down and enjoyed watching the others as they played.

For the next little while, the woods were filled with

laughter and gleeful squeals as the children jumped about splashing and playing. When the girls stomped their feet and water flew everywhere, Bessie and LaVeeta waded away in a futile attempt to keep their dresses dry. Even Glover couldn't resist slipping off his loafers and cooling his little piggies.

Judging the hour of the day by the sun lowering in the western sky, he knew that it was getting late. Amid protests, Glover insisted that they get back to the house in case Auntie needed help with the babies.

Climbing the steps to a small porch on the back of the house, Molly opened the screen door and led the way into the kitchen.

As they approached the front room, they heard voices. One voice clearly belonged to Auntie; the other was a man's raucous voice. Glover quickly stepped in front of everyone. Entering the room, he saw Auntie holding Baby Jack. A tall man with flaming red hair and beard, dressed in bib overalls with no shirt underneath, was bouncing Baby Jim Ed in his arms.

Turning to greet Glover, the man immediately stuck out his hand and introduced himself.

"Coggins Campbell," he said with a smile that covered most of his face. His piercing sky-blue eyes, shaded by bushy red eyebrows, sparkled as he spoke.

"Just call me Cam. I'm your next door neighbor, neighbor." He nodded his head to the right. Glover assumed that this indicated that he lived in the house that was barely visible through the woods.

Marianne reached for Jim Ed as he leaned toward her with outstretched arms. Although she was only eleven years old, she handled the babies as competently as any of the adults.

Auntie quickly filled in gaps by repeating all that Cam

147

had told her – he was widowed three years ago. His grown children lived nearby. He was a carpenter by trade. And he was hoping that they were buying the property. He needed a neighbor.

"I've not fully decided, although it seems likely that this'll be our future home. All votes haven't been counted." Glover grinned.

Simultaneously, Doris, Bessie, LaVeeta, and the kids raised a hand high above their heads and chimed in, "We already love this place." Glover glanced at Auntie – she raised her hand although she hadn't seen much past the front rooms. Looked like all the votes *were* in. They were willing to pitch in, roll up their sleeves, and make Doris and Glover's dream come true.

Cam and Glover walked outside while the women took one last tour of the house, and Bessie showed Auntie the grounds out back.

Pointing in the direction of his house, Cam led Glover to a narrow path through the woods that connected the two properties.

"I knew the Tiffins for more'n fifteen years. We kept this path worn bare when Horace was sick. His wife Tillie came to get he'p when he'd fall. Had dropsy. Poor fellow's legs were as big as tree trunks."

"Sorry to hear that." Glover walked toward the path. "That 'xplains why the house hasn't been kept up."

"I added that bathroom on the back of the house 'bout four years ago when Horace got to where he couldn't make it to the outhouse. I knew an inside bathroom would he'p them out." Cam turned toward a commotion in the front yard.

The women were trying to soothe twins that were screaming like babies will when they are hungry and sleepy. The

148

two cranky baby boys prompted everyone to say their farewells and head toward Cherry Street.

"Y'all call on me to he'p any way that I can, if y'all decide to move in. I can drive that ol' long-bed pickup truck to town and load it with furniture." He pointed to his truck parked behind Lulu. There was that half-mile spread of pearly teeth peeking through a bush of red whiskers.

"Well," Glover said as he pumped Cam's large, calloused hand, "we're off to a good start. Good neighbors make good friends."

*

It was a done deal! Glover and Doris were officially homeowners! Hallelujah!

With the house and land in the Daniels' name, the women lost no time packing and were ready to move lickety-split.

Early on Saturday morning, Buddy, Cam, Marvin Stoddard, Buddy's brother Axel, and Cam's look-alike son Thane arrived at the house on Cherry Street, ready to load furniture and belongings into five pick-up trucks. They were hoping to get everything in one trip. Glover would drive Lulu, packed to the gills, and they would load Bessie's car too.

The previous week, Avis had come to help Auntie and LaVeeta scrub the new house inside and out. Glover had put down in the kitchen and bathroom vibrant patterned linoleum – red, yellow, and green triangles like rubber bands on a dappled gray background. Cam had insisted on pitching in to help paint the bedrooms. Buddy had helped Glover sand and shellac canary-yellow knotty pine floors until they looked better than

149

brand-new. LaVeeta had spent the better part of a day scrubbing white metal kitchen cabinets and polishing the chrome hardware until it gleamed. Everything was ready for moving day.

At 6:00 on the morning of the move, Auntie baked a batch of biscuits, fried sausage patties, and made enough coffee for everyone. Bessie and LaVeeta contributed cinnamon rolls from Smoot's Bakery on 5th Street. Ann and Wally Smoot – Wally'd gained his skills as a baker when he was in the army – were known far and wide for their melt-in-your-mouth pastries.

Marianne kept the coffee pot perking. After filling Buddy's cup, she thought that she'd seen him take a flask out of his pocket and add something to the black brew. *Maybe not*, she thought, having not gotten a clear view. The workers made light work of the task at hand. They laughed and joked while loading furniture and boxes into the trucks. By 9:00, the house was empty, and the convoy headed north.

Hemmed in by furniture, black and white speckled Briscoe sat in the back of Cam's truck close to the cab so that Marianne could stick her arm out the window and hold onto a rope tied around his neck. Every once in a while the baffled pooch let loose with a loud "Wroof! Wroof!"

Bessie stayed to clean up anything that was left behind and return the door key to the landlord. They had searched for days, and nearly given up, until Glover dumped the kitchen junk-drawer into a cardboard box. There amongst a conglomeration of odds and ends lay the missing house key. A dingy, white shoelace serving as a key ring was the only reason they'd spotted it.

Avis and Edward Earl had taken the twins to their house on Friday and would bring them home on Sunday afternoon, making it easier on everyone to get things settled at the new location.

Unloading the trucks took more time than loading them. The furniture had to be placed and boxes put in appropriate rooms. The wringer washer had a new home on the back porch, located just outside the kitchen. Draining the washer tub would be much simpler because the water could drain directly into a trench and away from the house. Although, washing in the winter would be more inconvenient since the washer was outside. They would cross that bridge when they'd come to it.

By early afternoon, the June heat was inching the thermometer into the middle 90s. Bessie arrived with three large watermelons just as the last of the boxes were unloaded. The melons had been cooling overnight in a galvanized washtub, filled with ice that Mitch Chestnut had chipped and filled on Friday. This was his last ice delivery to the Cherry Street house. Mitch really hated to see them go. He wondered if they'd thought ahead that there was no ice delivery where they were moving, and they'd have to get an electric refrigerator or do without ice – a commodity that no Southerner could live without, being that iced tea was necessary for survival.

Cam and his son Thane went to get a wooden table they'd made from 2X4's and scrap lumber. They set it in the backyard underneath a shady oak and cut the melons on it. The hot, tired men ate cold watermelon slices as if gnawing corn off a cob, letting the juice run down their chin.

When the women weren't around, the men told jokes and laughed hysterically. Glover and Buddy told about when the home brew froze and spilled inside the bedroom wall. What had not been the least bit funny at the time had somehow now become hilarious!

Buddy slapped Glover on the back and said "Ya added

insult t' injury when ya poured out th' seven good quarts that didn't freeze."

"You know darn well I did you a favor. You'd prob'ly be in the penitentiary if it weren't for me."

"I'da prob'ly had some money in my pocket if I'da had 'nuff nerve t' make another batch." They all howled with laughter.

When any one of the ladies brought iced tea, the laughter and jokes ceased as the manners of Southern gentlemen took over, only to break out again when she was out of earshot.

Around noon the last helper had taken leave, after being thanked numerous times. As soon as Glover set the beds up, Doris and Amanda were going to take a short nap. Marianne and Molly were off to play in the creek.

"Take Briscoe with you. He'll scare off any snakes," said Glover.

"Keep him up near you. Be careful," Auntie cautioned.

The playful hound was glad to be out of his pen and free to run where he pleased. He would tag along with the girls and stay around the house during the day. For the first night or two Glover would put him in the abandoned outhouse to be sure that he didn't leave until he learned that this was his new home.

*

Coggins "Cam" Campbell was as pleased as Punch to have new neighbors. Had it been up to him, he couldn't have picked people that he liked any better than the Daniels family. Cam considered himself a good judge of character. He knew a good man when he saw one, and he suspected that Glover Daniels might even be the king of good men.

He perceived Glover's aunt as not only a lady, but also an attractive woman in a subdued, come-hither kind of way. Cam wished he knew her given name, but it would have been presumptuous of him to ask. She'd introduced herself to him as Auntie; so far, he'd not called her anything. He wondered if she'd been married. There were a lot of things that he would like to know, but a gentleman did not ask a lady such questions. Glover would have the answers, but Cam didn't want to offend anyone by being too forward or personal. He could not get the image of her in a pale yellow blouse – a shade lighter than her honey-colored hair – out of his mind. Her skin was like peaches-and-cream and her voice – that sounded to him like angel whispers – resonated in his mind's ears. Not that he was aware of ever actually having heard an angel whisper.

Unbeknownst to Cam, a relationship with a man was not only at the very bottom of Auntie's wish list; it wasn't even on the list.

Cam Campbell was 62 years old, although he looked and acted ten years younger. His forty-three-year marriage had ended when his wife Elizabeth died from complications caused by diabetes. Their sons Chalmer, Thane, and Delmus (aka Chip), and their families, lived nearby on land that Cam had given them. In fact, the whole community was filled with Campbell offspring of one sort or another – whether sons, brothers, aunts, uncles, or cousins.

Cam, a master carpenter, was in a position to pick and choose jobs, since he needed very little money to live on.

Apple, peach, and pecan orchards on his sixty acres of land yielded a bounty of fruit and nuts each year. A chicken house, hedged by a wire fence, was home to thirty or so hens, providing eggs. At the first winter cold snap, Cam and his boys'

153

butchered hogs, and one of the sons raised cattle, so there was never a shortage of meat.

All in all, Cam had everything that he needed to live comfortably. Although better off than most men, Cam lacked one thing. He was lonely, and he yearned for a wife.

The community of Campbell's Corner had been so named because of generations of Campbells that had lived and raised their families there. The road that ran in front of Glover's and Cam's property was named Campbell Cove Road. On a hill, not far away, stood Campbell Baptist Church overlooking a slew of Campbells planted in Campbell Cemetery. Campbell's Christmas Tree Farm raised cedar trees, and Campbell's Dairy manufactured a full line of cultured dairy products.

The proud Campbell clan could trace their ancestry back to Scotland, County Argyll, in the fifteenth century. Cam was named Coggins as a result of the boastful attitude of his father Angus. Maureen Campbell, Cam's mother, was a Coggins before she married. Having grown so tired of the highfalutin ways of the Campbell clan, she said, "They think that a Campbell hung the moon."

She decided to give Cam her family name, for it was her strong opinion that a Coggins could outclass a Campbell any day.

*

Glover was riding high with big plans for the last six months of 1950. And those plans included a television set. The Philco was paid for, and the furniture store would finance a TV. Also, he was on a short waiting list for a telephone. The fabulous '50s were unfolding, and Glover Daniels had never had it so good.

Chapter Seven
The Fourth of July

Glover turned the tuning knob on the Philco back and forth across the dial hoping to find a news station. So far, he'd found more static than news.

On June 27, 1950, the hottest item in the news was the most recent military conflict in Korea. Hovering close to the radio, Glover twisted the dial, listening for a familiar voice – Drew Pearson, Edward R. Murrow, Walter Cronkite – just anybody reporting on the situation there.

After WWII, Glover'd closely followed the changes that had taken place in Korea. Japan surrendered to Allied troops in 1945 forfeiting rule over Korea, which they'd held since 1910. American administrators divided the peninsula along the 38th parallel: U.S. military troops occupying the southern half, Chinese and Soviet military forces occupying the northern half. A three-mile-wide demilitarized zone separating the two areas was a volatile hotspot due to cross-border skirmishes and raids.

Korea had become a pawn in a new era coined the Cold War. This terminology was used to label a real and dangerous power struggle between Capitalism and Communism, the United States and Soviet Russia. The Cold War was so named because it rarely featured direct military action – somewhat like a sullen standoff between feuding spouses.

In the case of players on the world stage, both sides possessed nuclear weapons: and their use would probably guarantee mutual destruction. The ideologies of both sides had become a tug of war between good and bad, godliness and ungodliness. The term Cold War represented a concept that did not fit what the world had known as war since war was first recorded in 2700 B.C. The average American was hard-pressed to define a Cold War, much less recognize one.

Cold or otherwise, just the thought of war threw Glover into a tizzy.

"Cam's grandsons are draft age," he said to Doris. "Buddy's brother is nineteen and will be called."

"What about Lester and Leonard?" asked Doris, referring to Avis and Edward Earl's sons.

"They'll go," he shook his head and continued. "I'm not willin' to lose any one of them, but I'm not so stupid that I think a war can be fought without losin' men. The whole thing stinks like a bucket of rotten fish! How can we go through another war?"

Finally! Glover stopped turning the radio dial at the sound of Walter Cronkite's voice. Cronkite reported that open warfare had broken out when North Korean forces invaded South Korea on the 25th of June. President Truman would dispatch Army and Navy troops to the region, the objective being to halt the invading troops and push them back across the neutral zone.

Cursing underneath his breath, Glover balled his fist and exclaimed, "Communist pigs!"

For the sake of his rising blood pressure, he switched the radio off and headed for the kitchen. He needed coffee.

Little did Glover know that his worst fears would come true. The conflict would continue to escalate, and one day after Glover and his family would attend a big shindig at Cam's on the 4th of July, Private Kenneth Shadrick would be the first of 36,940 Americans to lose their lives in Korea. Another 92,000 men would be wounded. 3,700 would be missing in action. And

156

4,400 would become prisoners of war.

*

A wooden ladder made from scrap two-by-fours leaned against the side of the house. Scared but fearless, Glover stood on the roof, remembering the time that he'd helped lay tar paper atop Zeke Dooley's old barn. After one careless misstep, Sonny Miller had slipped and tumbled down the slanted roof, frantically pawing for something to grab on to. The other men had hurried to the edge to look down, halfway expecting to see a pile of broken bones. Luckily, Sonny had landed in a water trough. With that in mind, Glover cautiously climbed to the highest gable and steadied himself by digging the soles of his boots against the rough shingles. His mission: to mount an antenna for the new television.

Spindly and awkward, the metal antenna perched atop a long pole looked like a huge fish's skeleton, minus the head and tail. Plopping the pole into a bracket he'd mounted, Glover connected lead-in wire to the antenna and strung it across the roof, down the side of the house, through an open window to the television. Then he connected it to the back of the set.

Marianne was called to stand outside near the ladder. Inside, white snowy-like dots, rapidly danced on the television screen, making Auntie woozy as she watched. Satisfied that the lead in wire was properly attached, Glover climbed back onto the roof to turn the antenna this way and that. The threesome worked in unison: Auntie hollered out the window to Marianne who hollered to Glover, as to whether there was more or less snow when he turned the antenna.

"It's worse, Glover. Turn it back the other way."

"It's worse, Daddy. Turn it back the other way."

"What?" Glover cupped his ear and leaned in her direction.

"The other way, Daddy, back like you had it, but not as far!" Marianne shouted at the top of her voice.

Back and forth – a little this way, a little that way – they worked to clear the snowy screen. When it was determined that the picture was clearer, he stopped turning the lanky antenna.

Auntie switched the dial to all three channels to see if there was a discernable picture. Tired of messing with a television set, Auntie declared that all channels were as clear as they were going to be.

"That looks pretty good. I don't think you'll get it any better!" yelled Auntie as loudly as she could.

"Daddy! Auntie says that's it. It's as good as it's gonna get."

"Not yet? Did you say that's it or not yet?"

"It's good! Done, Daddy! Quit!" Doing jumping jacks, Marianne screamed like the hometown team had scored and motioned for him to stop.

Glad for the good news, Glover cautiously made his way across the roof and down the ladder.

No use putting the ladder away – there would surely be more trips topside as, no doubt, the antenna would shift in the wind. Clarity of reception depended a great deal on the weather and the stability of the antenna. Every time there was excessive snow on the screen, a trip to the roof was required.

"I'm gonna leave this ladder up here. I'd better not catch any of y'all climbin' on it," he instructed Marianne as he headed inside. Glover said what he meant, and he meant what he said – and his children knew it. Not a one of them would go near that

158

ladder.

A brand new Admiral black-and-white, vacuum tube TV set with a 17-inch oval screen beamed from the confines of a handsome cabinet.

Cast aside to make place for the "magic box of moving images," the trusty Philco radio had been banished to a wall behind the dining room door. The Admiral TV claimed center stage on the only living room wall without a door or window, where it could be easily viewed from every chair.

Glover's family had never owned a more fascinating gadget. The children were constantly warned, "Don't sit too close. Move back. You'll be blind as a bat if you sit too close." The Lord only knows what this newfangled contraption would do to people in the long run!

Doris and Auntie loved daytime TV, although there was not a lot of time to sit and watch. Glover was glued to the news reports on ABC, CBS, and NBC at six and nine. He took turns looking at each channel, but his favorite commentator was John Cameron Swayze, hands down.

At times it seemed like aggravation outweighed entertainment. Frequently at a critical point in the show's plot, horizontal or vertical lines striped the screen. Other times, with no warning, the picture would begin to roll – over and over, round and round. Glover spent about as much time fiddling with the controls to regain focus and make necessary adjustments (plus making visits to the roof to point the antenna in the right direction) as he did actually watching television.

Whenever there was a reason to change channels, someone had to get up from his comfortable chair and manually select another program. Such inconveniences were small when compared to the delightful entertainment that was available at the click of a knob – game shows, variety shows, westerns, comedies, music, children's programs, and drama. Advertisements were often as entertaining as the regular shows. Profanity was strictly prohibited, suggestive or risqué material unheard of. Every program was suitable viewing for children, including octogenarians and all ages in between. All three networks played the National Anthem, had a poem about God, and then signed off the air from midnight until 6 a.m., leaving a black-and-white test pattern filling the screen.

Like most people, the Daniels family saw this clever invention as a means of entertainment. Little did they know that it would revolutionize the way people received information and understood the world.

*

The annual Campbell Fourth of July barbeque was in full swing. It was hotter'n blue blazes, but folks were accustomed to summers in the South. Guests from every neck of the woods began to arrive around four in the afternoon to enjoy festivities that would continue until ten o'clock or later.

Outside Campbell Castle, as Glover called it, freshly mown grass held a patchwork of blankets spread under every spot of shade. Folks were arranging pillows and chairs, placing diaper bags and baby strollers and other necessities as they set up temporary accommodations for the day. Some joined games in progress while others greeted friends and family.

Molly led the way, swinging a dozen yeast rolls tied up in a red-checkered dishtowel and carrying a cloth bag stuffed with hats, sunglasses, and three dozen more rolls. Following were Marianne, peeping over two folded quilts stacked in her outstretched arms, and Amanda, steadying a covered Pyrex dish full of green peas swimming in butter. Doris, with a diaper bag hung over each shoulder, carried Jack on her hip. Auntie kept pace, while balancing Jim Ed on two pillows bunched in her arms.

Glover (with Briscoe close on his heels) brought up the rear, as they all marched single-file along the trail from their house to Cam's. With his arms stretched forth like rails on a forklift, Glover held a sizable cardboard box containing a butter-pecan cake inside a cake carrier, a squash casserole, a bowl of green beans with pearl onions and new potatoes, and thirty-eight fried apple pies – there had been forty, but two had succumbed to Glover's lack of will power when it came to fried pies.

Fiery open pits behind Cam's two-story brick house infused the air with tantalizing smells of hickory smoke and barbeque sauce. Smoke tendrils rose from the pits like incense on an altar – slowly, steadily ascending from smoldering coals. Iron grids over the fire shelved sizzling meat bathed in thick, tangy, tomato sauce – pork shoulders; whole sides of ribs; plump, juicy hamburgers and hot dogs; and halved and quartered chickens. The roasting meat gave off a bouquet of nostril-tingling sensations that stimulated the salivary glands to near euphoric heights. Serious cooks fussed over the meat, swabbing it with mops made from shortened broom handles wrapped with clean strips of cotton cloth saturated in barbeque sauce. The red-hot coals spit and sputtered when sauce dripped on them.

"Happy Fourth of July!" The younger Campbell grandkids passed out small American flags to anyone ready to wave them overhead. Red, white, and blue swags covered the front porch from end to end. Even Cam's long-bed truck was decked from hood to tailgate with crepe paper streamers.

161

Ol' Glory, planted in the center of a bed of red and white petunias, flew high atop an iron flagpole. Cam's wife Elizabeth had lovingly stitched the flag. Since her passing it was always flown on the Fourth of July – not only for the occasion, but also in remembrance of her.

"Mercy! Look at this. We truly live in the land o' plenty," Cora Campbell said as she moved bowls around to make a spot for her famous macaroni and cheese. Unpainted wooden tables were laden with boo koos (beaucoups) of vegetables, either boiled, roasted, or fried. Plates of sliced, juicy red tomatoes brightened the array, lending a splash of color. Fried green tomatoes didn't add a lot of color, but no get-together was complete without them. And, of course, anybody who was somebody knew that no Southern smorgasbord could take place without wedges or muffins of cornbread and baskets of cloverleaf yeast rolls.

"I hope everybody and his brother didn't make a butter pecan cake," said Auntie as she surveyed the dessert tables.

"It won't matter if they did, Auntie," said Molly. "Yours'll be the best one." Molly knew. She had licked the icing bowl.

A quick check turned up one, but Auntie's soft swirls of cake frosting was different. The other cake was covered with pecan halves and just enough icing to keep them glued on. For those with a sweet tooth, a bakery shop display of triple- layered coconut, lemon, chocolate, and strawberry cakes were so picture perfect they almost looked too good to cut. Pyrex dishes of berry cobblers covered with crisp, sugar-sprinkled brown crusts begged to be scooped into a dish and topped with homemade ice cream.

Around back of the house near the kitchen door, Cam's

162

oldest son Chalmer and his wife Gladys were supervising the ice cream station. Vanilla was the most popular flavor, but some would add fresh peaches, pecans, or berries to a basic vanilla recipe. Eleven wooden ice cream freezers, packed tightly with heavily salted, chipped ice were being hand-cranked by anyone who would take a turn.

On the north side of the house, the horseshoe players gathered. The old timers − especially good players because the game of horseshoes had been around since horses first wore shoes − never missed ringing the fifteen-inch iron stake planted in the ground.

Boastful men engaged in the sport of arm wrestling manned five tables set up near the barn. The crowd cheered them on, and on the sly a few bets were placed. The winner was whoever overpowered his opponent two out of three tries.

Pickers tuned their banjos and guitars in the shade of the columned front porch.

"Here we go!" shouted Bedford McGregor, drawing his bow across the strings of his fiddle in a saw-like motion. Banjo player Robert Tomlin and guitar players David and Ralph Unger moved near and picked up the tune to "Foggy Mountain Breakdown."

Felton Toolan hurried out of the house lugging an upright bass that was so big and cumbersome it was like carrying a dead buffalo. "Hey, y'all! I didn't know we was startin'." Plopping the giant fiddle down near the banjo player, Felton picked up the tempo as his calloused fingers plucked the bass's taut strings, causing a deep, hoarse, plunk-plunk-plunking sound that served as a metronome for the other musicians.

The steady beat of the bass set feet happily tapping throughout the crowd. Joining the ensemble, handsome Lamar

Gorton, who'd gone for a drink, ran up on the porch and grabbed his mandolin from a wicker chair. Completing the ensemble, Lebron Campbell, who'd been standing near the flag pole flapping his gums with a few of his fishing buddies, pulled a harmonica out of his bib overalls pocket and hurried to join the others. Without missing a beat, he leaned in, slid the instrument under his bushy, black mustache, and blew into that French harp like he was trying to put out a fire.

Four couples – the women dressed in pretty full-skirted dresses with petticoats, the men decked out in western shirts and bolo ties – were greeting members of the cloggers' dance team. It was early and too hot for dancing until the sun began to go down. Everyone would eat first, and then the entertainment would begin.

On the south end of the yard, Thane's wife Virginia Ann counted burlap sacks for the sack race. She thought that she'd brought twenty, but could only find fifteen.

Collin and Craig, Cam's nineteen-year-old twin grandsons, handed out sparklers. "Y'all need to supervise the kids so they don't get burned," they reminded folks. The fizzy, sparkling things were fascinating to watch, but a threat to little fingers.

No Fourth of July barbeque would be complete without ice-cold watermelon. In the shade of the barn, a new metal horse trough held ten or twelve plump melons buried under a blanket of chipped ice.

Doris and Glover set the squirming twins on a quilt spread underneath a shade tree. Auntie bunched a pillow behind each one, knowing that the boys were just learning to sit alone and were prone to topple over. Doris sat down with the babies.

"Y'all want somethin' to drink?" Everybody did, so

Auntie took orders. "Come help me, Molly," she said, and they headed toward the food tables. Colorful soda bottle caps peeked from beds of chipped ice packed in galvanized washtubs. Thank goodness, someone had remembered to tie bottle openers to the tub handles. Two #22 Radio Flyer red wagons, the ones with wooden stake sides, were loaded with buckets of sweetened tea or lemonade. A long, thin handle of a tin dipper stuck out of each.

"Daddy, Daddy!" Amanda pulled on his pants leg. "Want to ride the ponies!" she pleaded.

Glover lifted Amanda to his shoulders and set off in a trot to find where pony rides were taking place. "Hold on, Mandy!" Glover shouted. Giggling, she wrapped her arms around his neck, while he held her dangling legs.

In addition to Bessie and LaVeeta, Buddy and his wife Evelyn were expected to arrive shortly. LaVeeta's sister Addie Maude was coming too, and afterward she was to spend the night with LaVeeta at Bessie's. LaVeeta was worried about Addie. The older sister hoped to find out how things were going for her little sister at school and at home.

Glover walked about greeting people.

"Wave to Mrs. Harbin," he said to Amanda. She loosened her grip on Glover to wave and smile as they approached the woman who cheerfully returned their greetings. He'd taught his children that it only takes a second to respectfully acknowledge a person's presence. "It don't cost you a penny to throw up your hand," he'd always say.

Cam and his boys had shopped several places to buy fireworks, even going to Georgia and Florida. His sons took pride in putting on a spectacular show from a wooden platform anchored in the middle of a nearby catfish pond. In past years

165

this had proven to be a safe place to ignite skyrockets, Roman candles, bottle rockets, and whatever they'd found that was new in the world of fireworks.

Cam spotted Glover and Amanda and hurried toward them. He slapped Glover on the back with one hand and shook hands vigorously with the other.

"Glad y'all came!" exclaimed the jolly redheaded man. Amanda ran over to give "Uncle" Cam a hug and scurried back to her place in line for a pony ride.

"Where's the rest of your brood?" asked Cam.

Auntie saw Glover pointing in their direction. Cam waved, and from her place on the quilt Auntie smiled and waved back. She didn't dislike Cam. It didn't seem possible that anyone could dislike him. But, something about him flustered her and stirred up feelings that were contrary to her gentle personality. She couldn't put her finger on just what triggered her emotions. Maybe she felt challenged – like he was questioning her life-style choices. Some people assumed that an old maid was unmarried because she couldn't snag a husband. Not the case with Auntie, who chose to be single. Although she'd given him no reason to think that she was interested in him, Cam saw no reason why she shouldn't be. Fact of the matter was, Auntie couldn't comfortably make heads or tails out of Cam Campbell. He was such a powerful presence. Cam talked louder, laughed longer, and had more energy than seemed natural. Her way of dealing with the situation was to not spend a lot of time thinking about him one way or the other.

Bessie, LaVeeta, and Addie weaved through the crowd and across the sprawling yard, heading toward tables to add their foodstuff.

"There they are," said LaVeeta, spotting Doris and the

babies. They greeted people as they made their way, each carrying chairs (that went to Bessie's bridge table) and a stack of paper fans they'd gotten at church. Thane saw them lugging the chairs and ran to help.

"Here, let me carry those," said Thane, as he reached for all four metal folding chairs. Truth be known, he wanted to find out if Miss Bessie had brought apple pies. She had. Six pies, to be exact. Thane made short work of his helpfulness and then made a bee line to the pies to save a couple of slices, lest they *get gone*.

A well-regarded and respected family − Rufus Jenkins and his wife Lettie, with three of their six children, including Mose their five-year-old adopted son − were scattering their belongings on a quilt spread in the shade of an ancient lily-flowering magnolia tree.

For more than fifteen years, the Jenkins family had farmed land directly behind Cam's and Glover's property. Their two older sons, married and with kids, lived nearby on acreage Rufus had given them. The fifty-something-year-old man was a good friend of the Campbell family and was becoming fast friends with Glover. Come spring, he would borrow a mule and plow from Rufus to break up his garden plot.

"I'll be glad t' he'p," said Rufus. "My mule Arrabella, she try the patience of Job, but she listen t' me. Takes a bit o' sweet talkin', but she listen. She don't take to nobody bossin' her 'round. Thanks she the boss. Pays off ta let 'er thank that," he added reflectively, rubbing his neatly trimmed, graying beard framing an ebony face. "We'll get dat field plowed th' first Satdee mornin' th' ground be dry."

By five o'clock everyone had arrived. Climbing up on the bed of his ol' red truck, Cam shouted into a bullhorn to

167

address the crowd. "Y'all ready? Lester Jelks and his boys been cookin' since Hector was a pup. Let's hear it for Lester 'n them."

The crowd whistled, clapped, and yelled as Lester and his five sons took a bow. When the applause died down, Cam continued.

"While I got your 'tention, let's say a blessin' over the food and thank God for this great country we live in." Handheld flags fluttered as gratitude filled patriotic hearts.

A hush spread as heads bowed and eyes closed. Cam's prayer was supported by a chorus of hearty amens.

"Some of y'all start at the food tables, and some of y'all go on back to the pits for meat so that the line'll be shorter."

He wasn't kidding himself. He knew that most would head for the barbeque pits.

A line, mostly women and children, crowded single file along each side of the food-laden tables. Paper plates were balanced precariously and piled high with a spoonful of this and that. (Some, not favoring flimsy paper products, had brought Melmac plastic plates with them.) Glover's goal was to sample a little of every dish.

The day was filled with sounds of laughter, babies crying, children playing, spoons clanking against glass bowls, and chipped ice tumbling into paper cups. Bottle caps popped and soda drinks fizzed, as friends invited friends to try their dish.

Glover sat on the quilt with Doris as she slowly ate.

"Love you," he leaned close to her ear and whispered.

"Ditto," she replied, her smile saying more than words could express.

Doris still worked on perfecting her coordination. It seemed like her hands moved slower than her brain told them to. In spite of this, she had improved by leaps and bounds. Not only was she gaining ground physically, but she'd also regained that mystic sparkle in her eyes. That sparkle, coupled with her sweet smile, never failed to make Glover feel as weak as watered-down soup.

While leaning back in folding chairs, delicately balancing plates on their laps, Bessie adjusted her straw hat, and LaVeeta removed her white plastic-rimmed, cat-eye sunglasses. Addie sat on a quilt near Marianne. Slowly but surely, the shy teenager with dark-brown skin and eyes the shade of antique brass, seemed to be warming up to everyone. Little more than a child, thirteen-year-old Addie was struggling with myriad emotions, stemming from mistreatment by her mother. Going the second mile, Marianne and Rufus and Lettie's daughters had all reached out to befriend her.

If Bessie and LaVeeta had their druthers, Addie would never go back to her mother's house. Bessie's heart was breaking for Addie to know that she was loved and accepted. LaVeeta understood how insensitive and demanding their mother could be, and she knew that things were certain to get worse for her sister in the near future.

Dimpled shade from a giant oak danced over Jack and Jim Ed as they slept on a butterfly-patterned quilt, their bottles propped on a folded diaper. Doris fanned the twins with a paper fan, cooling them and at the same time shooing the flies and mosquitoes away. She never tired of looking at her babies. They were precious, clothed in white cloth diapers fastened with large silver safety pins. She smiled as she looked at tiny heads with sweaty brown hair jutting in every direction. *Their hair looks like a porky pine*, she thought. Just admiring them filled her with a sense of fullness and satisfaction that she'd never known before. They were her miracle babies, and that she was there with them was a bigger miracle.

Auntie was talking with Bessie when Cam appeared balancing a loaded plate of food in each hand. "Got room for one more?" he asked.

"Sit here," said Molly. She vacated one of the chairs so that Cam sat across from Auntie.

Crossing his long legs, Cam made a table of sorts. As he enjoyed the potato salad, he overheard Bessie speak to Auntie, calling her Janet.

Janet. Cam was beside himself. The name fit her perfectly, he thought, as it echoed in his mind. The Daniels family had lived next door for a month, and this was the first time he'd heard anyone call her anything other than Auntie.

He casually lifted his paper cup filled with tea, swirling the ice as he shook the cup, and took a sip.

Nonchalantly, he said, "I didn't know your given name. May I call you Janet?"

Well, of all the nerve! Auntie thought. Should she interpret this as forwardness or friendliness? Auntie was a single woman, and Cam was a single man. He just needed to mind his manners! It's probably just as well that before she could open her mouth to answer, Bessie spoke up.

"Cam, do you have any acreage that you're willin' to sell?"

Well, that certainly steered the conversation in a new direction!

Forks were suspended in midair as everyone listened. "Possibly," answered Cam. "Who'd the buyer be?"

"Me," replied Bessie. "I've been thinking about selling my house and moving from town. With the money from the sale, I could have a small house built. I don't need a house as big as

170

mine for just myself."

Polio had stolen Bessie's and her husband Edgar's only child Nathaniel. Hearts broken, they'd clung to each other and somehow made it through. Then five years after their dreadful loss, just as they'd begun to live again, Bessie was once more dealt a devastating blow. Her beloved Edgar suffered a fatal stroke. For sentimental reasons, she'd kept the big house they'd built as newlyweds. An older sister once lived nearby, but she'd recently moved to Arkansas, leaving another void to be filled.

Glover, Doris, and the girls had become family to Bessie Pearl, and although she would never say anything and risk hurting their feelings, their move had left her lonely and unsettled. She especially missed the children. Now, all she wanted was something comfortable, easy to keep clean, and close to the people she loved.

"Actually, I've been thinking about a change ever since I first saw the property on Campbell Cove Road," she said as she speared an olive rolling around her paper plate.

"Let me think it over. I'm sure I can come up with the right place to build a house for you. I'll get back to you in a day or two an' we'll talk 'bout it," Cam thoughtfully replied.

Auntie gathered her plate and napkin, climbed on her high horse, and said with some asperity, "Excuse me." Startled by Cam's outspoken announcement that he wanted to be on a first name basis, she felt not only embarrassed but also very uncomfortable. As far as she was concerned, as long as Cam called her Auntie they were only considered friendly acquaintances – and she wanted no more than that. This man whom she barely knew was knocking on the door of her comfort zone, and he was no more welcome than a bill collector.

Lord, have mercy! Talk about as brazen as a harlot in a

white wedding dress! And then Bessie's little nugget of surprise! Auntie needed a large slice of cure-all – chocolate cake, that is. She made a beeline to the dessert table.

When she returned, Marianne was taking pictures with her new Kodak Brownie camera.

"It's tricky business gettin' the fi'm undone just enough to fit without exposin' it to light," she explained. After removing the top portion of the case, she had to loosen one end on a roll of film and then thread it onto a spool. Marianne had ruined two rolls trying to get the end that attached to the empty spool wound onto it.

Looking through the viewfinder, the novice photographer focused on LaVeeta and Addie as they stared expressionless in her direction. "Y'all look like you're havin' teeth pulled. Smile!" Marianne directed. The sisters responded with a display of gleaming white teeth from ear to ear.

Bessie and Auntie smiled and said "cheese" when Marianne turned the camera toward them.

"Mama. Daddy. Y'all snuggle up an' I'll take your picture." Doris and Glover leaned close together as the shutter clicked. She took photos of the babies sleeping and one of Cam holding Amanda. "Y'all both look like a couple o' Chessie cats," she laughed.

If she's thinkin' of takin' up picture takin', she'll need to keep her comments to herself, thought Molly. "Get one of me, Sissy." Molly smiled, and wondered what Miss Smarty-pants picture taker would have to say next.

In what seemed like the blink of an eye, Marianne had taken all twelve shots. She would ask Bessie to take the film to the drugstore downtown tomorrow. In about two weeks they'd be thumbing through black-and-white glossy prints – that is, if they *took.* More often than not, there were more undeveloped snapshots than ones with subject matter.

A crowd was gathering round the front porch as folks gravitated toward the sound of music, dropping paper plates and cups in randomly placed trashcans on the way.

Eight dancers formed a square. A caller belted out instructions into a bullhorn, setting feet clicking and skirts bouncing, as the dancers kept time to lively music. Buddy and his wife Evelyn obeyed the caller's cues to do-si-do, promenade, and allemande to the left. They were members of the *Swingers,* a local square dance group that performed at the drop of a hat. Buddy, Evelyn and fellow hoofers put on a crowd-pleasing show.

"I wish I'd gotten Miss Evelyn and Mr. Buddy's picture while they're all decked out in their dancin' clothes. Next time I'm bringin' lots of rolls of fi'm," Marianne lamented. She needn't blame herself for wasted film. Loading those darn cameras was next to impossible.

While some sat on the ground enjoying the music, others stood, clapping their hands and tapping their feet. Gran and Pop MacDonald, both in their eighties, locked arms and pranced around as spryly as their arthritic joints would allow. After nearly half an hour, tired but exhilarated, the eight members of the *Swingers* headed to get something to wet their whistles. Fresh as daisies, the cloggers formed a line side by side.

Clogging, also called hillbilly tap-dancing, is a folk dance with roots reaching back to Scotch-Irish heritage. Truth of the matter is, it's basically "foot stomping" in time to fast music. The cloggers danced a jig while some of the crowd meandered toward ample shade, now that the sun was setting. Some of the older folks – used to taking an afternoon nap – had found a place to get comfortable and snooze off too much barbeque and ice cream.

Occasional breezes stirred the heat. Soon the dancers joined others that sat idly, waiting for fireworks to begin. Some folks went for a second round of desserts and drinks – Lord only knows how they found room for another bite of anything.

Slowly but surely, darkness chased the sun as it slithered toward the horizon. An early star appeared here and there in the darkening heavens; a hush grew over the crowd.

Tired children rubbed sleepy eyes, trying to stay awake to see the fireworks. Soon as it was dark and no one would see, several men discretely loosened their belts or unbuttoned their britches, glad to breathe easier. Darting silhouettes in the dim light were from a few milling about as they searched for the perfect spot to get the best view of the fireworks show. Glover leaned against a sapling with Doris resting against his shoulder; the kids sprawled on the quilt.

Cam returned to sit with the Daniels family. He wanted to sit near Janet, but outgoing, boisterous Cam was too shy. There was something about her that made him feel like a man and at the same time feel like a little boy. It seemed to him that either she welcomed his company, or she wanted to snatch him bald headed. Frankly, he wasn't sure just where he stood with her, especially on this day.

Mosquitoes were having a heyday. Doris had buttered the twins with lotion that Auntie made from the leaves of a citronella geranium, mineral oil, a dash of lemon oil and musk. They were slick babies, but at least they weren't being eaten alive.

"Anybody want to spare themselves from bein' supper for these bloodthirsty pests?" Auntie asked. She applied oil to herself and other family members, and then passed the lotion around.

Soon, brilliant showers of sparks illuminated the darkness as kids waved sparklers back and forth. Each sparkled a few seconds before it fizzled out. The children loved it! It was *big doings* handling anything on fire.

A three-quarter moon, suspended in a cloudless sky, cast a creamy, yellow glow. Suddenly silence was shattered by a loud "BANG!" that sounded like a blast from a shotgun. Swift swooshing sounds followed – and then, splendiferous explosions of color. With each bang and swoosh, sparkles of red, yellow, and green, sprinkled like vibrant raindrops.

Then another,

and another,

and another,

until the heavens were ablaze with bursts of color and trailing smoke.

How could anything be so exciting and at the same time so soothing? Only beauty has the ability to do that.

For the better part of half an hour, a kaleidoscope of color overtook the ebony sky. Alas, as suddenly as it had started – and much too soon – the "heavenlies" returned to a pastoral pace. What a grandiose ending to a jam-packed day of food and activity! A day not soon forgotten.

By the light of the moon, partygoers began to gather their belongings to head for home.

Earlier in the evening, LaVeeta and Addie had joined Rufus and Lettie. LaVeeta liked the Jenkins kids, especially Mose. She saw in Lettie and Rufus a husband and wife that were kind to one another and to their children. Mose was an adorable five-year-old to whom LaVeeta was immediately drawn, and it seemed that he latched on to her right away. She couldn't put her finger on what caused the twinkle in his big brown eyes. That was because she'd not known happiness nor seen it shine from the inside out.

Preparing to leave, Lettie and LaVeeta searched for items scattered about the quilt, aided by the light of a weak battery-powered flashlight held by Rufus. LaVeeta looked around for Addie.

She was nowhere to be seen.

"Where's Addie?" she asked the others.

After calling her name with no response, Rufus suggested, "She prob'ly done gone back to where Mr. Glover at. Maybe even she sittin' in Miss Bessie's car."

Gut-wrenching fear gripped LaVeeta as she scurried to Bessie's side.

"Miss Bessie! You seen Addie?" she excitedly asked.

"No, wasn't she with you?" Bessie shook her head from side to side. "Has anyone seen Addie lately?" she asked the others.

No one knew of Addie's whereabouts.

Everyone spread out to search for her, calling her name and asking others if they'd seen her.

No one had.

Marianne ran to Bessie's car − no Addie there.

LaVeeta was shaking from head to toe as she called for her sister through broken tears. Inconsolable, LaVeeta was left in Bessie and Doris's care, while Glover hurried through the darkness to find Cam.

After hearing that Addie was missing, Cam grabbed the bullhorn, hopped on the truck bed, and shouted into the thing.

"Addie Johnson, meet your sister in the parkin' area

176

immediately," Cam repeated several times.

Most people had already gone, but the few that remained searched every conceivable place that she might be.

When the crowd was reduced to a handful, and the only car left in the parking area was Bessie's, LaVeeta slumped to the ground, her face buried in her hands.

Her worse fears had become a reality.

"No, No," she sobbed over and over. "Addie's run away. I jus' know it! I knew it'd come t' this. She's threatened t' leave, an' now she's done it. I jus' know it; I jus' know it. I feel it in my bones! She couldn't've gotten far in the dark."

"Bessie, drive us to our house an' let me get Lulu. You search back toward town, an' I'll go down 'round Rufus's house. Maybe somebody's seen her." Glover shouted orders as he headed for the parking lot.

He knew that finding her in the dark would be about as likely as a blind man spotting a four leaf clover in a clover patch.

177

Chapter Eight
Dear Addie

Glover stood outside the chicken-wire fence, watching the hens aimlessly scratch and peck around in the dirt.

Eight Rhode Island reds and one cocky rooster were the latest addition to the Daniels family. The old outhouse had been converted into a nesting area for the hens, and each had lived up to Glover's expectations as prolific layers.

After frequent and lengthy instructions, Briscoe no longer barked at the chickens, although it was with obvious restraint on his part.

It had been two days since Addie's disappearance.

LaVeeta'd visited her mother, hoping to find out if she'd heard from her missing daughter. In an effort to meet Hester on good terms, LaVeeta had taken fresh vegetables from Cam's garden and a pie that Bessie'd baked.

"I need t' talk t' Addie. She home?"

"I don't know where she be, an' I don't care." Skinny as a rail and as unkept as a backroom closet, Hester snapped at LaVeeta.

With a leering smirk, Hester cursed and called Addie terrible names saying that she hadn't seen her in a couple of days.

"She ain't never been nothin' but trouble t' me. I can slap her jaws 'til my hand hurt, but she don't never hear nothin' I tole her. Good riddance! I hope she done run t' th' moon. She be doin' us all a favor!"

Balling her fist and biting her lip, LaVeeta glared at Hester. Knowing that there was nothing more to say, she turned quickly, blinking back tears, and hurried out the door – so thankful that she had somewhere to go. She'd found a safe place to land from the hate and bitterness that she'd known all her life.

Thinking over LaVeeta's account of her visit with Hester left Glover feeling angry, tired, and befuddled. He stared blankly at the hens – seeing, not seeing – for what seemed like an eternity. Finally he turned and began to walk slowly in no particular direction. Since he no longer walked to the foundry, he'd taken to strolling on his five acres of land each day, with his dog alongside, to unwind and to catch up on his thinking.

Glover hadn't gotten much sleep since the 4th of July. The frustration was in having to admit that he didn't know how to go about finding Addie.

Although he had racked his brain until it throbbed like a hammered thumb, he drew a blank, which compelled him to confront the bare face fact that the only thing left to do was to wait.

He hated, loathed, and despised waiting.

How could he just wait when this intense need to protect Addie was gnawing from within like a rat closed up in a wooden box? An eruption of anger arose from a raw place in the depths of his soul. *For God's sake, she's just turned thirteen! She's little more than a baby. Anybody with even half a brain knows that grown-ups are supposed to protect children! Everyone – myself most of all – has failed little Addie.* Thoughts of her crying out for help, hoping that someone would come to her rescue, were tearing him apart.

Fighting off an all-consuming sadness that sought to overpower him, Glover walked past the chicken pen toward the

179

woods beyond. He surveyed the towering trees shading thick undergrowth, the blooming cannas by the propane tank, the rose bushes growing near the house. A strong drive to search for Addie, anywhere, everywhere – whether it made sense to look there or not – left him eyeing the surroundings as if he would miraculously spot her, even though he knew that she was nowhere near. He felt sure of that.

Sometimes he felt so strong and sure of himself. Sometimes he felt so small, so helpless. As bereft as he was feeling, he felt it was his duty to appear strong for the others. He was their leader, and leaders stayed strong, or at least they put on a good face.

He walked, and he prayed. Glover was no fool. He knew the source of his strength. When his back was against the wall, he turned to that source on whom he could always depend.

He talked to his God as if they were standing face to face. He poured out his heart and asked that Addie would be safe and that they might find her very soon. Teary-eyed, with an aching heart rapidly pounding in his chest, Glover surrendered to a sense of relief as he gave his worse fears to his Maker and his Friend.

Not since Doris's dance with death had Glover felt so desperate. When he tried to encourage himself by remembering all the hard times that he had conquered, his fear of Addie being abused or harmed was greater than his efforts to rally a new round of courage. One thing he knew for sure: the odds were stacked against a dark-skinned girl child, even under the best of circumstances.

While talking to God had certainly strengthened his inner man and given him a feeling that his load was lightened, waiting was no easier. At least, someone in a better position to

180

fix this situation had been consulted.

Glover quickened his pace and headed for the house. Once inside, he stopped in the kitchen and poured himself the last cup of coffee. It was as old as Methuselah, and as stale as Aunt Effie's underwear. That mattered little to Glover. He wouldn't care if the coffee had gotten so thick that he had to spread it on bread. Coffee was coffee. He loved how it smelled, how it tasted, and how it looked.

Centered on a small table just inside the dining room, the telephone held its post, like a Buckingham Palace sentry guard. Glover pulled up a chair, sat his cup on the table, and dialed Bessie's number. The barbeque had been on Tuesday. It was now late Thursday.

"Hey, Bess. Just checkin' to see if you've heard anythin'. Doris and the others are over at Lettie's pickin' cucumbers, an' I thought I'd take the time to check with you."

"No, I'm sorry to say I haven't. I talked to Rufus and Lettie. They've asked around, but the folks in the colored community don't know anything either. It does seem definite that Addie's not around here anywhere." She cleared her throat and sniffed. "I'll bring LaVeeta out in the morning to stay through the weekend and give Janet a break from the babies. While I'm there I'm meeting Cam to talk about buying land to build a house on. He has something in mind. I'm anxious to get the ball rolling on this. In the meantime, let me know if you hear anything 'bout Addie and I'll do the same."

Replacing the receiver in its cradle, Glover propped his elbows on his knees and held his head in his hands. Solemnly staring at a pine knot in the wood flooring, he felt his shoulders tense. Willing himself to relax, he took a deep breath, closed his eyes, and listened. Sleepless nights and worry had left him

181

feeling like he'd walked to Atlanta and back. Resting momentarily seemed to help. Eyes still closed, he drank in the silence of the empty house.

A little tune was stirring somewhere deep down in his soul, and before long he rose from the chair and stepped into the living room. Outside the picture window, amongst a sea of dahlias in an overcrowded flowerbed, several bees criss-crossed from the bronze-colored blooms to the yellow ones. Engaged and amused by the work-driven little yellow and black drones, Glover began to whistle. His love and talent for whistling often served as a reservoir of renewal – sometimes mending brokenness, other times lifting his spirits to new heights when he thought that he could not go on another step.

Pastor Willcott once said, "Each person has a trigger of strength that only God can pull. And pull it He does. Always at exactly the right time."

Glover felt that he'd identified the trigger that had been given him; it was the ability to whistle better than a black-capped Chickadee. He had long ago learned to not resist but allow this gift to do its work.

Choosing not to dwell on thoughts of how a little girl might be handling big problems, he picked up his empty cup and headed for the kitchen.

Dumping wet grounds from the percolator basket into a pan where scraps for the chickens were saved, he tried to remember how many cups of coffee he'd drunk since breakfast.

After a quick tally, he decided to wait until later to make another pot. He needed to go outside and work on the footing for the brick that he would lay to underpin the house. *Stay busy, stay busy* was his mantra until he could find a clue that would lead him to Addie.

182

Vacation was scheduled to begin next week. He always took the second week in July as vacation time, although he'd never had a *real, sure 'nuff* vacation.

Maybe he would take the kids to the lake a couple of times during the week. One night he and Doris might go to Birmingham and eat at Morrison's Cafeteria. Maybe even take in a movie.

In years past, they'd ridden the train to Bainbridge, Georgia, to visit cousins and called that a vacation. It seemed a sure thing that they'd have no break from work if they took two five-month-old babies on a train, or even in a car. Following a short discussion, it had been decided by unanimous vote that they'd wait until the boys were older to venture toward Georgia again.

He'd made arrangements for delivery of used brick to be dumped in the side yard. After much thought, Glover'd decided that the best spot to pile the brick would be under a shade tree, near the house. It just made sense. The shade would serve to keep him cooler as he sat and cleaned the brick; being close to the house would mean less work carrying the brick to the work site.

A contractor, tearing down a building near the foundry, had gladly given the bricks to Glover. Of course, each was bordered with dried mortar. Most were still bonded in sections of three or four rows. Some had broken into small parts or single brick, but all had to be cleaned before they could be reused.

Glover planned to spend his vacation cleaning old brick.

*

183

Bessie and LaVeeta arrived at the Daniels house around 8 a.m. on an already muggy July day – LaVeeta staying over the weekend, Bessie meeting with Cam at nine that Friday morning.

Bessie Pearl parked her car at Glover's and walked along the path through the woods to Cam's house, carrying a 7-Up pound cake with lemon drizzle.

Just as her pink polished nail pointed to the buzzer, Cam opened the door.

"Well, come in. Come in, little lady," charmed Cam.

Bessie stepped inside and glanced around the roomy foyer. A sense of grandeur and a feeling of familial warmth radiated from brick walls and a brick floor, accented with repeating bright colors in a patterned runner rug. She faced a French-style half-table centered on the wall opposite a curved staircase. A magnificent wood-and-brass Venetian mirror reflected light from three electric candles inside a single coach lamp dangling from the coffered ceiling. Short little Bessie could barely see herself in the mirror over a floral arrangement taking up most of the table, barely leaving room for massive candle sticks nursing chunky white candles on each side of the greenery.

Whoa, thought Bessie. *Well, Cam, you ol' coot!* His overalls and down-home ways were a sharp contrast to the style and character of his home.

Cam took the cake and led the way into the parlor.

"How'd you know pound cake is my favorite dessert? I can just 'bout guarantee this won't make it much past supper time." Taking the cake to the kitchen, he left Bessie to survey the room.

Somewhat bedazzled, she reverently ran her fingertips over aged ivory keys smiling from a rosewood box piano, careful

184

not to push them down. She sat down on the ornate piano stool and took her time soaking in the grandeur of the room, concluding that it had the look of an Old World turn-of-the-century mansion. As she contemplated which century, she glanced between her polished white pumps and visually traced a mesmerizing pattern in the loveliest Persian rug she'd ever seen. Not since her and Wes's summer trip to Morocco had she seen such gorgeous work. Everything in the room was exquisite, from ginger-colored walls tastefully adorned with fabulous artwork to an intricately carved marble mantel. Tufted Victorian-style sofas, flanked by Rococo Revival side chairs, were charmingly grouped throughout the room. Quickly scanning the paintings, she did a double take darting back to an ornate frame. Moving closer, her eyes grew large as she recognized the work. During vacations to Europe while she, a teacher, and Wes, a principal, were out of school during the summer months, she'd had the privilege of spending long, relaxing hours in the Louvre on several occasions.

"Make yourself at home," Cam said, startling her.

"Cam, is this an authentic Rembrandt etching?" It was all she could do to maintain her composure.

"It is," he stated matter-of-factly.

Totally complacent, he casually pointed toward the dining room and then the library, saying that there was a Van Gogh, a Vermeer, and a Degas – as if every household in America had such a collection.

"I'm on a tight schedule t'day, but come again, an' I'll show you the rest of the house. It's mostly filled with a jumble of mine an' Elizabeth's family's hand-me-downs."

Hand-me-downs? You own a museum quality art collection!

185

Her thoughts were interrupted when Cam spoke again.

"I've been thinkin' 'bout it, an' I've picked a lot that I think will be just perfect for you. The land backs up to Glover's property, an' one side borders the property of Rufus and Lettie Jenkins. There's a graveled road runnin' in front with easy access to Campbell Cove Road."

"Sounds perfect. When can I see it?"

"Right now."

He fished his truck keys from a bowl atop a five-tiered étagère juxtaposed with old and new porcelain figurines. Gently placing his hand on her shoulder, he guided her back through the foyer and out to the front porch.

"Where can I get house plans? Are you interested in building the house?" she asked, climbing in Cam's truck after he'd pushed a pile of papers to the middle of the seat.

Her goal was to be in the new house before Thanksgiving. "I think the house can be finished by then, if we start soon. Together we can pencil-in some house plans." Cam stated. He would draw as she specified her preferences and together they'd work out details as they went along. He'd built so many houses that blueprints were stamped on his brain.

Bessie was excited to see the possible building site – and glad to have her attention focused on something other than Addie's whereabouts.

Cam pulled onto the main road and drove a little past Glover's house, then turned right. After going less than half a mile down a narrow gravel road lined on each side with dense woods, Cam pulled over and parked the truck.

Pointing out white wooden stakes that marked 100 feet along the roadway, he explained, "The property is 215 feet deep. That would make the lot just a smidgen shy of half an acre. If we center the house on the land, you'll have nice front an' back yards."

Unlocking the truck's tailgate and dropping it with a bang, he extended a hand toward Bessie. Six-foot four inches tall and as strong as a bull, Cam lifted little five-foot-three Bessie onto the truck bed as if she were light as a toe sack of Idaho potatoes.

With one giant step, he stood beside her, pointing to the right. "Look for Glover's house."

Sure enough, Glover's television antenna could be seen towering above the thicket.

Cam pointed to the left. "Look over here – right over that stand of young pines."

Bessie could see the roof on a large red barn that she knew belonged to Rufus Jenkins.

"We can cut a path from the new house to each of their houses right through the woods. You'll have neighbors, an' at the same time, you'll have privacy."

Delight threw Bessie off guard as she clapped her hands and squealed like a piglet. Embarrassed at her spontaneous reaction – after all, she was a mature, sensible woman – she quickly put on her official business face. God forbid that Cam think she was childish.

Cam, amused by her little girl response, stepped off the truck and lifted her down. Becoming very professional sounding after seeing the red blush on her cheeks, he hoped to save her any further embarrassment. They lingered and talked for a while about the things that Bessie wanted built into the house, as he jotted notes in a pocket-sized notebook with the stub of a yellow pencil.

They agreed on a price and a time-line and plotted their

187

next move to get the ball rolling.

"I'll list my house with Marvin Stoddard. He already has a buyer in mind."

"Good. We'll go on an' get the trees an' brush cleared from the lot."

"Leave me plenty of shade trees both in front and back."

"I will. You can come an' mark the ones you want saved. We need t' work next week on the plans so I can get the house staked out. Otis O'Leary can draw up the paper work an' get the legal stuff sorted out. I'll call him early next week."

Back inside the truck, they headed to drop Bessie off at Glover's house. Cam nervously cleared his throat and steered the conversation in a different direction. Somewhat timidly, he told Bessie that he would like to be on friendlier terms with Janet and asked her advice on how he should go about it.

Poor Cam, thought Bessie. *How can I tell him that he's barking at the moon?*

Relying on her better judgment, Bessie decided that it was not her place to tell him anything.

"My only advice would be to be honest with Janet. Just ask her if you might talk privately. Tell her your intentions. Honesty is always the best policy."

Cam nodded in agreement but doubted that he would ever work up enough courage to ask her. Seemed like she could be a tad persnickety, and he didn't want to make a wrong move and put more distance between them.

For the time being Bessie Pearl Pennycutt had more to think about than Cam's love life.

At least the plans to sell her house and build another would help take her mind off Addie. When she thought about where the child might be, Bessie's stomach knotted up like a prizefighter's fist, and she was weak with worry. Until they found Addie, it was best if Bessie stayed busy to keep her mind occupied.

*

Slowly pushing the porch swing with one foot, LaVeeta watched as Amanda and Jim Ed sat in the playpen playing patty-cake, amid a flood of infantile joy. The screened porch that Glover had added to the front of the house was a perfect place to relax in the late afternoon. The house faced westward, presenting a spectacular view of the setting sun each day. On this day, the blazing ball of fire appeared to melt into a pine thicket across the street from the house. A veil of misty tears in LaVeeta's eyes dimmed the awesome beauty of an orange and yellow haze-streaked sky.

She had exhausted every possibility as to where Addie could have gone. She reasoned that it didn't seem probable that her sister could've run away without someone helping her. Addie had nowhere to go. She had no way to get anywhere. She had no money. She had never been out of Etowah County. LaVeeta's final conclusion was that there had to be someone with Addie.

LaMarcus was first to come to mind, but LaVeeta had no way of knowing that he was involved. Without knowing where he was, there was no way to contact him. But, deep down in her gut, she knew that her good-for-nothing brother was up to something. Wanting to tell Glover her fears, she waited for the right time to discuss her suspicions with him.

189

Chips of mortar flicked about like sparks off an anvil as Glover, sprawled atop a pile of brick, swung a ball peen hammer. No sooner had the load of bricks arrived than he'd tackled the task of removing hardened mortar and breaking apart with a sledgehammer the sections with rows intact. He worked brick by brick – only 500 or so to go – methodically chipping concrete from the edges.

When a brick was ready for fresh mortar, Glover tossed it into a pile. Glancing over his shoulder to check the new pile of cleaned brick, he only counted a dozen or so, although it seemed he'd been working forever and a day. *Oh, Lord, what have I gotten myself into?*

Whistlin' "Stardust," Glover rhythmically pecked in tune at the dried concrete. He envisioned bricks, all neatly stacked in rows, firmly set in place as underpinning around the house. Glancing across the yard to the bumpy driveway, he imagined a wide, level, gray-graveled drive flanked along each side with colorful, blooming flowerbeds. Other than the people he loved, his dreams were the sweetest things he knew. He planned on living in this house for the rest of his life, and he intended to make as many improvements as were needed. That was his plan. Of course, one never knows what a day may bring forth.

Whap! The screen door slammed behind LaVeeta, Molly, and Amanda running down the steps and into the yard, sloshing soapy water over the sides of a bowl. LaVeeta dipped a wire wand in to coat it with suds and then blew gently, releasing a spray of bubbles that floated aimlessly mere seconds before bursting. Molly, not content with a few bubbles, swung her wand producing a mini-galaxy of delicate air balls.

Leaving the children to play, LaVeeta edged toward the pile of bricks.

Carefully making her way up the mound near Glover, she asked, "Gotta minute?"

"Sure, get a load off your mind."

As far as LaVeeta was concerned, Glover Daniels was the closest thing to a perfect man that she knew. She trusted him explicitly and admired how hard he worked and loved his family.

She stacked a few bricks side by side to form a makeshift seat. "I been thinkin'," she backed up and sat down. "You prob'ly already figured somebody had t' he'p Addie. She had nowhere t' go. No money. She scared o' her own shadow. There ain't no way she do this by herse'f. It scare me t' think 'bout it, but I wouldn't be s'prised if LaMarcus not mixed up in this somehow."

Her suspicions concerning her brother were a definite possibility, one that Glover had indeed already considered. He felt both angry and uneasy at the mere thought of LaMarcus returning and coaxing Addie into leaving with him. Or maybe he forced her to go.

"Could be, Veeta. But I hope not."

In light of LaVeeta's concerns, Glover considered calling the police. He hesitated because their involvement would likely cause as many problems as it remedied. The chances that they'd look for a girl whose skin wasn't white as snow were slim. Very slim. Maybe, not even a shred of a chance. Even so, Rufus had talked to Sheriff Tubbs about Addie, and he'd said that he would do what he could.

"Let's give it a little more time. We'll find her," Glover assured LaVeeta, although he had not a clue as to how this would be accomplished. But he felt down in his bones that they would find Addie – one way or the other.

*

As soon as Marvin Stoddard had placed a "For Sale" sign in Bessie's front yard, his phone began to ring. Two parties had inquired, and Marvin was bringing a perspective buyer at 2 p.m. The house was spotless, and Bessie'd made two pies so that the aroma of cinnamon and apples would make the place seem homey. If someone right-on-the-spot decided to buy the house, they might leave with their own personal apple pie in hand. No guarantee, but that could happen. An arrangement of fresh cut dahlias, zinnias, roses, and day lilies towered above silver candlesticks on the dining room table, adding a special touch. Bessie would be so thrilled if the house sold that she might even throw in the flower arrangement.

She had just filled her cup with piping-hot orange pekoe tea when the telephone rang.

"Hello," she said in her politest telephone voice.

"I have a collect call from Addie Johnson. Will you accept the charges?" asked the operator.

"Yes, operator. Yes!"said Bessie. "Addie! Addie! Where are you?"

The only sound Bessie heard was soft sobbing. And then a woman's voice came on the line.

"Hello. This Miss Bessie?" inquired the stranger.

"Yes, this is Bessie. To whom am I speaking?"

In a whispered tone the woman said, "Addie need he'p. She need t' git outta here. She want t' come there. Can you come git 'er?"

192

"Yes. Where is she?"

"Chicago," whispered the woman.

Chicago! Bessie Pearl grasped the arm of the chair to steady herself. *How far is it to Chicago? It has to be over 500 miles.*

"We'll come to get her. Tell me where to come," said Bessie without a second's hesitation.

"I know a man. He drive a truck an' can bring 'er far as Evansville on Mondee. He won't wait on you. You *have* t' be there. They's a truck stop called Frankie's on Hwy. 41. Be there at noon on Mondee."

"Evansville? Where is Evansville?" asked Bessie, jotting down the information on a note pad next to the telephone.

"Indiana," the woman whispered.

"We'll be in a gray Chevy or a black Ford sedan. Is Addie all right? Has she been hurt?" asked Bessie.

"Well, she ain't as good as she should be, but I take as gooda care of 'er as I can." The woman's voice was barely audible.

"What is your name? How can I ever thank you?"

"Jes try to he'p this chil' git over all this. She don't deserve all that done happen to 'er."

There was a click, followed by the droning hum of the dial tone.

To lessen the risk of chipping her nails, Bessie quickly spun the rotary dial with the eraser end of the pencil. *Have I dialed the right number? Oh Lord, I hope so.*

Auntie answered, and Bessie told her of the phone call revealing Addie's whereabouts. A loud thud crackled through the dropped receiver as it struck the telephone table.

"Glover! Glover!" Auntie shouted as she ran to the back

door and rushed out. Taking the steps two at a time, Auntie raced to the brick pile.

"Bessie," she said, gasping for breath, "On the phone. Got news 'bout Addie."

Within seconds Glover was on the line.

"Hey, Bess. What's this I hear?"

Bessie repeated word for word her conversation with the whispering woman. Neither Bessie nor Glover had a clue as to exactly where Evansville, Indiana, was – much less how long it would take to get there.

Glover took the lead. "I'll go down to the Shell station an' get maps of Bama and Tennessee."

Gas stations gave away maps, but he doubted that any in their part of the woods would have a map of Kentucky or Indiana. It stood to reason that if they could get through Tennessee they could find maps to guide them the rest of the way.

"I'll call you soon as I figure out where we need to go an' how to get there. Pack what you'll need, an' we'll leave early. Talk to you later."

He hung up the phone, and forgetting that Doris and the babies were sleeping, shouted "Thank you, Lord!" on his way outside to tell LaVeeta.

She'd taken the children to throw scraps in the chicken pen and hadn't heard Auntie tell Glover about the phone call. But she knew that something good had happened when she saw Glover jump over five steps from the porch to the ground while loudly calling her name. Running toward him, he grabbed her and swung her round and round.

When she heard the good news, tiny LaVeeta took off running across the yard. She clapped her hands, laughing and sobbing at the same time, bouncing about like a chicken with its head cut off. Hardly weighing 90 pounds soaking wet, with soft brown eyes and a broad smile to match her gentle spirit, LaVeeta ran to the children and grasped their hands, leading them in a ring-around-the-Rosie dance.

Glover threw back his head and laughed as he watched the ring of dancers prancing and squealing with joy.

Hallelujah! Oh happy day!

*

"Here's the plan," he'd told Bessie on the phone. "We'll drive to Evansville, or as close we can get, in a day. We can spend the night in the car. Early Monday mornin' we'll find the truck stop an' wait there 'til noon."

Lulu's headlights darted about in pitch-black darkness as Glover made his way along Campbell's Cove Road to the blacktop. Adrenaline pumping, hopes high, Glover and LaVeeta pulled up in front of Bessie's house at 4:00 on Sunday morning.

By the dim glow of the porch light, Bessie carefully made her way down the front steps and along the sidewalk leading to the driveway. She was carrying a picnic basket filled with sandwiches and sweets, and a thermos of coffee squeezed in the crook of her arm.

"LaVeeta," she said over her shoulder, putting the basket in the back floorboard. "Run inside and get four pillows off the beds, please."

"Yessum." LaVeeta hurried up the front steps.

"We brought water, Bess. Auntie packed us some sausage biscuits too."

Within a few minutes they were settled, raring to go, and

195

braced for a long ride. Glover pulled away from the curb and pointed the car north toward Nashville. Bessie, acting as navigator, shined her key chain flashlight on an Alabama map so she could be sure that they stayed on the right road. Stretching out in Lulu's back seat, LaVeeta bunched a pillow behind her head and closed her eyes.

"We don't need a map to get to Nashville." Glover turned the corner and headed out of town. "'Member when we went to the Grand Ole Opry that Saturday night? I'll never forget Minnie Pearl an' Little Jimmy Dickens. An' I haven't forgotten how to get back there either."

"Okay." She ignored him and continued to look at the map. She'd yet to meet a man that didn't need a woman's input when it came to staying on the right road.

Soon it would be daylight. They hoped to make good time before the heat of the day and traffic picked up. Being as it was Sunday, there would be fewer people out and about.

All roads to Indiana were two-lanes. Glover knew that if he got behind some local yokel with a pickup full o' younguns out for a Sunday ride, he could only hope to find a straight stretch where he could safely pass. The roads were narrow and winding; top speed was around 50 m.p.h.

A glimpse into the future would have told the Alabama travelers they'd have access to an easier route in not too many years to come. In 1956, President Dwight Eisenhower would get the ball rolling on the construction of an Interstate System. It would take 35 years to complete the original portion to the tune of $425 billion dollars before the network was finished. Not only would the interstate system forever change the way people traveled, but it would also become a part of American culture. The roads that Glover drove on this trip would become the scenic, out-of-the-way back roads of the future.

But that was for another day. This July morning was sultry before Mr. Sunshine ever peeped over the horizon, and the temperature would continue to rise like a French soufflé as the day unfolded. The little black Ford cruised along on shallow-shouldered roads. Lulu's black paint absorbed the sun's rays, and by midmorning the asphalt would be scorching hot. Warm air blowing in the open windows dried perspiration on foreheads and faces; but did nothing for sweaty clothes stuck to backs and bottoms.

With more cars on the roads, small towns saw a way to pad city coffers with fines from speeding tickets. Speed traps in every little pig trail of a town slowed the travelers and contributed to a heap o' aggravation.

They'd embarked on a long, hot trip. So be it. Nothing mattered as long as they brought Addie home safe and sound.

*

Glancing in the hall mirror, Cam admired his trimmed beard and eyebrows, considering himself a handsome man. That was a correct assumption – if you liked redheaded, ruddy Scottish men.

Decked out in sharp-creased khaki trousers and a blue-checkered, short-sleeved shirt, he smoothed his collar and looked down at bright copper pennies stuck in brown, polished loafers. Pink cheeks peeking above his beard were damp with Old Spice after-shave lotion, even though he hadn't shaved in years. Talking to his reflection in the mirror, he nervously rehearsed what he'd say to Janet when she answered the door.

He hoped that *she and nobody else* would answer the

door. If not, he knew that he'd feel awkward asking for her. Maybe he wouldn't just come right out and ask for *her*. Maybe he would act like he came for some reason other than to see Janet. He needed a Plan B.

This courtin' stuff could make a fellow break out in hives, he thought as he scratched underneath his collarbone. Or, maybe it was his allergies to certain flowers. He'd picked a small bouquet of daisies and tied the stems together with a narrow blue ribbon he'd taken off a box of cigars. He was going for it lock, stock, and barrel. If she laughed at him, so be it. His patience was wearing thin, and he could see that there was nothing to be gained from beating around the bush any longer.

It was Sunday afternoon, and in keeping with the habits of locals who considered it a treat to eat store-bought ice cream, he intended to ask Janet to go with him to Wren's Ice Cream Parlor for a cone. His favorite flavor was grape. Nobody else made grape-flavored – just Wren's. Visualizing the purple, frozen treat piled high on a crisp wafer cone, he steered the truck into Glover's driveway. Lo and behold! There sat Janet alone on the front porch swing. This had to be a Godsend; it was too good to be a coincidence.

He parked the truck and grabbed the bouquet, shaking loose a few petals as he shoved it behind his back. Carefully pulling the screen door open, Cam grinned like a child on Christmas morning.

Janet stood and greeted him with a smile. Making some bumbling remark about pretty flowers for a pretty lady, with a sudden jerk, he extended the bouquet in her direction as a few more petals went flying. She hesitated for a second, and then took it. "Thanks," she said in barely more than a whisper and quickly sat back down.

Well, so far, so good, thought Cam. *At least she didn't throw them at me.*

He heard himself asking if she would like to go for ice cream, but he was so nervous that it could have been someone else speaking. No, it must have been him, because she smiled and looked into his blue eyes.

"I can't leave Doris alone with five children. Marianne is a capable helper, but I just feel better if I know that an adult is nearby. Glover and LaVeeta are on the road to Indiana. There is no one else to help Doris. But, thank you, maybe another time."

When one is backed into a corner, sometimes one acts impetuously, and therefore, not always wisely. Before he knew it, he'd blurted out, "I'm invitin' ever'body t' go t' Wren's for ice cream. Ever'body. Doris. The kids. Ever'body."

With a delightful clap of her hands – more petals flew – Janet sprang from the swing, sending it swaying this way and that, as she hurried inside to round up the troops.

She disappeared inside the house, frayed bouquet in hand, while Cam stood on the porch, shaking his head in bewilderment.

He didn't know whether to laugh or cry. What just happened? How had he lost control of the situation, if in fact he'd ever had control?

He wanted to treat Janet to ice cream. Just Janet. Only Janet. Not the entire population of the South.

Realizing that it was too late to change things, he consoled himself. "Oh well, it's a start," he spoke softly. "At least she didn't say no, an' she did take the flowers."

Within a matter of minutes, the dusty red pickup bounced along the road toward town. Doris and Janet were in front, each holding a twin. Marianne, Molly, and Amanda were seated in the bed of the truck.

The children had been sternly instructed, "Sit with your back against the cab o' the truck and **do not** stand up while the truck is movin'."

Same warning, different truck ride – as if they were dumb enough to stand up in a moving vehicle. Marianne turned her head so that no one could see and rolled her eyes. She dare not let anyone see her. Eye rolling or shoulder shrugging (seen as a sign of disrespect) could get a youngster in a lot of trouble.

In a somewhat befuddled state of mind, Cam grumbled to himself as he drove toward town.

This wasn't exactly the outing that he'd planned.

Come to think of it, it had been a long stretch since he'd courted. But he would have bet his last nickel that normal, everyday courtin' was between two people, not eight.

*

Bright sunrays beamed through Lulu's windshield. Bessie was awake, although her throbbing head felt like all five of Big Ben's bells were counting off the midnight hour. Folded in a scrunched fetal position, LaVeeta slept soundly in the corner of the backseat, a pillow wadded behind her head. Glover'd been awake since four o'clock, just as he was every morning. He'd never understood why anyone needed a watch to know the hour of the day when they could simply listen to their body rhythms.

Shortly after crossing into Indiana the previous night, Glover had spotted a side road and decided it was worthy of exploration. To their delight they'd found that it led to a pecan grove. By the light of an apple-slice moon and the car headlights, he selected a level place beneath leafy, nutty trees and parked for

200

the night. Weary to the bone, they'd made themselves as comfortable as their situation would permit and were soon asleep.

Motels were few and far between, not that Glover would've felt comfortable paying for a place to stay, when stopping in a pasture or a pine thicket was perfectly acceptable in 1950. Travelers often slept in their cars or camped in the woods on their journey.

Mosquitoes were ever present, and no one had thought to bring Auntie's mosquito repellant. Rolling the car windows up at night had helped cut down on the number of bloodthirsty pests and assured that small woods creatures wouldn't crawl inside in search of a place to snuggle. No sooner were the windows rolled up until someone would mutter, "Air. We need some air." Soon as they were rolled down someone would say, "The mosquitoes are eatin' me up!" Glover didn't open his eyes, or hardly even miss a snore, when he'd reached over and cranked the handle to raise or lower the window on demand.

It was a new day and a beautiful morning to boot. Anxious to find the truck stop, unbridled anticipation stirred all three troupers on their mission to bring Addie 'home. After making a trip into the woods to answer the call of nature, the threesome freshened up as best they could.

A six-inch, leafless twig from a sweet gum bush, once skinned on one end and julienned into feathered bristles by Glover's pocketknife, became a toothbrush. Glover pulled a neatly folded wax paper pouch filled with baking soda from his pocket. He dipped the twig-brush in the soda and scrubbed his teeth. No, it wasn't Colgate and a soft bristle brush, but the results were somewhat the same. Morning mouth was chased away.

Glover shuffled through trash in the floorboard and came up with a tepid, leftover Coca-Cola.

"There's water, Glover," Bessie offered as he put the bottle to his lips.

"I know it." He took a swig of the drink and swished it in his mouth. Spitting in a bush, he grinned. "Um-um-good. Nothing like baking soda an' coke for a mouthwash. An' a throwaway toothbrush. You got to keep up with a wet toothbrush. Not me."

"Oh, dear Lord. Men!" She shook her head as LaVeeta laughed.

They washed their faces with water that Bessie poured over their hands from a Mason jar, and then dried off on whatever they could find. LaVeeta scrounged around in the picnic basket for leftovers. She offered to pass around a few limp sandwich halves, broken crackers, and a banana, prematurely ripened by sweltering temperatures the previous day.

"If y'all want to, let's leave this stuff for the raccoons. We can find somewhere to eat once we get to town." Without a single "yea" or "nay", LaVeeta turned the basket upside down and dumped the food on the ground. She was glad to hear that there were better prospects for breakfast.

Glover, carefully maneuvered around a sharp rock in the road — grateful that he'd not run over it in the dark. He steered back to Highway 41 and turned toward Evansville. Dust and road grime on Lulu's smooth black finish were streaked from a light shower that had passed through just before dawn. The rain had done little, if anything, to wash away an army of splattered bugs peppering the windshield.

Apparently, they were farther from Evansville than they'd thought. In the darkness it'd been difficult to find a place to stop, much less judge distances.

Rounding a steep curve twenty or so miles down the road, they spotted a welcomed sign announcing they'd reached the city limits of Evansville. A round of shouts and applause broke out from Lulu's passengers. Afraid they'd go too far or waste time looking for the truck stop, they pulled into the first service station they came across. The Texaco attendant filled the tank with gasoline, while a young boy mostly rearranged bug remains in a feeble attempt to clean the windshield. Momentarily looking at Bessie through the smeared glass with a "that's good enough" expression on his face, he raised the hood to check the oil.

"You know where Frankie's Truck Stop is?" asked Glover. The man filling the tank shook his head no. The freckled-face boy said, "No," wiped his snotty nose on the bug cleaning rag, and then pointed to a man in greasy coveralls with a tattered red cloth hanging out of his back pocket. Glover approached the man whose name, according to embroidery on his shirt pocket, was Duncan Duckett. The resident mechanic on duty was familiar with Frankie's Truck Stop. He reached behind to retrieve the faded scrap of towel, wiped his greasy hands, and mopped his sweaty forehead. Then he stuck out his right hand for Glover to shake.

"Sure, I know Frankie's. Get back to the road, turn right, and go about five miles or so. Look for a street sign that says Button Willow Road. Frankie's is on the right about half a mile past that sign. You can't miss it unless you go blind between here and there." He cut loose with a hearty howl as Glover struggled to see the humor. "They got a good breakfast in their coffee shop."

That did it! When Glover heard the word coffee, he was

renewed with an extra measure of urgency to find Frankie's as quickly as Lulu could scoot down the road.

Following Duncan's directions to a tee, they soon spotted a building with a sign above a faded green door that read: **Fill Up Your Truck & Your Belly At Frankie's**. Neither flaking paint, patches on the roof, or plate glass windows hazy with road grime improved Frankie's curb appeal. An expansive unpaved area for parking stretched from the building to the highway.

In spite of the rundown conditions, the parking lot was covered with trucks. Every truck driver in the area must have headed to this place to fill up the tank with gas and his belly with a good breakfast.

Glover went inside and ordered coffee and food to take out. He wasn't sure what the policy for dark-skinned folks was in Indiana, but there was no way that he and Bessie would go inside to eat if LaVeeta wasn't allowed. While Glover was gone, Bessie moved Lulu to a shady spot at the edge of the parking lot.

Appetites were whetted as the aroma of biscuits, bacon, and gravy filled the car when Bessie opened brown paper bags. The food was different from what they were accustomed to – the biscuits were denser, the gravy was browner, the bacon leaner. But, when push came to shove, different mattered little to this hungry crew. They dove in, and only after the food was gone did they offer critiques.

"Some sorghum syrup would perk this up a bunch," said Glover as he captured stray biscuit crumbs from his shirt, popped them into his mouth, and chased them down with coffee that was strong enough to dissolve rust.

"If I write out my biscuit recipe, will you slip it under their door?" Bessie's head hurt, and she felt that biscuits heavy as

204

lead deserved an equally heavy dose of sarcasm. She'd eaten two, and they had filled an empty stomach, but that was all. Yummy satisfaction was the missing element — those Indiana biscuits were not Alabama biscuits by a long shot.

"They be good to shine patent leather shoes with," commented LaVeeta from the back seat. She'd rubbed many a pair of patent shoes with a biscuit until she could see herself in them.

"True," Bessie casually nodded.

"One time we had a hog named Maurice that wouldn't eat cornbread, but he loved stale biscuits an' any kind o' white bread. My sister worked at a bakery, an' she'd bring home leftover cakes an' rolls an' stuff like that. We'd soak it in water for four or five days 'til it soured an' stank to high heaven. I had to hold my breath when I poured the slop in the trough. I'm tellin' you what, that pig loved sour bread. It'll fatten 'em up in a hurry, too," Glover grinned.

"True." Bessie casually nodded, although she'd never slopped a hog in her life.

"Well, I don't know nothin' 'bout feedin' no pigs," LaVeeta added. "But, I can tell you it be the gospel truth that you can make a patent leather shoe shine real good with a biscuit. The greasier the biscuit, the better the shine."

"True," repeated Bessie.

When they'd finished eating, they settled down to wait. No one was sure how they would know which truck Addie would be in, but with three of them watching, surely they would spot it. As time ticked closer toward noon, they would move Lulu from the shade of a tall oak tree to a more obvious spot, closer to the highway where they could see and be seen.

205

*

Marvin Stoddard was pleased to have a buyer for Bessie's house. He'd tried to get her on the phone all day to tell her the good news but had gotten no answer. The Bainbright family had seen the property and fallen in love with it. Monday morning they planned to come to Marvin's office and leave earnest money. Ray Bainbright's wife Nancy said, "I can think of no better place to raise our children."

There was one small glitch in this nearly perfect transaction. They wanted to occupy the premises before school started in September. The fly in the ointment was that Bessie Pearl's new house wouldn't be completed by then.

Marvin was anxious to find out if this was a deal breaker for Bessie; both he and a wishful family hoped not.

*

Bessie, unlike Glover, felt that she needed to wear a watch. Although endowed with a slight ability to occasionally peer into the future – these rare insights usually preceded an epic occurrence and were, so far, limited to three or four times – she felt that glancing at the watch on her wrist was much quicker and more accurate than Glover's faith in his circadian clock. She looked admiringly at her tiny, 14K gold Gruen wristwatch.

Bessie smiled, thinking that in twenty years, the faithful little timekeeper had been to the jeweler for repairs only once. Relieved that the hour of their appointment had arrived, and at the same time apprehensive at the possibility of an unwanted outcome, Bessie stared at golden watch hands – both pointing to the number twelve.

206

She held her wrist in front of Glover's face and pointed. He squinted to see that it was straight-up-and-down noon.

He too felt emotions that ranged from relief – perhaps the waiting was over – to apprehension. Maybe Addie wasn't coming.

A steady stream of trucks during the morning hours had slowed to one every now and then. Surely that would make it easier to spot the truck they were to meet.

Glover backed up to lean against the front fender of the car, crossed his ankles, and plunged his hands deep inside the pockets of his beige linen dress pants. Sweat had fastened his white shirt to his back. His thick coal-black hair, plastered with a pomade of Brylcreem, glistened in the bright sunlight.

He'd moved Lulu nearer the highway so they could be clearly seen by trucks pulling off the road. Bessie, dressed in a red dotted-swiss blouse and a white piqué skirt, sat sideways on the passenger seat, her sandaled feet dangling several inches from the ground. The open doors would have been perfect for channeling a breeze, had there been a whisper of moving air. Ruthless heat had stifled even the faintest gust.

Bessie cooled her face by waving a map of Indiana as fast as her tiny wrist could fan it. Strands of hair, that she'd twisted and pinned in the back, had come loose and hung in sweaty corkscrew curls on her neck. LaVeeta, in a red and yellow halter sundress, hung over the back seat with her chin propped on her arms; worry-wrinkled burrows filled with beads of sweat lined her forehead. Her stomach was rocking like a rowboat in the wake of an ocean liner.

A large tanker truck pulled off the highway and sidled close to an eighteen-wheeler that idled impassively. A young man wearing a white T-shirt, with a pack of Lucky Strikes rolled up in the right sleeve, jumped from the tanker to the ground –

207

never looking in their direction – and headed for the restaurant.

Locals were beginning to gather at the eatery for lunch. The Alabama travelers were antsy, drained from the heat, and more than a little tired. It was a well-known fact that sleeping in a car, while halfway sitting and halfway slumping, was hardly the ideal setting for a restful night.

12:10 p.m. – Glover nervously asked for suggestions. Should they move the car to another spot? Should LaVeeta stand outside so that Addie could see her when the truck arrived? Only talking to release tension, he knew the answers to his questions before he asked them. Neither Bessie nor LaVeeta answered him, anyway. There was nothing they needed to do differently. As painful as it was, their only option was to stay put and wait.

12:25 p.m. – Everyone was beginning to feel a twinge of disappointment and a boatload of frustration. No one wanted to say anything that would discourage the others, but finally when she could stand it no longer, LaVeeta broke the silence.

"What if they don't come?" she whined.

Glover tried to show optimism, but he knew there was a very real possibility that they had driven a long way for nothing.

"The driver mighta got a late start," he said.

Bessie quickly chimed in, "He may've had a flat tire or other trouble with the truck."

LaVeeta was in no mood to be comforted. Taking a deep breath as if about to reply, she instead began to sob. Bessie patted her shoulder in a feeble attempt to make things better.

12:47 p.m. – Deflated with disappointment, their last spark of hope was dwindling.

Just as Glover was about to say that they should move to the shade, a dilapidated pickup truck loaded to the hilt with watermelons and cantaloupes bounced off the asphalt, stirring up a cloud of dust as it sped into the parking lot.

An elderly, gray-haired man wearing a sweat soaked, tattered hat steered the truck alongside Lulu, slapped on the brakes, and skidded to a stop. When the dust cleared, he looked out the window and nodded to Glover.

LaVeeta shot out of the car like a bullet and ran to the passenger door of the truck, Bessie right on her heels.

A solemn, tear-stained face stared out the window.

"Addie! Addie! You awright?" LaVeeta said through sobs of relief as she opened the door and helped her sister out of the antiquated truck. She and Bessie embraced Addie with the happiness and fervency one experiences when finding someone or something that has been lost. LaVeeta grabbed Addie's hand and quickly led her toward Lulu. Addie stumbled after her as Bessie turned to close the truck door.

"Much obliged," said Glover to the driver who was short on words but had an ample supply of impatience. He grunted, and with a jerking motion shifted into first gear. The dusty, dented truck lunged forward as Bessie jumped out of the way. The old man leaned across and slammed the door as he pulled back onto the highway. Through the dust Glover could see a bushel basket of melons teetering and a tumbling cantaloupe take a dive and splat on the gravel. As quickly as the old truck had appeared, it was out of sight.

The sisters huddled in the backseat, holding hands. LaVeeta wept as she cradled her little sister in her arms. Addie looked down at her lap and only muttered when anyone said something to her.

Everyone welcomed her, but no one questioned her as to where she'd been or what had happened. Addie's sad expression and unresponsiveness spoke volumes as to what she'd experienced. She was wearing the same cotton blouse and knee-length circular skirt that she'd worn to the barbeque. After a week, they had taken on a life of their own in the form of dirt, stains, and a distinct odor. LaVeeta, always apt to think ahead, had brought clean clothes that she would offer her sister later. But the fact of the matter was that they were so relieved to have Addie with them again it didn't matter how she looked or smelled.

"I'll take the first shift," said Bessie. She'd decided to give Glover a break; maybe he could catch a wink or two before driving later in the afternoon. She steered Lulu onto Highway 41 in the direction from which they'd come. They waved out the windows when Bessie tooted the horn as they breezed past Duncan Duckett, who was airing up an Oldsmobile's tires.

With every mile they put behind them, any lingering apprehensiveness waned, like morning dew on a summer day. Hot, balmy air, blowing in the window, loosened a strand of greased hair that flipped and flopped across Glover's forehead, like a catfish out of water. Grateful, happy, and relieved, he was soon merrily whistling *Amazing Grace"* as he watched Lulu hug the centerline. Bessie started to hum and before long in her lovely soprano voice, she sang the lyrics.

Amazing grace! How sweet the sound
That saved a wretch like me!
I once was lost, but now am found;
Was blind, but now I see.

Addie felt relaxation calming the tenseness in her body as she rested her head on LaVeeta's shoulder. An overwhelming weariness replaced the fear and tension that had driven her for

210

many days. Knowing that she was safe, she closed her eyes, swollen and bloodshot from sleeplessness and too many tears, and soundly slept.

About the time that they'd crossed a short stretch of Kentucky and entered Tennessee, the scorching heat began to lessen. The sun was setting, and soon the asphalt would begin to cool. Thank God. A break from the heat was a welcomed relief. They hoped to make it near Nashville before stopping for the night. Although Glover doubted they'd make it that far, he never said so.

On the way to Indiana, they'd read the Burma-Shave signs posted along the highway. Because they'd been burdened with worry for Addie, the clever sayings – posted to remind travelers that they needed to try Burma-Shave's brushless shaving cream – had brought them little more than a chuckle. Now heading back to Alabama with Addie safely in their charge, the signs brought hoots of laughter. Glover read the words posted along the shoulder of the road as Lulu sped past:

"Hardly a driver / Is now alive / Who passed / On hills / At 75 / Burma-Shave.

Don't Stick Your Elbow/ Out So Far/ It May Go Home/ In Another Car/ Burma-Shave.

Trains Don't Wander/ All Over The Map/'Cause Nobody Sits/In The Engineer's Lap/Burma-Shave.

"Let's find a place to get a bite to eat." They hadn't eaten since Frankie's, and Glover's stomach was rubbing his backbone. He also wanted to drive. In his estimation, Bessie could knock it up a notch or two. As slow as she drove they'd be a week getting home.

"Reckon that cafe will do?" Glover pointed to a small building just ahead. Bessie pulled into the parking lot of the Red

Top Café while Glover took orders for hamburgers and Coca-colas. LaVeeta had her own money and insisted on paying for the food.

"Mr. Glover, please git us some Baby Ruths, too." She dug in her coin purse for an extra quarter. This was a call for celebration, and Baby Ruth candy bars – at five cents each – would do the trick.

Back on the road once again, the well-fed sojourners traveled until it was time to stop for the night.

*

A plan had been stirring in Lettie's heart and mind since she'd heard from Rufus that Glover and Bessie were traveling to Indiana to get Addie. She'd spent a day and a night stewing over an idea that she could not get out of her head – try as she may. When she was sure that it was the thing to do, she would talk to Rufus.

Balancing a straight-back chair on its hind legs, Lettie, pretty as she'd been as a young bride, sat under a shade tree snapping green beans from a bowl in her lap. Throwing bean bits and strings on the ground for the banty chickens that pecked about her feet, she felt that her thoughts were becoming a workable plan.

Rufus Jenkins, seven years older than Lettie, was a good husband and father. She and Rufus had raised two fine boys, who'd married and given them three grandchildren. Three kids were still at home – Eleanor was fifteen, Daisy twelve, and Daniel ten.

Five years ago, they'd taken in an infant boy, named him Mose, and raised him as their own. At the time, their youngest

212

child Daniel was five and almost ready to start school. They didn't need – nor could they afford – a new baby.

Neither could they say no when Sheriff Vernon Tubbs paid a call. She would never forget that day:

"Hey, Lettie Belle. Rufus." The sheriff tipped his hat as he sauntered up the front porch steps, leaving the door to his patrol car standing wide open.

"Mornin' Sheff." Lettie smiled and nodded as the sheriff and Rufus shook hands. "C'mon up here an' sit awhil'. Lettie's got coffee an' biscuits. You et?" asked Rufus.

"Not yet. Don't mind if I do join you, but Lettie don't you go to no trouble."

"Now you know you ain't no trouble. Sit down over there at the table, an' I be rite back."

Lettie wiped her hands on her apron and headed inside. As barefoot as a rabbit, she was dressed in a white sleeveless blouse and knee-length, cotton calico skirt. Glancing in the mirror over the sofa, she patted down her hair and slid on a pair of sandals she'd left by the doorway to the kitchen. For a second she considered putting on her gold hoop earrings, being as it was the sheriff that was visiting, then decided better of it.

Soon the three friends sat on the porch of the whitewashed house at a wooden spool table, drinking coffee and munching hot biscuits drizzled with tupelo honey. Lettie had long suspected that the sheriff was motivated by his love for tupelo honey to amble by their house as often as he did when he was in their area. Rufus's brother Amos came every summer from Wewahitchka, Florida, bringing gifts of the unique buttery-tasting honey from his hives.

"What bring you out our way, Constable?" asked Rufus as Sheriff Tubbs spread honey on his third buttered biscuit.

213

"Well, I'm in a bit of a pickle. Somethin's happened, and I need some help. I been thinkin' an' thinkin' who mite be able to step in an' turn a bad sitchuation into somethin' good. If you can't help, then I understand."

"What you mean?" asked Lettie.

"You won't b'lieve this, but some kids out in a vacant lot found a newborn. In a shoebox, no less."

Lettie's mouth fell open, and Rufus's eyes were as round as an owl's.

"What'cha mean? A live baby?"

"Sho'nuff." The sheriff drank the last swallow of coffee from his cup and then continued. "Little boy. He's ten weeks old now. Been up at Holy Name o' Jesus Hospital all this time. He weighed somewhere 'round three pounds when they found 'im. More than once, we thought he'd die, but the little fellow has more fight in 'im than Joe Louis."

Lettie refilled his cup as he continued. "You know they call Joe the 'Brown Bomber', so we just been callin' this little fighter Bomber. Been lookin' for 'im a home. Folks that take 'im can give 'im a proper name."

"Who deese folks?" asked Rufus.

"Well, to date they aren't any folks. I was kinda hopin' y'all mite think 'bout takin' 'im in. The County can help a little bit with the money part for the first year. I don't know anybody else that I'd feel good 'bout leavin' 'im with. Y'all think 'bout it an' let me know soon as you can. Go down to the hospital and ask for Gladys Stillwell. Tell 'er that I sent you. She'll show Bomber to you. Think 'bout it, will you? Jus' think 'bout it."

Full of coffee and honeyed biscuits, he'd excused himself and headed his black-and-white toward town. Although the sheriff's visit had taken place five years back, it seemed like

214

yesterday to Lettie.

Absentmindedly flicking a wormy bean to a banty hen circling her chair, she remembered the first time she'd seen the tiny baby with large brown eyes innocently studying her face.

If she'd had her druthers, back then there was no way that she would have taken on an infant. The last thing in this world that she'd wanted to do was wash diapers and go through years of teaching a child how to behave, to obey, and to love himself and others. But none of that mattered, because it had been love at first sight once they'd decided to go and see the baby − for both her and Rufus.

They named their newest son Moses, like Moses in the Bible. Their Moses, whom they'd nicknamed Mose, was found in a shoebox − not a basket − but nonetheless, rescued to be raised in a good home.

Now, once again, there was a child that needed a home. She and Rufus didn't need another child any more than they'd needed another when they took in Mose. Nor could they really afford to feed and clothe anyone else.

These would be the first points that Rufus would bring up when she approached him about taking Addie in to stay with them. Lettie could read his mind like a book − fortunately, there were only three or four chapters. She could also change his mind when she wanted to − one of the perks of being married for almost twenty-two years.

It had been Lettie's experience that it is always easier to get into things than it is to get out of them. She needed to be absolutely sure that she could see it all the way through with a youngster that needed more love and patience than most. There would be no turning back, for she had no intention of hurting Addie more by returning her to Bessie when things got tough.

She knew that there would be issues with discipline and building trust.

Snapping the last bean, she had both arrived at a place of peace concerning the matter and made up her mind. And once her mind was made up, there was no changing it. She knew that she could handle Addie and make a difference in her life.

Now, she had to convince Rufus.

*

Glover's head had fallen into an awkward position during the night, causing a painful crick in his neck. He opened his eyes, grasped the steering wheel, and winced as he turned his head. This was not good. He still had several hours to drive before they got to Gadsden.

Twisting his head from side to side, he glanced through the windshield.

Jumpin' Jehosafats! He nearly jumped out of his skin!

Directly in front of Lulu's hood ornament, a man stood motionless.

Dismissing a sharp pain in his shoulder, Glover quickly opened the car door, sprang from the driver's seat, and rushed toward the stranger, all the while explaining that they were traveling and had stopped for the night.

"Howdy. Howdy. Hope we're not trespassin'. Been to Evansville. On the way back to Bama." Smiling, Glover extended his right hand as he approached the unexpected visitor.

Tall, slim, with a hint of hillbilly, the man grinned and reached to shake Glover's hand. He held a 12-gauge double-barreled shotgun in the crook of his left arm. At his bare feet lay the saddest looking bloodhound that Glover had ever seen. The dog was the color of rust, with black patches around his nose and on the tips of his ears, and one round spot on his back. The big-boned hound, with a distinctive houndy odor, looked to weigh about eighty pounds.

The stranger's bony, bare shoulders served as hangers for a pair of denim bib overalls; a well-worn red baseball cap, turned backwards, covered all but a few stray wisps of stringy blonde hair. The man looked to be about forty years old and was as friendly as a speckled pup.

Without a moment's hesitation, Glover continued, "We'll be leavin' soon. We want to get home an' get a bath an' drink a gallon o' iced tea."

"Billy George Jones," the fellow introduced himself. "But call me Coot. My daddy nicknamed me after a Florida Cooter turtle. Always said I was so slow he had t' set pegs t' see me move." He chuckled as slowly as he talked.

Pointing with the barrel of his gun, he showed Glover the deflating front tire on the passenger side of the car. A quick glance and Glover knew that there was no doubt about it. The tire was low on air.

"I reckon you done picked up a nail not far back. Come on up t' the house, an' we'll fix it. It mite take a minute t' find a patch kit, but just foller me." Coot slowly pointed the barrel of the gun toward a small, weathered house, the early morning sun beaming off its tin roof. Barely visible in the distance, the house was perched on top of a hill at the far end of a flat green meadow.

Glover didn't want any trouble.

He knew that narrow-minded people were as much a part of the South as people who had good sense. Sometimes it seemed they made up the majority.

Hesitating, then carefully choosing his words, Glover said, "I got two colored girls with us. That a problem for you?"

The man threw back his head and laughed. "Lord, no," he said. "Marmie Watson lives o'er yonder hill. She comes t' cook for us. She'll make y'all breakfast an' talk them girls' ears off."

Coot and his dog cut through the woods, while Glover drove along the dirt road that led past the meadow and ascended to the top of the hill. He thought that they would have to wait, but to his surprise, both Coot and his sad-sack dog were standing in the front yard as Lulu rolled to a stop. *Must know a short cut,* Glover reasoned. Anxious to move around, Bessie, LaVeeta, and Addie piled out of the cramped car, stretching and yawning as they looked around.

Whap! The screen door to the never-painted dwelling slapped shut, and a short, pleasant-looking woman (who weighed 250 pounds if she weighed an ounce) waddled to the edge of the porch. Bright blue eyes lit up with excitement as she wiped her hands on a purple calico apron that clearly had once been a flour sack. She was barefoot and had her dishwater blonde hair pulled back into a ponytail.

"Howdy! Welcome! Welcome!" Smiling, she shouted and waved both hands. A space between her front teeth was wide enough to drive a truck through.

Two midnight-black Labrador retrievers came running from behind the house at breakneck speed, barking for all they were worth. The woman on the porch hollered "Shut-up, You Two!" And they did. It would later be revealed that their names were You and Two. They'd been raised together since they were puppies and were always side-by-side. Someone had called them You Two, and the names had stuck.

218

Once inside, introductions were given all around.

"My name's Glenda. I'm Coot's better half." She winked at her husband causing an ah-shucks grin to creep across his face.

A tall, dark chocolate-colored woman, who looked to be in her early seventies — although there was not a wrinkle on her face — came from the kitchen. She was wiping her hands on the hem of an apron that was strewn with printed bright-red cherries and covered most of her faded blue dress. A pair of leather loafers, with the back part cut away, flopped on her feet as she rushed into the room.

"Let me introduce Marmie Watson." Glenda reached for the woman's hand and held it tightly. "She's fixin' to put breakfast on the table. Marmie, can you put another cup o' water in the soup?"

"Sho' can. You folks hungry?" Kinky, gray hair framed her face with its sunny smile.

Bessie was tempted to say, "No, we're not hungry — ravenous is more like it." Instead, always one to mind her manners, and not wanting to seem over anxious, Bessie said, "Breakfast sounds divine. How can we help?"

Looking around, Glover saw that the homey house mimicked the smiles of its occupants. The little house was clean as a whistle, tastefully but sparsely furnished, and smelling good with the aroma of sizzling bacon and pork sausage.

Glancing into a hazy mirror hanging above the couch, Bessie winced at her reflection. *Dear God. I look like death warmed over.* "May I use your facilities?" Bessie asked.

Glenda let out a jovial laugh and put her arm around Bessie's shoulder. Steering her toward the kitchen door, she pointed to the back porch.

219

"Just foller that trail t' the *facilities*."

"Oh, thank you so much." Bessie acted as if she'd never seen an indoor bathroom and was perfectly comfortable using a toilet that was little more than a hole in the ground. At this point she couldn't be choosy anyway. Hurrying along, she snapped the screen door shut and followed a trodden dirt path that led to a three-foot-square building peppered with knotholes. Tall grass bordering the path parted as You and Two playfully appeared, quickly falling in line behind Bessie single file. They stationed themselves, one on each side of the door, and sat down to wait once Bessie held her nose and went inside.

Glover followed Coot to a barn that leaned perilously to the left, to search for a repair kit. LaVeeta asked Marmie if she could help with breakfast, and Addie sat down at the kitchen table.

"Them are the biggest biscuits I ever seen," LaVeeta commented as she stared at a flat iron griddle loaded with nine unbaked biscuits, neatly aligned in rows of three. Marmie welcomed LaVeeta's help.

"Git a dozen eggs from off dat she'f an' break 'em in dat orange bowl." Marmie opened the door to the cast-iron cook stove and added a stick of wood on the grate.

"Chil', what you been doin' since school be out?" Marmie tried to engage Addie in conversation, but Addie looked at her hands folded in her lap and mostly shook her head every now and then. Marmie wrinkled her forehead and looked over her gold-rimmed spectacles. "Laud, Laud, somethin' terrible done happen to dis chil'," she muttered to herself as she stirred grits into a pot of boiling water.

Bessie, hoping that breakfast was ready, returned to find Glenda in the living room. Eyeing a colorful afghan that was

220

spread across the back of the sofa, Bessie knew right away that they were sister crocheters – a bond that only they understood. The women talked about their accomplishments with everything from afghans to baby sweaters to tablecloths and bedspreads. Glenda proudly displayed an afghan with a stitch that she called broomstick lace. Bessie was beside herself. She'd not heard of this stitch, so Glenda got out her sawed-off broomstick and showed Bessie how to weave yarn around it with a crochet hook.

"I can't wait to get home and start on a spread for my bed. It'll be something special for my new house. Thank you, Glenda. I've never seen broomstick lace." Bessie scribbled down the exact sequence of stitches on the back of an envelope she had in her pocketbook.

"Gimme a minute." Glenda left the room to return with a mound of blue and white woven yarn in her arms.

"Oh, Glenda! How lovely!" exclaimed Bessie as her new friend unfurled a broomstick lace coverlet. Bessie fingered the intricately woven loops of yarn with admiration.

"Idn't blue your favorite color?" Glenda remembered this from earlier in their conversation.

"It is. I'm doing my new bedroom in blue. Maybe I'll accent with yellow. Maybe rose."

"Well, spruce it up with this spread." Glenda grinned so big that Bessie imagined that such enormous smiles were the culprits responsible for the gap between her teeth.

"Oh, thank you, Glenda! Thank you ever so much. But, I'll be glad to buy it from you." *Lord only knows how many hours of work have gone into this,* thought Bessie.

Glenda's smile quickly faded. "Now don't go an' hurt my feelin's. Friends don't sell things t' each other, not when they's a blessing for sharing."

221

"I would *never* want to hurt your feelings. It is my pleasure to own such a beautiful piece of work, and I will treasure it always. Thank you, Glenda." She embraced the dear, sweet woman's ample being, even planting a kiss on her chubby cheek.

In a corner of the tipsy barn, Glover and Coot jacked up Lulu and removed her tire. That was the easy part. Getting the tire off the rim and the tube out without puncturing it further took some know-how. After several tries, out popped the tube with no apparent additional tears.

Glover swung the collapsed tire tube over his arm and followed Coot.

"I got a wash tub full o' rainwater 'round back o' the barn," Coot said over his shoulder, as he led the way through freshly mown grass.

Taking a box of Ivory Snow Flakes off a shelf, Coot sprinkled the soap into a galvanized washtub that had collected rainwater. He stuck his long, bony fingers in the clear water, swirling and squishing until the flakes were dissolved.

"Now we jus' got t' let them bubbles bust an' the water settle down." He reached for the tube.

Glover stepped closer. It would take an eagle eye to find the puncture in the wreath of black rubber.

Neither spoke a word as Coot slowly rotated the nearly deflated tube in the soapy water, gently squeezing it.

"I'll blow it up a little," said Glover as he took the tube and stuck the air valve in his mouth. He blew as hard as he could, causing his eyes to bulge and the veins at his temples to puff up like popped corn. After half a dozen blows, Coot took the tube, inserted the valve in his mouth, and blew for all he was worth.

222

"This'll take all day an' we gonna blow our brains out. 'Sides, we don't have no way of holdin' the value stem down. Let me hunt for a bicycle pump. They's one 'round here somewhere. I seen it not long ago. We got goats that git in here an' eat ever'thin' in sight. Hope they ain't chewed it up."

A short search produced a battered but not chewed-up pump. They connected the hose to the tube and pumped the plunger rapidly.

"Try it now." Glover prepared to watch like an owl eyeing a field mouse. Just as they heard Marmie's call, tiny bubbles floated on the water.

"There it is!" They both shouted at the same time. Coot dried the punctured place, and then he drew a circle with leftover barn-red paint and hung the tube on a wheelbarrow's handle to dry.

Marmie hollered at full lung capacity as she rang an iron bell hanging near the front door of the house that was suspended several feet off the ground on pillars of fieldstones. "Y'all come'n git it!" she shouted, unnerving the serene setting. The sad-looking bloodhound sleeping near the door raised his twitching nose, sniffed, then closed his eyes and returned to wherever sleeping dogs go.

"That's Roger," Glenda said nodding toward the dog. "He don't hunt no more." *Did he ever?* thought Bessie, having a hard time visualizing Roger in motion.

Glenda unfurled a tablecloth, that was starched stiff enough to stand through a torrential downpour, and flung it over a wooden table spanning the front porch. She'd insisted that cloth napkins match, although she had to search to come up with seven of the same. LaVeeta set the table with mismatched ironstone plates and mugs, just as Bessie had taught her. The table could not have looked nicer – shabby/chic before its time.

Hanging baskets spilling over with pink, white, and yellow petunias swung from rusty, bent nails. Swayed by a gentle morning breeze, sprawling ferns, crowded in dented washtubs on legs made from scrap lumber, trailed over the porch railing.

It was the perfect setting for breakfast on a spectacular summer day. The view from the porch to the valley below, alive with activity, was something to behold!

A white-tailed buck, a doe, and a fawn grazed on a deer-breakfast of clover while being serenaded with bird music. Oodles of mission-driven bees hovered over unsuspecting patches of wildflowers; each bee selected a blossom in full bloom, and then unabashedly – in broad daylight – robbed it of its pollen. The sun, bathing the valley with warmth, sipped droplets of early morning dew besprinkling the meadow.

"I'm so glad y'all stopped by. It thrills my heart t' be able t' share breckfas' with y'all on this beautiful day," said Glenda, carrying a platter piled high with crisped bacon and browned sausage patties in one hand, and a bright blue-striped bowl filled with scrambled eggs and sharp cheddar cheese in the other.

"I believe dat eggs wid cheese is like a hug wid a squeeze," laughed Marmie, as she added a plate of fried red new potatoes mixed with green onions, and a bowl brimming with buttered grits.

"I don't tell ever'body my secret for good grits, but I done tole LaVeeta, so I mite as well tell y'all too. I adds in milk toward da end. Start out cookin' 'em in water. Add yo' milk towards da end. You has t' simmer 'em real slow, but dat makes 'em creamy." Marmie smiled and chuckled as Bessie took her envelope, designated for note taking, out of her pocket and jotted

224

down that little tip.

Addie shyly stood in the doorway holding the pièce de résistance – cathead biscuits the size of a cat's head – bundled in a red-checkered dishcloth, and nestled inside a breadbasket woven from grapevines.

Glover Daniels' heart was overflowing with joy. How grateful he was to have so much! There was no doubt in his mind that surely he was the most blessed man in the entire world, Addie was safe and back with them, there was enough food before him to feed an army, and he was among both old and new friends. They were good friends, the kind of friends that practice love on a daily basis. Surely it didn't get any better than this.

Everyone bowed their heads and closed their eyes as Coot offered a blessing.

"Lord God, thanks for this food an' for these good fr'ends t' share it with. Git 'em home safe an' sound, if ya don't mind. Thank ya ag'in, Lord, for all ya bless us with. I'm askin' this in Jesus name. Amen." And so be it. "Amen," the others chimed in.

Glover sliced a biscuit and slathered it with home-churned butter. On one half he centered a sausage pattie and balanced two slices of bacon on top. On the other half, he drizzled cane syrup. What to do with the grits was a no-brainer – a puddle of grits always made a perfect nest for scrambled eggs. Easing a spoonful of potatoes and onions covered with sausage gravy into his mouth, he chewed slowly while contentedly gazing at the Tennessee countryside.

Beautiful Tennessee! In light of good company and the fabulous meal before them, the beauty of the meadow took on an even more delightful aura.

The others agreed when he stated, "Too bad that

ever'body don't understand that life is better b'tween two slices of bread." They all laughed when Coot added, "Or maybe a cathead biscuit."

*

When Rufus heard Lettie's proposal to give Addie a home, he had to bite his tongue to keep from laughing. She need not know that he'd already considered taking Addie into their family, but he felt that it was a man's duty to be stubborn. And he surely couldn't let his wife think that she was ruling the roost, although in a roundabout way she did. And both he and she knew it.

Lettie had carefully chosen what she thought would be the right time to talk about opening their home to a child that needed love. Five years ago, they'd taken Moses in, and now she felt a twinge of guilt in asking Rufus to provide for another child. Rufus worked hard and asked for little. Another mouth to feed added up to more responsibility for folks that were already overloaded. But she knew Rufus. He had a good heart, and he was strong and kind.

She had made chicken croquettes with a cream sauce, mashed potatoes, and plump green peas – Rufus's favorite supper. Strawberry shortcake would seal the deal.

Lettie was prepared for Rufus to play her like a Fender guitar. He never just said-so on any matter and got it over with. No, he had to stretch it out over several days and leave her waiting for his decision. Most of the time, she knew what he would choose before he did; still he would string her along before giving an answer.

Rufus knew she had already made up her mind. He

226

could play along and act like he was indecisive; but before she ever brought up the subject, he'd been thinking about where Addie would live. He knew that if she went back to her house Hester would beat her within an inch of her life. He'd known Hester Johnson for a lot of years and he wouldn't put anything past her. Glover, Doris, and Bessie would do their best to take care of Addie, but they had their hands full already. Glover and Doris had five children, two of them babies. Bessie was building a house and would soon be moving, and LaVeeta was so young and needed to take care of herself. Rufus had wondered if he and Lettie might be the best choice of caretakers to help Addie heal and grow. He wanted her to develop into a stable, decent young woman.

Much to Lettie's surprise, without a second's hesitation, Rufus said, "Sho'nuff. We give it our bes' shot."

Lo and behold! If this man was trying to drive her stark raving mad, he was doing a stellar job of it!

*

Glenda's son came to take her to his house to baby-sit her three grandchildren while her son and daughter-in-law worked. Glenda had insisted that Bessie stretch out across her bed and rest while Glover and Coot worked on the tire. Which she did, and was asleep before she got her eyes closed good.

Soon as the breakfast dishes were washed and put away, LaVeeta used the hand pump at the kitchen sink to fill a red-rimmed enamel basin with water. Being careful not to splash water on the floor, she took baby steps as she carried the basin toward the back porch. Everyone had washed up before breakfast; even so, she knew she'd feel better if she could

227

remove a little more of two days of sweat and road dust. She'd planned to ask Addie to join her – Lord knows she needed to – but Marmie had whispered, "I'd like t' talk t' da chil' alone."

The gentle, wise woman came to make breakfast three days a week for Coot and Glenda. Sometimes Marmie ironed or helped do the washing, because Glenda had arthritis in her hands and scrubbing clothes on a washboard was almost more than she could handle. Nonetheless, she could do her part by building a fire under the black iron wash pot to boil the towels, sheets, and underwear to whiten them. In return, Coot and Glenda helped Marmie and her husband, who had lost a leg in a logging accident two or three years back. Coot kept their grass mowed and went once a day to slop Harland and Henrietta, their morbidly obese hogs. After the first heavy frost, H. and H. would be part of the breakfast fixin's – fried and sandwiched in a biscuit.

Marmie put her arm around Addie and whispered, "Come walk wid me thru th' woods t' my house."

Addie didn't want to go, but Marmie coaxed her saying, "I needs somebody to he'p me cross a narrow bridge o'er th' creek."

As they walked, Marmie told Addie that she knew that something bad had happened. She knew because when she was a girl the same thing had happened to her. Although Marmie didn't know the details, she had a pretty good idea what had taken place.

Not far down the footpath through the woods, they sat down to rest on a fallen pine tree and Addie, feeling that what she said was safe with Marmie, confided in her.

"My brother LaMarcus sent a man that he knew t' bring me to Chicago. I was goin' home the day before the party at Mr.

Campbell's, an' a man came out from behin' the bushes near our house an' called my name. He tol' me that LaMarcus sent him t' git me." Her chin quivered as her eyes began to tear.

"He said I'd have my own room, an' LaMarcus had me a job at a res'rant there. He promised lots o' good things an' the best part was that I wouldn't never have t' see Mama again.

"He said LaMarcus done made it good an' lived in a nice house an' wanted me t' come an' stay with him. He showed me two bus tickets he had in his pocket."

Addie dropped her head and softly sobbed at the thought of living with her mother. Every day had been filled with conflict that kept her hurt, angry, confused, and in tears. Dreading the day when Hester would make her quit school, she wanted to get away; but she didn't know how.

"This sounded like it mite be somethin' better. Wouldn't take much to be better'n puttin' up with Mama," she defended her choice to go with the man. Addie couldn't leave until after the barbeque; she'd promised LaVeeta that she would go with her.

"Durin' the fireworks, I sneaked away. This guy – his name Damon. He was waitin' for me behin' Miss Bessie's car. We caught the midnight bus to Chicago at the Trailways dee-po. It was a long way. When we fin'lly got there, he took me to a hotel room where we met LaMarcus. The place was filthy an' LaMarcus was dog drunk. He always drunk. I don't know why I thought he wouldn't be." Disappointed in herself, she had to stop for a minute to regain enough composure to finish telling Marmie her story.

"He lied to me! I shoulda knowed he was lyin'! I felt so stupid an' I was so scared! Before I ever got there, LaMarcus done sold me to this ol' man. Sold me! Like he owned me! Mean as Mama is, she ain't never sold me to nobody!"

229

Marmie's heart was close to breaking when she heard the anger and hurt in the young girl's voice.

"LaMarcus kep' hittin' me. He said that a virgin had bought him top dollar. I don't even know what he talkin' 'bout."

"Now, now," whispered Marmie as she patted Addie's hand.

"I didn't know what to do. I couldn't stop cryin'. I tried, but I jes couldn't. LaMarcus kept hittin' me. He pulled my hair. He twisted my arm. I thought he was gonna break it. The more he hollered at me to stop cryin', the more I couldn't stop. Then, I got sick an' throwed up all over ever'thin' – LaMarcus too. He was so mad he was fit to be tied. He woulda hit me ag'in, but he wanted to git away from me 'fore I throwed up ag'in. He said he woulda had his way with me – whatever that means – but then I'd be worthless to him. More worthless than I already is.

"They called a woman to come an' git me. She was 'posed to watch me 'til LaMarcus could figure out what to do next. Her name's Mariah. If I hadn't met her, I don't know what they woulda done to me."

"Thank you, Lord Jesus, for Mariah," Marmie whispered to herself. Marmie could only conclude that Mariah surely knew that she would be held accountable, but had chosen to not allow a frightened little girl to be used by evil men.

"I tol' Mariah to call Miss Bessie. I didn't know nobody else to call. Mariah made a deal with a man she knew who went to Indiana ever week to pick up watermelons."

Addie explained to Marmie that she had been reunited with her sister the day before. Feeling some relief from telling someone what had happened; she hung her head and sobbed as if her heart were broken. Marmie let her cry for a while, and then she reached over and lifted Addie's head.

230

Speaking slowly and softly, she looked over her spectacles into Addie's sore eyes and said, "Listen t' me chil'. An' you listen real good. Listen like you ain't never listen t' nobody b'fore. You don't ever let no man outdo you! Never! Sometime it mite feel like he got da upper hand, but dey ain't no man in dis wurl smarter than you is. Not even one."

Choosing her words carefully, she continued, "We has t' let hurts make us stronger. Dat's what we do wid 'em. We lets' 'em make us stronger. Da smartest an' strongest people in da wurl is da ones dat knowed what to do wid hurts. I knows 'xactly what you talkin' 'bout, cause I had pretty much da same thang happen t' me. What is *is*. Dat's all dey is to it. Short an' sweet. Don't fret over what you can't change. What's done's done. You got yo' whole life ahead o' you. Can you swim, Addie?"

"Yessum," came a whispered reply.

"Well den, you know dat if you cain't swim, you gonna drown out in deep water. It's da same way wid da hard thangs in life. Jus' like you swim outta deep water 'til you gits yo' feet on da ground, you move on from hurts an' pain 'til you gits sure-footed ag'in."

Marmie shook her head and went on. "If you don't look hard times in da eye an' stare 'em down, you'll drown in se'f-pity. Oh, you still be 'live. But you mite as well be dead for all da good yo' life gonna 'mount to.

"You got people dat love you. Look here who's done come all dis way t' git you. Who done dat? Yo' mama not gonna do dat. Yo' brother ain't gonna do dat. Dees folks did dat. Dey's all dat matters. Dey gonna he'p you, an' you gonna put dis whole thang b'hind you." Marmie pulled Addie to her breast and cradled her head.

Addie didn't have a word to say. She was out of words,

out of explanations, out of answers, out of tears. Marmie lifted Addie's head and again looked deep into her eyes. "Don't never tell nobody else what happened. You got to move on. Don't waste yo' time going o'er an' o'er it. Right now! Dis da end o' dis! *Today* is yo first day. It's a good day. You understand?" Addie wiped her eyes with the end of her skirt and nodded her head yes.

"Now let me see a smile on dat pretty face o' yorn. C'mon now. C'mon. Marmie ain't gonna have no mo' o' dis." Love radiated from her smile as she gently stroked Addie's cheek.

Addie had listened to every word. This woman was the mother that Addie had always wanted. She was the grandmother that Addie wished she had. If Marmie could be this sweet and strong after going through horrible experiences, then Addie knew that she could too. Hurt tugged at her heart, but Marmie had said that hurt can make a person stronger.

"I want to be strong like you, Miss Marmie. I want to please these folks who came to git me. My sister care 'bout me an' I'm so sorry I ran away."

For the very first time in her life, Addie felt that she might be of some value. That's what real love does. It makes a person know that they are valued.

Somewhere deep down in Addie's soul, a surge of fresh hope breached the dam of fear and frustration. Strength flooded her being.

"I have to be strong an' smart. I have to take care of myse'f," she whispered to Marmie, but even more so to herself.

There was no need for any further talk. It was settled within Addie, and Marmie recognized the breakthrough. Holding hands, they silently continued along the narrow path until they came to the wooden bridge. Taking the lead, Addie turned to walk backwards, steadying Marmie as they took baby steps along the planked overpass. Midway, they paused to look over the railing at water trekking along the creek bed.

Marmie went on and on about the cramped passageway. "I always wonder why dis bridge hadn't been built wider. It seem t' me some skinny person done come up wid dis bridge buildin' plan." Then as if the reason for constructing the bridge, barely wide enough for any person, had been divinely revealed to her, she clapped her hands and said, "Or, maybe dey only had a li'l bit o' lumber."

She threw her head back and laughed till she shook. Marmie's hearty laughter, rattling through the silent woods, was infectious. Addie chuckled. Chuckles bubbled into laughter, and soon Addie laughed so hard that tears trickled down her cheeks. The two doubled over, sides aching, trying to catch their breaths.

The jovial sounds were like straw brooms whisking away any residual hurt feelings and sadness. The phenomenon of laughter had freed Addie's bruised soul once and for all. The tears that freely flowed were no longer tears of sadness and grief, but tears of relief and happiness.

Light-headed and filled with joy, they continued their walk. The warmth of the sun felt good as it dried their tear-stained faces.

A blue jay grasping an acorn in its beak flew over.

"Did you know jays store nuts jus' like squirrels do?" Marmie pointed as the bird seesawed on the tip of a pine branch where it had landed.

Edging their way along the foot-trodden trail, Marmie began to hum the tune to "This Little Light of Mine." And then her rich alto voice rose, filling the air with music as she belted out, "I'm gonna let it shine, let it shine, let it shine."

She smiled at Addie. "Chil', you let it shine. Darlin', you let yo lite shine. I be prayin' fo' you. I'll never stop."

At a fork in the trail, Addie turned back, and Marmie continued to her house. Before parting, Marmie hugged and squeezed Addie long and hard. The tight hug infused warmth into the girl's bruised spirit like a blazing fireplace on an icy morning. She had never had anyone to comfort or care for her as Marmie had.

With tears in her eyes, the wise, compassionate woman told the fragile young girl once more to never look back. Addie promised Marmie that she wouldn't, kissed her cheek, and told her good-bye.

When Addie reached the Jones' house she found the others waiting for her. After a trip to the facilities and a drink of well water, Addie was good to go. She'd changed into clean clothes that LaVeeta had lent her. The tube was patched, and Lulu was ready to roll; Bessie and LaVeeta were refreshed and ready to ride. Glover felt like he was on top of the world, even though sleeping in a car had left his neck as stiff as Uncle Martin's peg leg.

Bessie offered to sit in the backseat with Addie to give LaVeeta a turn up front, but LaVeeta wanted to sit near her sister. Right away, she had sensed that Marmie had reached Addie, and things were on the mend. When all were seated, and Glover was about to crank Lulu, Addie softly spoke one sentence to the others. One sentence was all she could manage without falling apart.

"Mr. Glover, Miss Bessie, LaVeeta, thank you."

As soon as Glover put the car in gear, You and Two sprang into action. Lulu slowly rolled forward, the dogs trotting

234

ahead instead of behind the car. "What kinda dog leads instead of chases a car?" Glover said as he hung his head out the window, trying to dodge the frisky canines. They all laughed and waved as Coot slowly waved back. Lazy Roger, lying at his master's feet, couldn't be bothered to run or bark, it had taken far too much energy to follow Coot into the yard. Glover tooted the horn, and Lulu stirred up a storm of dust as they headed down the hill.

"Next stop Campbell's Corner, Alabama!" shouted Glover as he steered the car onto the highway.

Chapter Nine
Love Conquers All

Glover thought that probably fewer people had participated in building the Pyramids than had worked on cleaning brick for underpinning the house. Cam and his sons, Rufus and his sons, most of the members of Glover's family, and Buddy and his brother – to name a few – had at one time or another sat on the pile of brick and chipped away at mortar. When anyone had any time to spare, they'd donated their muscle power to the brick project. At last, a pile of concrete chips had been dumped behind the chicken house to be used when needed to fill in ruts in the driveway, and the bricks were neatly stacked. Rufus had helped prepare the footing so that all that was left to do was to lay brick. Glover was anxious to bring this business to an end.

Even though it was late August, the weather was more like mid-July – hot and sticky. After work each day, Glover was busy by five or six each afternoon laying brick. Sweat trickled down his shirtless back, his well-developed biceps flexing as he mixed small batches of mortar in the wheelbarrow. Buttering the brick and carefully leveling each one, Glover worked persistently row after row.

It was shoutin' time when the last brick was in place. One would think that Glover had hit the jackpot by the way he carried on, glad to see an end to the tedious, exhausting work. The finished product was a beautiful red brick wall surrounding the framed house from the ground up to the bottom row of planking. Leftover bricks were loaded in the wheelbarrow and moved to the backyard. There they were stacked to wait until some Saturday, when they would be transformed into a barbeque pit big enough to cook an elephant.

Now that he'd finished the underpinning, he'd have more time to help on Bessie's house. Construction was going according to plan, and Cam was pretty sure they'd have the house ready for Bessie by the middle of November.

Auntie was excitedly making plans to take a break the first week in September and visit long time friends in Chattanooga. Cam had volunteered to drive her there, as he needed to come back through Ft. Payne to check at a salvage yard that he'd heard about for a certain fixture needed in Bessie's house.

At first, Janet wasn't considering taking him up on his offer, but her dislike for riding trains was making the decision to accept easier. The three hour trip would give them time to get more personally acquainted – not that she wanted to be more than friends.

Cam thought that he'd died and gone to heaven when Janet agreed to allow him to drive her to Tennessee. This seemed too good to be true, and he halfway expected her to change her mind. If she didn't cancel, they'd have three hours together. Other than the first day when they had met, there had never been another moment when just the two of them had time to spend alone. This could be his one and only shot at winning her hand.

*

Addie seemed to be happy and doing well – as well as one could starting life at thirteen. She never returned to her mother's house, and Hester never looked for her. Lettie Jenkins asked Addie to stay with them a few days to get to know Eleanor and Daisy. Those few days set a pattern. Soon Addie became

237

friends with the girls, who made her feel like one of the Jenkins family. Having a home, a real home, took a little getting used to, but it was a dream come true. At least once a week, Addie spent the night with LaVeeta and Bessie; every now and then LaVeeta spent the night at the Jenkins house. She and her sister had a lot of lost time to make up now that they were in an environment that favored trust and love. Mose took to both sisters. They read to him and taught him to count, and every now and then he would tag along when Addie spent the night with LaVeeta. They had not a clue that Moses was actually their brother, and it would be many years before LaVeeta would discover how fate had brought them all together.

In the fall Addie would go to school with the Jenkins kids. Bessie was helping her with reading and math. She was so far behind, and Bessie didn't want her to be held back another year. Bessie Pearl had pulled a few strings, called in a few favors, and made arrangements for LaVeeta to be tested to bring her up to the grade that she would have been in had she not quit school. Smart girl that she was, with Bessie's tutoring, LaVeeta should pass with flying colors.

When anyone asked Addie how she'd gotten to Chicago or what had happened, she volunteered not a word of information. She would simply say, "Miss Marmie say don't ever look back – jes' keep on keepin' on."

*

At first, Bessie hesitated when Cam offered her living quarters while he worked on her new house. Who'd ever heard of such? What would people think? She didn't want to give anyone room to talk.

238

After pondering the situation throughout several sleepless nights, she realized that moving into the upper floor of Cam's house was the perfect solution to her problem.

"Strike while the iron is hot" had always been her motto. Marvin had a buyer for her house, and she needed to make the sale; it just made good sense to take Cam up on his offer. Moving in with Cam would, no doubt, open the door for gossip and speculation.

Bessie had a long talk with herself and concluded that it was as plain as the nose on any face that she was no spring chick, and as far as she knew, her reputation was spotless. Surely, when people factored in these obvious details, they would not draw any unfavorable conclusions. The truth of the matter was, at sixty-one years of age, she was not looking for male companionship; and although it was common knowledge to everyone but Janet that Cam was looking for a wife, he wasn't looking in Bessie's direction. Only thoughts of Janet plucked at his heartstrings. After considerable deliberation, Bessie'd settled into a peaceful place within herself, putting aside what anyone might think or say.

"An outside entrance from the back of the house to the upstairs makes living at Cam's house like having a private apartment. Besides, it'll only be for a little more than two months," Bessie explained to Janet.

"I have no objections," said Janet. "Matter of fact, I'm lookin' forward to you livin' next door."

There was plenty of room in Cam's house for Bessie. In fact, there was room enough for three or four Bessies. And he had space in the barns to store her furniture.

"I haven't seen the upstairs. Cam is waiting for me. Let's go see what I'm getting into. Come with me, Janet." Bessie needed all the encouragement she could get. This was a big step. Moving into the house with a man that she barely knew was not something that her Mother would have approved. Or anyone else in her family, for that matter.

"Let's go." Janet went to tell Doris that she would be right back.

The two made their way through the path to Cam's sprawling brick house. Cam, sitting on the front porch with an attention addicted yellow cat named PatMore in his lap, waved as he saw the ladies coming across the yard.

"Let's go 'round back so you can see the outside entrance." He led the way to the side yard. "The stairs are not steep an' there's a landin' half-way up."

Opening the door, Cam suggested that Bessie and Janet explore the upstairs alone. "I'm not goin' up. I've seen it one or two times before," he joked. "Pick out any bedroom that you like, Bessie. The whole floor is yours. If you need anythin', just let it be known. Your wish is my command." He was talking to Bessie but looking over her head at Janet. Janet was admiring the quarter-sawn oak staircase.

Bessie led the way, stopping to admire a stained glass window at the landing.

The upper floor housed four spacious bedrooms, each with an adjoining alcove that served as a sitting room.

Sotto voce, Bessie said, "Have you ever seen anything like this?" Peeking in the first bedroom that they came to, they saw a towering Cuban mahogany, four-poster bed reaching toward twelve-foot ceilings.

"Look at the gooseneck rocker. It's like Doris's, only fancier," Janet commented as she sat down in the chair. She pushed off and listened to the sound of worn rockers faintly

240

creaking. Bessie was looking at her reflection in a hand mirror she'd spotted on top of an Eastlake dresser. She loved mother-of-pearl, and both the mirror and matching hairbrush had M.O.P. handles.

"Come look." Bessie bent over a skirted dressing table. A mirrored tray reflected a montage of antique crystal perfume bottles, some topped with ornate stoppers. The ladies spritzed a sweet-stink and giggled like little girls.

"Heavens to Betsy! Stale! Lord only knows how old this perfume is." Janet continued to squeeze a tiny bulb with her thumb and index finger, aiming at an earlobe.

"Doesn't matter. It prob'ly doesn't smell like it did when it was new, but it's still pretty potent. We're going to smell like a shameless hussy off a Paris street corner late at night, if you know what I mean." Bessie laughed as Janet blushed at a mental image of a French lady of the evening.

Eyeing a tooled leather dressing screen, Bessie darted behind the accordion panels and beckoned Janet to follow. Janet, usually levelheaded and sensible, let playfulness get the best of her and joined Bessie in a game of "What shall we wear to dinner?"

"Oh, dahlin', do hand me my string o' pearls. Shall I wear the tiara an' diamond drop earrings too?"

"Why not both, dearie? An' a ring for every finger." Janet stretched forth her hands and spread her fingers apart.

Good thing Cam wasn't watching, or anybody else for that matter. They'd think Bessie and Janet had taken leave of their senses. Even the women felt silly, although they were having jolly good fun. And, times were few and far between when, at their age, they could become little girls again.

In a bedroom furnished with heavy, dark Empire-style

241

furniture, a green marbled fireplace surround, and floor-to-ceiling bookshelves behind glass doors, Bessie was drawn to a copper-lined humidor nestled beside an oversized, leather chair. It proved to be home to six or seven carved pipes, each exuding the unmistakable odor of pipe tobacco. Opening its door, both women slowly inhaled the sweet scent.

"Reminds me of my favorite uncle. He used to get his pipe tobacco from Carolina. Smelled like fruit and vanilla," Bessie reminisced.

The other bedrooms housed tall Edwardian armoires with mirrored doors and several oval Cheval mirrors, all reflecting light from an abundance of tall windows. Delicate, colorful Tiffany shades accented brass lamps like cherries on top of sundaes. In the sitting rooms, Thonet chairs – their artfully bent twigs forming curved backs and arms – were dressed in printed chintz cushions and soft velvet pillows.

The women found themselves tiptoeing along the wide hallway that connected the rooms. There was no one to disturb – the grandeur of the place just seemed to say *"tiptoe."*

One of Bessie's favorite places was the roomy bath. A stained glass window, depicting scenes of the Scottish Highlands, served as a backdrop for an oversized claw-foot tub embellished with gold faucets.

"Janet, would it be a bit snobbish for me to imagine curling up in that calico chaise lounge and taking a nap after a long, hot bubble bath?" She pointed next to an ebony Queen Anne dresser.

"Not if I can sneak over once in a while and do the same."

Bessie Pearl Pennycutt loved everything about this house. Everything – bar none. She noticed each etched-glass transom above the doorways and admired wallpaper prints ranging from pale yellow with tiny bouquets of violets to scenes of foxhunts on hunter green backgrounds. Flipping switches to set dangling crystal chandeliers shimmering with light was like opening a gift and finding a treasure inside. Bessie thought that maybe her favorite things were the yards of plush silks and linens, flowing from coffered ceilings to puddle on the floor underneath each window. Maybe not. It would be hard to choose a favorite thing in the castle-like fortress that Cam's grandfather had built in 1850. The furnishings had come through both Cam's and Elizabeth's families throughout the last century, most of them originated in Scotland.

"Does Cam have a housekeeper?" Janet knew that this was too much house for a man to keep. There wasn't a speck of dust anywhere.

"Kristalene comes on Saturdays. She cleans, does the laundry, and cooks a few things for Cam to have later in the week. Actually, to hear him tell it, he's a pretty good cook and doesn't need someone to help on a daily basis." Bessie recalled information that Cam had given her on her first visit to the house.

"Kristalene?"

"She kept house for Cam's wife. He said that she is like family. Has a husband named Otto, if I remember correctly. I think he said that all their kids are grown and gone. I don't really know her. Just know what Cam told me."

Bessie stopped in the doorway to the corner bedroom.

"Janet, I think I'll take this room."

She chose the bedroom cloaked with powder-blue toile wallpaper, a quilted blue satin comforter, almond-colored French-style furniture, and a perfect view of tea roses near the

243

ornamental garden pond out back.

"Oh, Bess! Look at this!" Janet hurried toward the dresser. Amid scattered tortoise shell brushes and combs, there sat a porcelain music box. When Bessie raised the lid, a small white dove with outstretched wings, grasping a red rose in its beak, spun round and round to the tune of an old Irish folk song. "The Last Rose of Summer" played softly, tinkling like gentle breeze-blown crystal wind chimes. She remembered her mother humming this song to her when she was a child. There was something strangely hypnotic about the box. Drifting back in time, she closed her eyes and listened to the melody. *This must be an omen. It's Mother's stamp of approval,* thought Bessie.

"This is more than I could ever have hoped for. As you well know, Veeta is a compulsive house cleaner. Neat should be her middle name. She'll think she's died and gone to heaven when she sees all these do-dads that she can dust. But how will I ever be able to leave all this?"

Realizing that it would be easy to like Cam's home far too much, Bessie cautioned herself not to get too settled or too attached.

She suspected that would be much easier said than done.

*

On Friday, September 1, 1950, Janet carefully placed the last few folded items lying on the bed into her suitcase. Cam would be coming to get her within the next hour to drive her to Chattanooga. Her childhood friend Laura had invited her to a Labor Day cookout on Monday and to stay until the following weekend. Laura's husband Dewey had grown up on Lookout Mountain and knew the history of the Battle of Chickamauga

244

(fought for two days in September 1863) like he'd been an eyewitness. He never tired of telling how this bloody battle marked the end of a Union offensive in southeastern Tennessee and north Georgia. Janet chuckled as she pictured Laura rolling her eyes as Dewey led them through the battle for the umpteenth time.

Cam was to pick Janet up at 9 a.m. She hoped that there would be little awkwardness between the two of them. Never would she have agreed to this, if it weren't that she so disliked traveling by train. The monotonous rhythm of the wheels got on her nerves, not to mention that it seemed like it took forever and a day to get anywhere.

Next door at Cam's house, Bessie was making her way to the kitchen. She'd risen early, spent an hour reading from Psalms, and was anxious to start the day on a positive note and a good cup of coffee. Descending the back staircase that led to the kitchen, she could hear Cam clinking dishes and running water in the roomy farmhouse sink.

Usually Bessie waited until Cam had eaten breakfast and the kitchen was vacant, but she knew that he'd be leaving to take Janet to Chattanooga, and Bessie needed to ask a question.

Cam quickly glanced toward the stairway when he heard Bessie's bedroom slippers scuffing across the hardwood floor. Chewing a bite of buttered toast, he turned to see her standing in the doorway, wrapped in a floor-length, pale blue chenille bathrobe cinched tightly at her waist.

An unintentional pleasant look of surprise flashed across his face, while quite unrepentantly, his heart skipped half a beat. Momentarily, his breath was literally taken away, and a sense of warmth oozed over him like honey on a hot biscuit.

He could not have been more startled by his reaction.

245

"Mornin', little blue bird", he stammered as he pulled out a chair and motioned for her to sit down. The morning sunlight streaming through the windows lit up her shapely silhouette. An unexpected feast for his eyes, he was surprised at how fresh and lovely Bessie appeared first thing in the morning.

She was an attractive woman, slightly plump, but in a good way — full figured might be a truer description. Delicate facial features — twinkling eyes and pouty lips — complimented her usually jovial expression. She'd twisted her salt-and-pepper hair in the back and then piled it on top of her head. Curly tendrils, with minds of their own, had escaped from bobby pins to dangle here and there around her face.

Quickly, Cam turned toward the cabinet, rattling cups before choosing one. As he tilted the percolator, hot brown liquid splashed on the cup's rim, splattering onto the countertop. Nervously, he grabbed a dishcloth to sop it up. Steadying his hand, he reached for another cup, sat it on a saucer, and carefully filled it to the brim.

He extended the cup of steaming coffee, turning toward Bessie, with a nervous smile twitching at the corners of his mouth.

"Thank you. And forgive me, Cam, if I'm intruding." Bessie smiled and sat down at the table. Dropping a sugar cube into the cup, she watched as it dove to the bottom.

"I hope that I'm not behaving improperly, but I need to be sure that we're on the same page 'bout the paint that I'm getting for the house. As you know, exterior paint is $3.29 a gallon." She sipped the hot brew. It was a shade stronger than she made coffee, and she wished she had an iced cinnamon roll for dipping to cut the stoutness. Bessie added, "At that exorbitant price I don't want to get more than we need."

246

Staring blankly into his coffee, Cam eased into the chair across the table. What in tarnation was going on with him? Meeting her gaze from underneath shaggy brows, he looked into her azure blue eyes and slowly sipped his coffee, lost in thought.

He was thinking that they'd gotten to know one another well. Bessie was agreeable and easy to work for. He'd found her to be witty and very intelligent. She knew what she wanted at the new house, but she was also open to suggestions. Bessie'd made his job as builder a pleasant task – this wasn't easy to do, considering all the headaches, pitfalls, and set backs that accompany building a structure from the ground up.

He'd made no secret of the fact that he was lonely. Oh, he didn't kid himself; he knew that there would never be another Elizabeth. The love of his life had staked claim to his very being, and he'd gladly given her full ownership – lock, stock, and barrel. She'd taken the deed to his heart to her grave, and he would never love again with that all-consuming kind of love. But he missed the presence of a woman. He missed the warmth that only a woman can bring to a house, a home – to his self, his soul, and his spirit. Love wears many masks. He yearned for the kind of love that seeks a needy heart and consoles it with gentle care and companionship.

"Cam."

The sound of her voice snapped him back to the moment.

"Yes. Yes, Bessie. Just drifted off there for a few seconds. My brain doesn't fire on all cylinders 'til I get a couple o' cupsa coffee under my belt. Sorry. Get whatever color you like. It'll prob'bly take at least five gallons of the primary color and two for the trim. Weren't you thinkin' 'bout blue?"

"White for the house and blue for trim."

When Bessie understood exactly what kind and how much paint that she needed to buy – and her cup was empty – she felt that she needed to go so that Cam could get on his way.

"Have a safe trip, and a good day." She pushed the chair away from the table and extended her cup in his direction. "May I take a refill?"

Cam filled the cup, careful not to spill any this time. He muttered something about her having a good day too, and watched as she dropped two sugar cubes in the cup, gave a quick stir, then headed upstairs.

*

Sunrays scorched the hood and cab on the northbound truck as it rolled along Highway 11, bound for the Tennessee state line. Conversation between Cam and Janet was at first somewhat strained, but the farther they traveled the more comfortable they became. Janet laughed easily as she told cute tales of Jack and Jim Ed.

"The babies are a laugh a minute," she chuckled as she remembered when they first began to crawl. "Jim Ed is the more outgoin' of the two. Jack mimics his brother. There is no mistakin' who is leadin' and who is followin'".

Gazing out the window at the green rolling hills, Janet realized that with little or no effort, she could talk about the twins all the way to Chattanooga. Yet, she didn't want to hog the conversation or seem insensitive.

Minding her manners, she said to Cam, "Tell me 'bout your family."

A proud grandpa doesn't have to be coaxed to brag about his grandkids. Anxious to share, Cam began, "I got three grandsons an' six granddaughters. Two of my grandsons, Craig an' Collin, are old enough for the draft. Craig's been called, but Collin didn't pass the army physical. He's more than a little nearsighted."

Cam grew quiet for several minutes, swallowed hard, and continued.

"I worry 'bout Craig. He'll be goin' to Korea in a few weeks. If they'd take me, I'd go in his place. I just have to believe that he'll be all right an' come home without a scratch. I can't deal with the thought of anythin' happenin' to him." And Cam knew that even if Craig returned without a scatch that would not mean that war had not changed him.

"We'll trust that he'll return safely," Janet said, quickly steering the subject in a cheerier direction.

"Tell me 'bout your granddaughters." It was Cam's turn to monopolize the conversation. One by one, he told of each young lady's attributes, from the oldest (who was twenty) to the youngest (who'd just turned twelve).

Familiarity lessened tension, and after an hour or so, Cam mustered up enough courage to ask the question that had been on his mind for a while.

"Would you like to go out to supper an' a movie when you get back?" Sweat dampened his upper lip beneath a row of red bristles as he waited for her answer. It seemed like half an hour went by before she timidly replied.

"I'll think 'bout it while I'm gone. I don't want to hurt or mislead you, Cam. I really like you, but I haven't thought a lot about a relationship with anyone. I'm satisfied with my life and the choices I've made. Really, I am."

Exercising his right to selective hearing, Cam ignored her, as men following their feelings for a woman are prone to do.

"All I ask is that you give it some time. I've had feelin's

for you since the first day we met while you were watchin' after the boys when the others were lookin' at the property."

Flattered, Janet felt a school girlish blush spreading to her cheeks. Cam carefully slid his hand across the seat and brushed her hand. She hesitated for a second and then moved her hand and rested it in her lap.

Cam felt that he'd said enough. No use pushing his luck. He changed the subject to the progress on Bessie's house.

When he told that Bessie was getting paint for the exterior, a mental image of her standing in the kitchen doorway, bright-eyed and bushy-tailed, flashed across his mind. New feelings stirred once more as he recalled that morning. It was as if this were the first time he'd really seen her.

Hell's bells! What's wrong with me? Is Bessie gettin' under my skin? He liked and respected her, but theirs was *only* a business arrangement. What was happening to him? Cam quickly changed the subject to sightseeing in Chattanooga.

"Been to Rock City or Ruby Falls?"

"More than once. That cave is cold an' wet. I didn't like being underground. From Rock City you can see seven states. Or so they say. I'm not sure I located two, much less seven."

They both laughed. Cam could relate. He had enjoyed the view from cliffs high above Chattanooga, but couldn't tell as he'd gazed across the vast plain where one state ended and another started.

The red truck followed a narrow, winding road along the banks of the Tennessee River as they neared the city. Janet fumbled in her pocketbook to find a scrap of paper with scribbled directions to the place where they'd agreed to meet. Laura had suggested a well-known spot that was easy to find – the Krystal restaurant on the corner of Seventh and Cherry

Streets.

Shortly before noon Laura pulled alongside them in the parking lot.

"Janet, bless your heart, you look wonderful!" exclaimed Laura as she threw her arms around her friend.

"Not as good as you do. I love your hairdo! Bangs look so good on you."

She introduced Cam, who offered to treat the ladies to a hot meal inside Krystal. As they ate little Krystal burgers and drank Cokes at the first Krystal, they had no way of knowing that in the future drive-through windows would be part of every Krystal – all 420 locations in 11 states.

Cam ordered the signature cake donuts for dessert. Janet was a little embarrassed that he ate six and then ordered eight more to take with him to eat on the way home. But then, the man was as tall as a silo, and he exerted more energy than a team of oxen.

Janet and Laura bid Cam farewell and went on their way, chattering like children at recess.

Heading back down Highway 11 toward Ft. Payne, Alabama, Cam pondered the morning's events. He'd been caught off guard with new, unsolicited feelings toward Bessie, and he wasn't even a little bit happy about it. Just when he thought that he might be making some progress with Janet, he couldn't get Bessie off his mind.

*

Standing with his hands thrust deep into his pockets and his fedora snug on his head, Glover gazed into clear, cool water meandering along the winding creek bed. Whirlpools of thoughts mimicked the swirls and ripples created as water parted, making

251

its way around moss-covered rocks. Minnows and small bream hitched a free ride as they were swept along.

The woods were ablaze with color. It was the first of November, and trees were doing that wonderful thing they do – rust, scarlet, and gold leaves, like flags of surrender signaling the end of another sweltering season. Someone once said, "Fall is a Southerner's compensation for having survived summer."

He spotted a familiar, large gray boulder, smooth on top – a perfect resting place. Having brushed the fallen leaves away, he scooted back and let his legs dangle.

An eerie cocoon of quietness shrouded the woodsy thicket, disturbed intermittently by faint fluttering, as another leaf swirled to the ground, or by dried leaves crackling as acorn-foraging squirrels rearranged them. Glover found the sweet solitude of nature like music to his ears.

Damp, mossy, earthy smells filled the air. Taking deep breaths, Glover melted into a state of beatitude – his spirit catching the drift of an unseen, unspoken presence.

From deep within, the words of a familiar hymn stirred – a hymn he'd sung all of his life.

He began to whistle softly as praise bubbled forth like an Artesian well. It was indeed well with his soul.

Events of the past year paraded in his thoughts. He smiled. "I could call 1950 the year of surprises," he said to his audience, a bushy-tailed squirrel set to sprint at the first hint of danger.

More often than not it had seemed that he could not work hard enough or do enough to see any real financial gain. He'd dreamed big dreams, but only hoped – not expected – for them to come true.

With Doris's inheritance from her mother, they'd gotten

252

the break that changed their lives. When he thought of himself as being husband to the love of his life, the father of five children, a property and car owner − as well as having a multitude of friends − he felt like the luckiest man in the world.

Glover had learned that there is power in satisfaction. *Bein' satisfied deep down inside when I know I've done my best gives me a sense of freedom. Oh, the power of satisfaction!* He thought. He was also aware that to whom much is given, much is required; and he gladly accepted his responsibility to reach out to others.

Sliding off the rock, he rustled the fallen leaves with his boot, like a child splashing in a mud puddle. The few remaining leaves on the trees rattled as squirrels scurried. Soon winter's rain and ice would blend the leaves into part of the forest floor forever.

I think I'll walk over to Bessie's after I get a cup o' coffee an' check on progress there, he thought, making his way back along the creek bank.

The house needed a few minor things before Bessie could move in. Glover would be finishing the trim molding around the doors and installing shoe molding along the baseboards. Although he'd been up since before dawn, he decided that he would go to the new house after supper and work until bedtime.

*

Turning sharply into the graveled parking lot, Glover jockeyed between a new pickup truck and a beat-up Hudson with a bashed-in bumper, and braked Lulu to a stop. Switching the headlights off, he grasped the handle of his lunch box, left Lulu in the dark, and slowly walked toward a naked bulb burning over the entrance door to the pipe foundry.

As he had done countless times before, he headed toward the timekeeper's desk. On this new day, Junior was especially chipper for so early in the morning, although he'd been up all night. His daughter had given birth to a baby boy a little after midnight. It was his seventh grandchild and first grandson. Glover joyfully patted him on the back and rapidly shook his hand, realizing that they were on shoutin' ground.

"Another Joe DiMaggio in the makin'."

"Could be," agreed the proud gran'papa.

Aiming for his usual spot on the shelf, Glover sat his lunch box down and carefully balanced his hat upon it. Admiring his well-worn fedora perched atop the box like a barn owl on a weather vane, he sighed in a gesture of homage. That silly hat was like a faithful friend that patiently waited for his return each day.

As much as he cherished the stillness and tranquility of a forest, he doted on the noise of the busy foundry.

When he was at the foundry, he was glad to be there. When he was at home, he was glad to be there. He loved his life. What did he have to complain about? Nothing. He was so thankful that his mother had taught him that attitude is everything.

This day was a good day.

Doris had cooked a pot of white butterbeans. That meant butterbean sandwiches for break or lunch, and that alone was enough to put a little zip in his step. Glover, feeling adventurous – and for the sake of variety – had vigorously shaken a ketchup bottle over the beans, splattering globs of sweet red sauce. No mayonnaise. A little variety was good for the soul.

Whistling "Stardust" softly, Glover went about his daily

254

routine until nine, when a familiar shrill signaled break time. Swinging his lunch box in stride, he went to the car to listen to the radio while he ate. Joe Rumore was broadcasting his show "Hi, Neighbor Time" from the Alabama State Fairgrounds.

The radio wouldn't come on.

"Dadnabbit!!" He pounded on the steering wheel with his fist and rapidly switched the dial on and off. *What now?*

It was probably just a loose wire; he would work on it on Saturday. He hoped that was all there was to it. Maybe Cam had a spare radio – he would check. If not, he would have to go to Tim's Car Accessories, buy a new radio and install it. *Oh well, you do what you have to do*, he consoled himself. He knew Tim. Tim would give him a good deal.

Settling his back against Lulu's sparsely padded seat, he held his butterbean sandwich in both hands and bit into it, savoring the delicious taste that totally rocked his soul. Why butterbean sandwiches weren't on every menu in every cafe in America was beyond him! If only the world knew what they were missing.

Chewing contentedly, his thoughts turned to Thanksgiving, just a couple of weeks away. This would be a Thanksgiving like they had never known. All their married life, they had gone to Doris's mother's house for a family gathering. Now that she had moved to Heaven, Avis and Edward Earl, Mary and Frank, Owen and Amy, and all their kids would come to Gadsden to spend the day with Glover and Doris.

The women had decided to try something new: a progressive dinner. Mary, ever open to anything new or challenging, had heard about it at the Women's Missionary luncheon. As best she could explain it, the idea was for each participating household to host one particular part of the

255

Thanksgiving meal.

It had been decided that they would have salads and finger foods (which amounted to tea-size pimento and cheese sandwiches on white bread) at Bessie's. Then they would walk to Cam's for turkey, dressing, and the trimmings. After the meal, the women planned to string garlands of cranberries and popcorn to decorate their Christmas trees, while the children made paper chains and ornaments from glue-covered pine cones sprinkled with glitter. The holiday festivities would conclude at Glover and Doris's house for dessert and coffee.

"We're gonna leave around 2:00 to hunt for a while," Glover added as plans for the day were coming together. (Cam, Thane, Edward Earl, Owen, Frank, and Glover were planning to hunt in woods nearby.)

"Y'all'll be back by dark, won't you?" asked Doris.

"Hope so. We'll plan to come back to our house. Have the coffee on. We'll be cold an' ready for cake and pie." Glover knew what Auntie was planning to bake, and among the plans being made were his personal plans to thoroughly enjoy several slices.

In addition to pumpkin and mincemeat pies, Auntie traditionally baked a six-layer coconut cake with seven-minute icing. She depended on Piggly Wiggly to stock fresh coconut from Florida for the holidays, and so far they'd not disappointed her. Auntie knew from experience that it would take longer to crack the coconuts than it took to bake the cake.

Anxious to try something new, the women were eager to try the progressive meal. The men were mostly confused and wondered why women were always changing things.

His thoughts jumped ahead to Christmas. "It'll be our first Christmas in our own home," he whispered. "In our own home. In our own home." Glover chuckled, as he tasted the words coating his tongue like melted chocolate. It was a dream come true. What could be better than standing in the middle of your dream?

Late in September, Doris and Auntie had put toys on lay-away at Sears to give them plenty of time to pay them off before Christmas. Molly was getting a bicycle, and Amanda had waited all year to tell Santa, when he stopped by Sears, that she wanted a Betsy Wetsy doll. Marianne was biding time 'til Santa brought her first pair of shoes with low high-heels, a pair of nylon stockings with seams up the back, and a garter belt. Dog-eared pages in the Sears catalog were a testament to her diligent search for just the right pair of shoes.

Glover had spotted a short, fat cedar not far from the creek that would be perfect for their Christmas tree. About two weeks before Christmas, he and the girls would cut it down with a handsaw. Even with daily watering, cedar trees tended to wilt, so best to wait as close to Christmas as he could. His nostrils twitched as he thought of waking each morning to a cedar-scented house.

Naked oak trees were laden with nests of mistletoe. Glover, a crack shot, planned to take his .22 rifle and dislodge roosting bunches of mistletoe with a fast-moving bullet. He may even be able to sell some to Stancil at the general store – those who had no way to get mistletoe out of trees would gladly pay for a sprig to hang in a doorway. From what he had spotted so far, there should be enough to keep Campbell's Corner residents kissing all year.

Two short shrills signaled that break time was half over. Swallowing the last bite of his sandwich, Glover slid down in the seat. He settled against Lulu's doorframe, closed his eyes, and

257

encouraged his thoughts to meander.

The house was finished, and he expected Bessie to move into it this week.

She would.

Glover had no way of knowing that she wouldn't live there long. The future held many changes for Glover, his family, and his friends.

Bessie Pearl Pennycutt would become Mrs. Coggins Campbell on Valentine's Day, 1951. She would sell the new house to Auntie, who had been sitting on a nest egg she'd inherited from her mother. Bessie would put the money from the sale of the house into a savings account for LaVeeta to go to college to earn her teaching degree. Talladega College was a fine school and LaVeeta would become a fine teacher. Addie would follow in her sister's footsteps and eventually work as a guidance counselor in the Birmingham public school system. Mose would go to school on an athletic scholarship, and in time play baseball in the minor leagues. As for LaMarcus, thank God, nobody would ever hear from him again.

The three Daniels girls would each marry well, and both Marianne and Molly would become teachers. After graduating from Judson College in Marion, Alabama, Amanda would become the wife of Alabama's lieutenant governor. (It would be rumored that Amanda's honey platinum blonde hair and charming ways tipped the scales for her husband in winning the election. Some would say that Glover started that rumor.)

Doris would surprise everyone by going to work after the twins graduated from high school and headed to Ole Miss. With no previous work experience, Doris would be hired at Campbell's Drug Store as a cashier. It would seem ridiculous to everyone that Doris could work outside the home; and bets, ranging from one week to one month, would be placed on how long she would last. She would last twelve years.

Glover's days as an ironworker were numbered. As more iron was imported from Japan, iron foundries would downsize over the next few years; the pipe shop on 12th Street would close forever in 1956. To make a living, Glover would work with Cam in the construction business and cut timber as a sideline.

The Daniels family would continue to grow and prosper in ways they'd never dreamed possible. Glover's children would never know the struggles he'd known. They would enjoy the benefits of education that had not been available to him. They would grow to appreciate that the strong, decent people they became was largely due to a hard-working man who married a sweet Southern Belle. A man that lived his life for his family, and an occasional butterbean sandwich.

The End

Recipes

Lettie's Chicken Croquettes with Cream Sauce

1 can of cream of chicken soup
1 ½ cups of finely chopped, cooked chicken
¼ cup of dry bread crumbs
2 tablespoons of minced celery
2 tablespoons of minced onion
¼ teaspoon of poultry seasoning
Additional breadcrumbs for coating
3 tablespoons of shortening
½ cup of milk
½ cup of green peas (optional)
½ teaspoon of black pepper (optional)

Combine 1/3 can of the chicken soup, chicken, ¼ cup of breadcrumbs and ¼ teaspoon poultry seasoning. Shape into 6 croquettes (cone shaped or patty shaped.) Roll in remaining breadcrumbs, chill for one hour. Remove from frig. Melt shortening in a skillet and brown croquettes (medium heat) on all sides. Drain on paper towel. In a small saucepan, combine the rest of the soup, milk, and a dash of poultry seasoning. Bring to a boil, add peas, turn the burner down, and continue to cook for one full minute. Serve over croquettes.

Auntie's Caramel Cake

Butter and flour three 9" cake pans

Make the cake:

1½ cups of granulated sugar
1cup of powdered sugar (confectioner)
½ cup of Crisco
½ cup of butter, softened
5 egg yolks
3 cups of all-purpose flour, sifted
3 teaspoons of baking powder
½ teaspoon of salt
1 ¼ cups of half and half
1 tablespoon of vanilla extract
5 egg whites
1 teaspoon cream of tartar

In an electric mixer bowl, add shortening and butter to sugars and cream well. Add egg yolks one at a time. Sift together dry ingredients. Combine milk and vanilla. Alternate dry ingredients with wet into sugar/butter mixture. Beat the egg whites, adding cream of tartar mid way, until stiff. Fold carefully into batter. Pour batter into pans, bake at 350 degrees for 35 - 40 minutes. Cool in pans for five minutes. Turn out onto wire racks.

Make the icing:

1 cup of butter
2 cup of brown sugar, tightly packed
½ cup of heavy cream
4 cups of powdered sugar
1 tablespoon vanilla
1 teaspoon cinnamon

Melt butter in a saucepan, add sugar and cook over low to medium heat for two minutes. Add cream and stir until mixture comes to a boil. Remove, cool, and then pour into a mixer bowl. Add powdered sugar gradually. Add vanilla and cinnamon. Mix on low speed for one minute. (If frosting is too thin, add more powdered sugar; too thick, add a tablespoon of cream until spreadable consistency.)

Spread frosting generously between layers and on sides of cake.

Bessie Pearl's Apple Pie

Prepare two 9" piecrusts

Ingredients:

2 unbaked piecrusts

3 medium to large granny smith apples
3 medium to large red delicious apples
2 tablespoons of all-purpose flour
1 cup of sugar
1 teaspoon of cinnamon
1 teaspoon of nutmeg
½ cup of apple jelly
½ cup of sugar
4 cups of apple juice
¼ stick of butter
1 egg white whisked with 1 tablespoon of water
sugar for sprinkling

Wash and peel apples, placing peels in a medium saucepan.

Core and slice apples (1/2 inch slices). Toss apple slices in a bowl with flour, ½ cup sugar, cinnamon, and nutmeg. Pour mixture into a pie crust (lightly butter bottom of pie pan to help the bottom crust to brown and not be soggy). Place in frig until needed.

To the peelings in a saucepan, add ½ cup of apple

jelly and ½ cup of sugar. Add apple juice, and water (if needed) until liquid is two inches over peelings. Cover, bring to a boil, lower heat and simmer until peelings are soft and liquid is reduced. When tender, remove from heat, cool, and then puree with an emulsifier or in a food processor to the consistency of applesauce. At this point, taste and stir in more apple jelly, if more sweetness is desired. Pour over apples in crust. Dot with pats of butter. Cover pie with top crust (cut an X to vent it) or lattice crust. Brush crust with egg white and water. Sprinkle with granulated or turbo sugar. Bake at 375 for 50-60 minutes on bottom oven rack. Cover edges with foil if browning too quickly. Serves 8.

Cathead Biscuits

(No catheads required)
Serves 8

Ingredients:

5 tablespoons of bacon drippings
5 tablespoons of melted butter
3 ½ cups of all-purpose flour
1 1/3 cups buttermilk
½ teaspoon salt
2 tablespoons of melted butter to brush tops

Heat oven to 375 degrees. Place flour and salt in a bowl. Stir in bacon drippings, butter, and buttermilk just until combined. Do not over mix. Turn dough onto a well-floured surface and knead two or three times. Divide into 8 equal portions and roll into balls. Flatten to ½ inch thickness. Brush tops with ½ of the butter. Bake at 375 for 30 minutes or until browned on a baking sheet or in an iron skillet. Brush again with remaining butter immediately after removing from the oven. Cool slightly before serving.

And now a Sneak Peek at the sequel to *Whistlin'*
Stardust by Sara McFerrin. Coming soon!

Chapter One
Dear Hearts and Gentle People

"Bess!"

Janet yelled up the stairs to her friend and neighbor. Just
as a cardboard box slid into view, Bessie Pearl stuck her head
around the corner.

"Just doing a walk-through. I think I have everything."
She hefted the box and started down the stairs.

"The car is packed to the gills. If there's more, we'll have
to come back," Janet said as she reached for a winter coat draped
across the top of the box.

Heading toward the back door, Bessie set the box down
and took a detour to the kitchen. "I want to check that the
percolator is off." She held the still-warm chrome coffee pot at
eye level, shaking it to determine what was left of the morning
brew.

"There's probably two cups here. You want to take a
break?"

"Let's get this stuff over to the new house. This is it.
We're done. Once we get this unloaded, it'll be dinnertime, and
we can make a fresh pot." It was as cold as a frog's foot outside,
and a hot drink sounded good to both women.

Janet's 5:00 a.m. breakfast was quickly wearing off. She glanced at her watch. It was almost noon, and they'd been at it since a little after 7:00.

Bessie Pearl's new house was finished and filled with furniture from Cam's barn, where it had been stored for the last 3 months. This would be her first night in the house that Cam, a friend and builder, had recently completed.

Stuffing the box into the backseat amongst clothes, books, and other boxes, Janet threw the coat on top and then slid into the passenger's seat. Peering over a table lamp perched on the seat between them, she looked at Bessie sitting behind the steering wheel, staring straight ahead, as if she were gaily skipping about in la-la land. After several seconds, Janet asked, "What's wrong? Tired?"

"Oh, I don't know. I have bittersweet feelings. I knew that it would be hard to leave this house. Cam was so gracious to offer me the upstairs while he worked on the new place. As you know, when my house sold, my choices were to move in with Cam or lose the buyers for the house on Cherry Street. So much has happened in so little time." She sighed and stared at nothing.

"Well, the good news is, Cam lives a stone's throw away. It's not like you'll never come here again." Janet felt her friend's sadness. Campbell's Castle, as many referred to it, was a sprawling brick two-story house, chock-full of priceless antiques, art, and Scottish heirlooms. It was home to red-haired Scotsman and widower Coggins "Cam" Campbell.

"I know it. I'm just being childish. And I am excited about setting up housekeeping in a brand new house. It's been a long time since I've had new everything." She cranked her '48 Chevy and slowly backed out of the driveway, weaving this way and that.

It was the second week in November, evidenced by treetops aglow with shades of rust, scarlet, and gold. Cam Campbell had promised her that he'd have the house finished by Thanksgiving, and he'd stayed true to his word. Campbell's Corner, Alabama, had a new resident; and, as 1950 was coming to a close, Bessie Pearl Pennycutt was starting a new chapter in her life at age 61. Retired school teacher, widow, and mentor to LaVeeta Johnson, a sweet, petite, brown-skinned, sixteen-year-old, Bessie had sold the home built by her beloved Edgar when they were newlyweds.

It was a gutsy move. But staying on Cherry Street, after long time friends and neighbors Glover and Doris Daniels and their five children had relocated, would have taken even more courage – more than she had to offer. Over many years, the Daniels family had become such an integral part of her life. She'd grown attached to Marianne, Molly, and Amanda, and the two newest additions to the Daniels household, twin baby boys. The children's grandmother had died a short time back, and Bessie hoped that she had helped fill that void. Because she had lost her only child to polio when he was young, these children were the closest she'd ever come to being a grandmother.

"Back up close to the porch, an' we'll pile everything there and take it in a little at a time." Janet got out to supervise the backing. Bessie was not known as one to do much driving in reverse. Forward, she was okay, but backwards – that was a whole *nuther* story. She'd often said, "If God intended for us to drive backwards, He'd have put eyes in the back of our heads."

Bessie pulled forward and back several times, finally ending up near the front steps. Near, but not close. She opened the trunk and handed Janet part of its contents, which Janet handed off to LaVeeta, who'd just opened the brand-spanking-new, bright-blue front door.

"Hey y'all. Let me get my coat on." She went inside with the first load and quickly returned, buttoning her saddle-brown wool coat. Pulling a plaid scarf out of the pocket, LaVeeta tied it over her head as she hurried down the steps.

"I got dinner ready. They's 'nuff for supper, if y'all want leftovers."

"Hallelujah!" Janet huffed up the steps carrying a box of books. "I'm ready. What're we havin'?"

LaVeeta took an overnight bag filled with hair-doing stuff from Bessie, and said as she passed Janet (who was headed back for another box), "Pork chops, mustard greens, stuffed eggs, cornbread, fried potatoes, an' peaches an' pound cake. I whipped up some cream for the cake."

"Everythin' but the kitchen sink. There'll be enough to send Cam a plate for his supper tonight," Janet commented over her shoulder.

"Ah, well. Maybe he can eat it for dinner tomorrow," Bessie hurried inside with the last armful of dresses on wire hangers and headed for the bedroom closet. Janet looked at LaVeeta. LaVeeta shrugged her shoulders and raised her eyebrows.

Once seated at the kitchen table, the women helped their plates, and slathered cornbread muffins with butter. "So, how is it that Cam won't need supper tonight? He goin' somewhere?"

Bessie had hoped that Janet would move on to something else. She really didn't want to discuss Cam or his supper plans.

The percolator bubbled on the countertop, audible over the sound of Roy Acuff bellowing from the radio that was turned down low. Bessie cut a chunk of pork chop, and aimlessly

271

swirled it in gravy and mustard greens juice. Placing it in her mouth, Bessie chewed slowly, as if she were counting the number of chews in each bite. LaVeeta put cake on each of three plates at the counter and spooned sliced, home-canned peaches while listening to the conversation.

"Well. What's the big mystery? Why'd you say that he wouldn't need supper tonight?"

Sheepishly, Bessie replied, "He thought it'd be nice if we had supper together, being as this was my last day there."

"Oh," said a surprised Janet.

"It's just a token of thanks. He's cooking for us. I need to thank him for all he's done. He's gone above and beyond to help me."

"And how is it that you'll be thanking him?" Janet took a dessert from LaVeeta and passed it to Bessie.

"Come on, Janet. It's nothing. Really. You've said time and again that you're not interested in him. He's chased you like a bloodhound on the heels of a fox. Don't make a mountain out of a molehill. It's just a show of friendship. LaVeeta, save these bones for Briscoe."

"Yessum, I will. He be out there on the porch come late in the day lookin' for handouts." Briscoe, a lively hound, lived at the Daniels's house at the end of the path leading from the back porch and through the woods.

"I'm not makin' a fuss," said Janet. "Lord knows, it would get him off my back. I don't dislike Cam. You know that. But even if I was lookin' for a man, which I never claimed to be, I'm not sure that I'd pick Cam. He's a little much sometimes − to put it mildly." Janet poured coffee and set a cup next to Bessie's plate. "You want coffee, Veeta?" She shook her head no.

"The dinner was delicious, Veeta. Thank you. We'll

272

finish it up tomorrow." A sugar cube dove to the bottom of Bessie's cup.

"Well, isn't he? Much, I mean?"

"We're all a little much from time to time, if you want to get right down to it. Supper is just an innocent attempt to further our friendship. That's all. I think he's enjoyed having company in that big, rambling house."

"We didn't really see much o' Mr. Cam. He pretty much be downstairs an' us upstairs. We come in an' out the back way. But least he know that livin', breathin' bodies be under the same roof he is. Y'all want more whip cream?" LaVeeta scraped up the last few spoonfuls of whipped cream into a pile in the bowl.

Janet extended her index finger. "Just a tad, right here. A dollop on my finger." Unwilling to chance it, LaVeeta handed her the bowl. Heaping a tablespoon high with sweet, fluffy cream, Janet ate it and then said, "Here, Veeta. Put the rest up. If you don't take this, I'll eat every bite. I'm tryin' to watch my weight."

Watch her weight! thought Bessie. *The woman could eat a side of beef and never gain an ounce. I can look at a cow in a field and gain a pound.*

"Remember the day you moved in over there, you said that it would be hard to leave when the time came. Looks like that prediction has come true." Janet licked the spoon.

"Well, it's not only the house I'll miss. There's something to be said about having a man in the house." Bessie couldn't believe that she'd heard those words come out of her mouth. Quickly she hoped to correct any false impression she'd made. "Don't read anything into that. I just mean that it's been a pleasant experience staying there."

LaVeeta stacked dishes in the sink and swished her

273

hands in warm, soapy water, making bubbles billow like a cloud. She'd been at Bessie's side since they'd met Cam. She was surely no expert on the subject, and nobody had asked for her input one way or the other. But it seemed to her that their friendship was mighty close to blossoming into something more.

*

Thane Campbell was the spitting image of his father Cam, minus the beard and mustache. After examining the lock on the chicken pen gate for the third time, he began to count bobbing, red-feathered heads.

"Final count twenty-two," he stated.

"Another one missing?" asked his wife, pretty, brown-haired, brown-eyed Virginia Ann Campbell.

"Yeah. That makes three. One a week for the last three weeks. Got my favorite hen Mona Lisa, this time. The one with a whop-sided, deformed comb that flops from one side to the other when she runs. Can't figure it out. If it were a possum, a coon, or anything else there'd be signs of a struggle. There's not a feather on the ground."

"Somebody's stealing them," she surmised.

"How? The dogs are out at night. Samson and Goliath walk the yard all night and sleep all day. Those dogs'd chew the ankles off anybody who'd come sneaking 'round here in the dark."

"Maybe it's somebody they know." Virginia Ann was trying to be helpful, although she really hadn't a clue as to why the hens were disappearing.

"Who? Who do we know that would steal chickens?"

In one last feeble attempt to come up with the right

answer, she said, "Maybe the hens are getting out somehow. I presume that you've checked for holes in the fence."

"First thing I did. They've all had their wings clipped, so they aren't flying over the fence. The gates locked, so nobody's letting them out. Me and Chalmer sat down here three or four nights and didn't see nothin' or nobody. You seen a drop in the number of eggs we're getting?"

"Well, of course, there are fewer eggs because they lay less this time of year. Be hard to tell if anybody's taking any. If chicken snakes were getting in the nest, there'd be shells left behind."

"Too cold for chicken snakes."

There was nothing that Thane disliked more than a low-down, lying, lizard of a chicken thief. He hoped that the culprit was four-legged, rather than two-legged.

"I'll call around and see if anybody else is missing anything. I've talked to Pa and Chalmer. They've got all their chickens."

Virginia Ann reached for Thane's hand and turned toward the path leading to the house. She knew that he would be on pins and needles until he found out what was going on. Of the three Campbell brothers, Thane was high-strung, and easily frustrated. Chalmer, the oldest, was a rock. Levelheaded, patient, and practical. And, unlike either of his brothers, Delmus (aka Chip), the youngest, was Mr. Charisma. Unrealistically optimistic, and as charming as a fairy tale prince.

*

Cam Campbell was so nervous that he was meeting himself coming. He had not expected to feel sad and unsettled about Bessie leaving his house and moving into her own. They had worked together for months, planning and building a three bedroom, one-bath, cottage-style house. He was glad to be finished, and glad that Bessie was so pleased with the end results. For several weeks he'd been dealing with unwelcome emotions when it came to Bessie. He was thinking of her far too often, and actually found himself missing her when they were apart. This unintended behavior kept his head spinning and his moods changing. He constantly questioned himself as to why he felt like he was losing someone that he'd never had to begin with.

Rushing into the bedroom for a last, quick glance in the full-length mirror on back of the door, he smoothed his red beard, and tucked his navy-blue, long-sleeved shirt neatly into navy trousers. *Maybe I need another color shirt,* he thought. *I look like a deliveryman.* He'd changed shirts three times, and truth be told, he didn't have but a couple more shirts that were suitable for this occasion.

He'd cooked a ham (that was his fourth choice, as menu plans changed several times.) Everything needed to be perfect. He didn't know why − it just did. It was *just Bessie* coming for supper. But, then again, it was *Bessie* that was coming for supper.

Cam was a man caught in an enigma. He'd thought that he had strong feelings for Janet, and Bessie was no more than a client who'd hired him to build a house. But somewhere along the way, quite unintentionally, Bessie had taken first place. And his thoughts about her had nothing to do with building a house. He had absolutely no idea how she felt about him. She'd been nothing but a lady, a pleasant business acquaintance, and one of the nicest people he'd ever known. His frustrations left him

276

feeling foolish. If he were perfectly honest with himself, neither Janet nor Bessie had shown any romantic interest in him. Sometimes he wondered if he was going through a midlife crisis, but then how could that be? – midlife at his age had long since come and gone.

"Kristalene. You need to leave before she gets here. Thanks for everything, and I won't forget to put ice cream on the apple pie." The aging housekeeper took one last glance at the dining room table. She'd set it with the good china and crystal goblets, and placed a folded napkin in both plates. Taking her coat off the coat tree near the back door, she pulled a scarf out of the pocket, effortlessly folded it in a triangle, and slung it over graying braided hair. She tied it snuggly under her chin before giving last minute instructions.

"The percolator be loaded an' ready to go. Don't plug it in 'til you ready to serve the pie."

"I'll remember. Thank you, Kristalene. I'd hate to think of life without you."

"Uh-huh. I know that be the truth. It be rough on you awright."

Cam chuckled. Little did she know how true her statement rang?

She said good night and hurried to the truck where her husband waited. He'd kept the motor running so that the heater would stay warm. Once inside, she looked at Otto, "I'm gonna tell you what. That man actin' like a lovesick cow."

"Well, a man need a woman. Miss Lizbeth been gone a while now. It time he look 'round an' see they somebody take a likin' to him."

Kristalene knew that he was right. She'd worked for Cam's wife for over twenty years and helped care for Elizabeth when she was deathly ill. The faithful housekeeper wasn't sure that she could behave graciously should there ever be a new mistress at the helm.

****

Please email the author at
saramcferrin@mediacombb.net to be notified when this sequel is
available.